Decided We Fall

Ra'Quann Randle-Bustamonte

DEDICATION

To my Homophilic Halfway House (You know who you are)
And my sweet home Alabama, who irked me enough I had to write
a book to relieve some of my annoyance.

CONTENTS

ONE

L ike the rest of the town, the memorial had seen better days. Days in which people came, looked around, and cared for her. She sat on the right side of a forgotten football field. Nature had long swept away the white lines that marked the field. The only things betraying its original purpose were the rusted goal posts on each end and the unkept track around it. The ever-collapsing stands protecting nature from human hands. The abandoned memorial defiantly stood at the end of a hill, guarding the quarter-mile road to an equally abandoned school. The name of the school was Calera High, long forgotten since the time Calera had integrated with neighboring towns to form the city Justice. There was nothing in the school, it was a shell of a place for learning; so condemned not even Lye could find a reason to stay there. The school was not the reason he had biked his way to Calera. The only thing that mattered was his abandoned memorial.

The yellow letters still shined in dull resilience to being forgotten; spelling out the words Roy Down Memorial. Plywood boards covered the windows;

continuing a job they started long before Lye was born. The doors had been chained for so long rust mended the links together. No one could look at the amount of rust without reassuring themselves they were updated on their shots. But that wasn't where Lye was heading. Lye pushed his bike under the nearest bush. This way, no one would see the light blue paint that alerted someone there was a trespasser. He wrapped his bike chain around his left forearm. In case someone tried to rob him, he held a weapon. As was habit, he looked around to make sure no one was looking at him, peering across the street beyond the train tracks for a hidden observer. Pleased he had seen no one, he continued toward the back of the memorial.

Lye felt the familiar feeling of adrenaline as he made his way toward the back of the door. Crossing the line from curious loiterer to felon always sent a wave of excitement up his spine. From pure conditioning, he looked up at the sky to see if there were any black birds. Only the clouds bore witness to what he was about to get himself into, but the clouds never cared. The presence of cops was lax in this area. Not due to the lack of crime; crime came out of the woodwork as soon as the sun went down. There was more money lost than earned watching over the poverty-stricken part of Justice.

Lye paused to look at the plywood-covered glass door as he reached the back of the memorial. He often daydreamed about the time where people would come into this place of reverence and simply look outside at the small wooden area through the double glass doors. Or about how many people stood at the miniature bridge barely outside the frame of vision of the doors. He shrugged his shoulders and continued his mission.

The amount of effort to make sure no one wanted to enter was the exact thing that piqued his interest as a boy. The bricks themselves cried out to him whenever he passed by, waiting to tell him a secret. The first time he had trespassed into this temple, it was on a dare. Bernabe had dared him two tamales he didn't have the guts to go inside this condemned building. Ever since he was nine, ever since that day, he couldn't help but return.

Lye stopped at the wooden door, tucked away into a corner, and froze. Something wasn't right. He didn't know what was wrong until he got down on one knee and pulled out his lockpicking kit. Given his keen eye and his frequent visits, he remembered everything about this door. More importantly, he knew everything about the lock. He remembered every scratch he had ever put on the lock. He could mark the oil stains his hands left on the door throughout the years. As he looked closer, he noticed more scratches on the lock than accounted for by him. He wasn't the only visitor to this condemned building. These scratches came from someone using a lockpick with amateur hands, someone other than him. The information pleased him instead of worried him. Whoever was entering this place was as much as a criminal as he was, and whoever was entering this place was acquiring small pieces of knowledge. The thought of someone else entering this oasis made him smile as he unlocked the door with practiced hands.

The creaking could have been heard in the dead of the night the first time he had opened this door. The renewed traffic ceased its unnecessary announcements. Once he opened the door, he replaced his lockpicking kit back into his bag and took out a flashlight. Lye looked inside the darkness, and the darkness looked back at him. He turned on the flashlight, grabbed his bag, and closed the door.

Any acknowledgement to the outside world was choked off as the door closed. The bricks of the memorial would not allow any outside interference to disrupt its slumber. Dust mites gleefully danced in the beam of the flashlight; welcoming Lye back into their care. Like fairies of tales long forgotten, they danced, willing to take the time to show the hero the right way to go. Lye bypassed the light switch; the memorial had not witnessed electricity to this place for decades.

Nine years ago, when he first walked into the pitch black of his memorial; it drenched him in terror. Now the same setting brought a feeling of companionship. It separated him from the outside world. The first room he walked into could have been used as a classroom. Tables of rotten wood were stacked alongside of chairs holding the same rust as the chains outside. A metallic taste hung in the air, along with it a dangerous feeling. As though too much inhalation of this room's air would cause problems. Lye reflexively put his sleeve over his mouth and squinted his eyes.

Lye opened one of the double doors and peered inside the sanctuary of the memorial. Dust had fallen in such quantities it created a barrier protecting everything from time itself. There had been several items showing people would frequent these walls. Lye had found the occasional hoodie or backpack or antique Android phone. Rows and rows of unnamed contraband sat on the shelves, all waiting their turn for Lye to crack their spines. Lye's repeated footsteps broke the blanket of dust on the floor, crisscrossing the sanctuary like ant trails to nourishment. The windows were boarded up, but they were boarded up in haste. The tops of the windows were free, allowing an inch of sunlight to create a stage for the dust mites to dance on. Sun bleached chairs greeted Lye as he decided which one to sit down in. He yawned, it was still pretty early in the morning, and this was the only time today he would be able to make it today.

The pulpit of the memorial sat in the center of the sanctuary. Lye dropped his backpack on the floor, the impact bringing a dust cloud to his knees with a PLOOF. Keeping his flashlight on the shelves of contraband, he began looking for the next item in his list. He came to the memorial at least twice a week, but the number of untouched contraband still overshadowed those he opened. Lye didn't know the proper name of such contraband, and he wasn't exactly sure spine was the right term for the part that always stood facing him. He only *called* them spines because that part of the contraband, like the spine of any animal, kept them erect. It connected the sheets of paper together. Lye grabbed the one closet to him. It was a thick article; the weight alone told him it would be an interesting adventure. Printed toward the bottom of the spine was the creator's name: William Shakespeare. The name filled him with guilt, and with guilt he put the contraband back and went to find something else.

All of this is illegal, he thought with a smirk. As a law abiding-citizen, *all* of this should give him a sense of guilt. It didn't, but it should. Lye grabbed another article of contraband. The creator's name was Edgar Allen Poe. Once he rightfully decided he felt no guilt, he went to the table and cracked the spine. Lye read the words with glee, digesting whatever amazing stories were typed on the paper.

This temple had birthed many things inside of Lye. He felt joy; he had cried looking into the forgotten worlds of contraband. His face always scrunched up as the word contraband went through his mind. Contraband couldn't have been the first names for such delights. He couldn't find the word, and he was sure if he said the word outside of this area he would be in trouble. He put his flashlight in his mouth in order to free both of his hands. He read for the better part of an hour, until his alarm went off on his phone. There was never any fear of someone outside hearing. The same bricks that kept sound outside also protected Lye from other ears. He took the article and put it back on a shelf. For a second, he contemplated, shaking the dust out of his afro as he bit down on his lip and his guilt. He grabbed the contraband created by Shakespeare and wiped the dust off the front cover.

He pulled out a lead box from his backpack. He found it on another of his childhood adventures with Bernabe. It was the right size to place an article of contraband in and walk around without some people noticing. While he frequented the shelves under the name fiction, his favorite section of his memorial was called non-fiction. Fiction gave him an array of emotions as he read them. The reoccurring feeling non-fiction gave him was anger.

His memorial had taught him many truths. He thought about those truths as he walked out of his memorial. Many of the facts he learned there differed from the facts he learned at school. The Common Connector didn't give him much of the information nor the stories his memorial held. He walked out of his sanctuary and made sure to lock the door behind him. Again, he looked toward the Alabama sky to make sure there were no black birds. Even the clouds had left him during his hour of reading. Like any good criminal, Lye looked around to see if he was being watched as he grabbed his bike. As he began to peddle home, he reflected over the things he learned in his memorial. There was always one truth that never strayed far from his mind. The biggest truth was about his government. About his government, he was sure of one thing:

His government taught him lies.

True to her legend, Mother Nature had started the day off with a muggy seventy degrees, even though he arrived at his memorial at five in the morning. The humidity didn't bother Lye; however, he rarely gave it any thought. The humidity would have to fight the sweat pools over his shirt and shorts before it mattered any bit to him. After a look over his shoulder, he peddled a little farther, all the more eager to get back to his house in order to get ready for school.

Lye rode his bike almost every day before school, and twice on the weekends. He peddled in the calmer parts of the city; the places where the stubbornness of country folk stopped the expansion of the city. This was especially true when he left his memorial, as it was safer to take the scenic route. Not even the muggy Alabama heat could dampen the beauty of the scene as he pedaled down county road one nineteen. Abandoned farms and hills painted the horizon, and there was not a care in the world. If he could stay in this part of the city for the rest of his life, he wouldn't mind.

Lye Davis enjoyed riding his bike. A more accurate description would be he preferred it. On a bike, there were far less distractions. There were no radios, no talking, no passengers. Only him and his mind. Most days it was a godsend. Some days...well some days were better than others. He quickly glanced at his watch and peddled even harder, blowing off the sweat accumulating on his top lip. Sooner than he would have hoped, the trees began to give way to buildings. At first it was just the occasional house, or an out of the way shop. Those gave way with more buildings, and more commotions and signs of civilizations. He passed the sign for the city of Justice, tipping his hat at the irony of the name.

The first reminder was the buzz of the mall area. Decades had passed since the greatest attraction to this part of town was the lonesome Wal-Mart. Those times were long gone. A mall, which held any wish someone could ever desire, was always open throughout any time of the day. People wanted to forget their lives no matter the time of the hour, and businesses were always ready to comply to their desire. People continued to get out of their cars and walk along the sidewalk as he peddled by. Some still yawning from waking so early. Some staggering as makeup ran from parting all through the night.

It was uncommon not to see the homeless on his way home. They migrated toward places they could sleep during the night and beg during the day. Lye tried his hardest not to dwell on the homeless scattered alongside the trash and smushed cigarette butts. He never knew where to direct that anger as his heart broke at the sight of those who no longer could care about what happened with themselves.

The second reminder was more ominous. The presence of civilization required a presence of authority, and within three minutes of biking through the area, the first drone appeared. During the introductions of these machines years ago, people would stop and watch them patrol with awe. People felt protected by the sight of the drones, nicknamed black birds because of the matte black paint they were covered in. Nowadays people quickly glanced at the black birds, and then looked away to something- anything- that would make them appear less guilty in the camera lenses of the drones. The amount of money needed to care for the drones were well into the billions. America could afford it, as she had long since stopped giving benefits for the less fortunate of her children. Money that should have went to help the single mother or disabled were used to enforce the all-seeing eye in the land of the free.

Justice Police Department went across each drone in bold white letters. The letters were in between the two torrents mounted on each drone. One of the requirements of growing up was to know which torrent carried non-lethal ammunition, and which one did not. Facing the drone's façade, the torrent on the left always looked better taken care of than the one on the right. The reason was simple: the ones on the left were used more frequently. The one on the right was only used at children who were unaware of the fact they committed a crime. The red camera on the drone watched all, saw all, and judged all. The number of cameras around the city contrasted drastically to the openness of the less civilized areas. Every streetlamp, corner, building, and walkway sheltered at least three cameras.

As Lye peddled past the Common Connector, he took a moment to take in the architecture. Not to admire, the building was made by someone who wanted to make an antient Greek temple, but never took the time to research one for their own knowledge. It was a sad imitation. Between the columns of the buildings waved several ten-foot banners. Much like the cameras, these banners were always in the corner of everyone's eye.

Instead of watching others, they told a message. The words "America is Great" hung heavily in golden letters, embedding themselves in the subconscious of anyone who dared look too much or too long. And everyone looked too much and too long. Copious amounts of imagination were wasted in naming the building.

Its function was to connect the common people, as it was the only route to getting information in the country that didn't come from word of mouth. It stood across the street from Justice High School. All forms of media, texts, movies, and the like were filtered through one of these buildings before it hit the masses.

Lye casted those thoughts out of his mind. It was still early in the morning, which meant the day still belonged to him. After a few minutes he turned toward the suburb where he lived. Each house had the exact same layout. No one could get to their house without paying close attention to the number of houses they already passed. Each house was painted with the same light blue paint with a red door, and each house contained three bedrooms and two baths. It was very easy to walk into the wrong house at times, and birthday parties always licked Lye with paranoia, as though someone came into his house when he was away and changed all the furniture.

The black sedan in the driveway announced his mother was home. The lack of a gray SUV announced his father wasn't. Lye rarely saw his father during the weekdays. On several occasions it took him days to notice his dad had cut his hair. Once it had taken him an entire month to realize his dad had decided to grow a beard.

Lye hopped off his bike and pushed it toward the

side of the house. There was no reason to worry about somebody stealing it; the drones had more than enough access to suburbia. He fumbled his keys out of his pocket and unlocked the front door. The lights were still off, but that didn't mean everyone was asleep. His mother had developed the uncanny ability to move around in pitch darkness without bumping into anything or anyone. A skill he was sad he didn't inherit but had long since realized it was for the best. A skill like that would only lead him to get into trouble.

"Hello." Said a voice in the living room, confirming his thoughts his mother might be up.

"Hey ma, good morning. How are you doing?" Lye asked between long draws of breath.

"You know, if you stopped smoking cigarettes, you wouldn't sound like a half-dying dog when you walked in the house." His mom quirked. Without seeing her face, Lye still knew she wore a smile as she looked in his direction. "I'm doing well though, I just came down to get my tablet." Lye heard her pick up what could only be the item in question. "Since you're up, I've been meaning to ask you, would you mind taking your sister to Michelle's birthday party Wednesday?"

"Uh, sure," he said absentmindedly, looking to find the light switch. Once he did, he squinted his eyes as the sudden change in the house. His mother- her task completed- started towards her bedroom. Like every master bedroom in the neighborhood, hers was the only bedroom on the ground floor. She still wore her black bathrobe; her hair wrapped in a silk scarf. She stopped halfway and smiled. Unlike her uncanny ability to move like a cat in the night, Lye inherited her mischievous smile, a smile that said she was up to something; that she wanted to play a game whether or not the other participants knew they were playing.

"Lye...what did I just ask you to do?" she asked.

Still in his absentminded state, Lye answered. "You wanted me to cut the grass tomorrow. . ." after looking at his mother's smile, he realized that must have been the wrong answer. "No wait, you wanted me to...take Courtney...to Michelle's house... for a slumber party? No, birthday party."

After he answered correctly, she promptly turned around and went to her room.

Lye grabbed a water bottle and went upstairs in order to take a shower. With his mother in her room, he had the house to himself for an hour before he had to get ready. A studious teenager would use the allotted time to catch up on classwork or homework. A more realistic teenager used the time for extra sleep. After a quick shower, and a small game of tug of war between him, his hair, and his pick, he climbed into his bed and went to sleep.

Only to wake up to the feeling he was being watched. Not by an intimate object, habitation had long since allowed him to ignore the camera in his bedroom. There was one in every room in the house besides the bathroom, as was standard in every almost house he had been in. Whatever was staring at him was a living creature. He opened one eye to see his little sister standing at the end of his bed. In one hand she held a comb, in the other she held hair grease.

"What time is it?" he groaned, checking his phone to see how long he slept. It was six-thirty. He had thirty minutes before he had to get ready for school.

"Can you put my hair in French braids? I'm not as good as you, neither is mom. And I want to look good today."

Lye heaved himself up to a sitting position and stretched, yawning unnecessarily to emphasize his sleep had been interrupted. "You want me to do your hair in thirty minutes? You don't think you're pushing it? I mean, I'm good, I'm just not sure I'm that good. I gotta ask, who are you trying to look good for?"

Courtney scrunched her face and tilted her head. It was a pointed question, but there was a lack of respect, nonetheless. "I'm trying to look good for myself." She asserted, putting her hand on her hip.

With a laugh Lye took a pillow off his bed and laid it on the floor. He scooted toward the side of his bed, so his feet were on the floor as Courtney flopped down on the pillow. With the skill acquired by having a little sister who insisted on having her hair done, he quickly braided her hair. Small conversation insured as he weaved his fingers, never forgetting to make the comment that she had given him such a small window of time to do so. She had woken him up from a nap, but Lye enjoyed the time he spent with his sister, even if it meant just braiding her hair.

"Okay, I'm done." He said, patting her hair to finalize his task. She hopped up with joy, hugged him, and kissed him on the cheek.

"Thank you, Lye, is there anything you need me to do?"

He stood up to stretch more and looked around his room. Just as the blueprints to the houses that neighbored him, his room looked like every other bedroom on the second floor of the house next to the staircase. He had a full bed, a dresser, and a wardrobe. Every room was expected to be kept in the greatest cleaning standard, expected being the definite word. There were two differences between his room and others. Having pictures in any place other than the common areas of the house was forbidden. On Lye's dresser sat a solitary picture, slightly faded and pressed from all the times he kept the picture in his back pocket when he was younger. In the picture sat two little boys. One little black boy with his hair in a mess. A Hispanic boy sat next to him with his arm around Lye's shoulder. Both were laughing with tamales hanging out of their mouth. The picture was taken on Bernabe's fifth birthday. Next to it stood two pill bottles.

"Um, no. I think I'm good for the day. Actually, if you could remind me to take you to the birthday party whenever, I would appreciate it. You know I'm likely to forget it." Lye walked toward his dresser and opened the pill bottles. He took one out of each bottle and cocked them back and looked back at his sister. "Also, I need you to get out of my room. I need to get dressed."

"What you need to do is do something with that nappy hair, one side of your fro is stuck to your head. To be real, your hair looks like your farmer remembered he left something in the oven in the middle of a sheering." Courtney laughed, and walked out.

Lye looked in the mirror; she was right. It was obvious he slept on his side. He hesitantly put on his school uniform. It was the same uniform he wore every day since kindergarten. The same color gray slacks, gray button up shirt, and red tie. He slung his backpack over his head and headed toward the bathroom to grab his pick. He resumed his game of tug of war with his hair as he walked down the stairs. Courtney had already dressed. She wore a white button-up shirt with a gray skirt, smiling as she looked at herself in the mirror. While looking in the mirror she fixed the armband she wore on her right arm. A red armband with a simple cross in the middle for everyone to see. The sight of it unsettled Lye, but he never brought it up to his sister.

"Is Mom taking you to school, or are you taking the bus?" Lye asked.

"How many times do I have to remind you, I'm in middle school now. I don't need anyone to take me to school."

Lye caught her eye and stood silently, waiting for her to continue.

"But in order to make her feel better, she will be taking me to school . . ." she added sheepishly.

As though the sound of her name was a spell of summoning, Mrs. Davis walked out her bedroom. She yawned, and seeing her children in the living room, she smiled. She had dressed since Lye took a nap; wearing simple jeans and a white t-shirt. She too wore the Christian armband. Lye didn't agree to such necessities.

She grabbed her wallet and pulled out a fifty and

handed it to Lye. "Don't forget, today is Tuesday." She said, before Lye had time to ask for the reason. She gave her children a hug and walked in the kitchen to make herself breakfast.

It was only early February, but Alabama never took the time to listen to more rational weather patterns. There was no need for a jacket as Lye walked outside and grabbed his bike. He stifled a yawn as he headed toward school. There was a difference in the commotion within the two hours. While it was true there was rarely a time where everyone was quiet in the city, there was a difference in the type of buzz that went on. Most of the sounds of loud music and partying had subdued in respect for those who were crawling out of their homes to go to work. Some people would wave at Lye as he passed their house. They had grown accustomed to seeing the boy with the bike. No matter the time of day; familiarity and southern hospitality required this of them. Lye didn't mind, he would wave back, as most of them did so with a tired smile.

It was the same thing every day, no matter the weather. Occasionally, Lye would count the time between the person at the end of the block getting inside their car and the person on the other end of the block opening their front door to head to work. Forty-seven seconds. It was the same forty-seven seconds every time. Like cogs in a machine, if they differed from the set schedule it meant something was wrong.

The school bus would always turn into his neighborhood at exactly ten minutes past seven. The bus driver would always give him a head nod of acknowledgement as they passed one another. Each day was the same.

And each day it irritated the hell out of him.

The grayness of Justice High School dominated over him as he parked his bike. It was the second semester of his senior year. Only his anticipation of finally leaving his prison kept him going on school days. The gray of his uniform was the same gray of the building. The crimson of his tie was the only thing separating him from his background.

He pulled his bike into the bike rack, bending down on one knee to chain his bike in place. Most of his peers whose parents could afford cars drove, and those who couldn't rode the bus. He had declined his parents' offer to buy him a car. While it wouldn't had put a dent into their budget, he preferred to ride. If there was an errand to be ran, he could always find a ride.

Lye stifled his umptieth yawn as he peered at the groggy assembly line of students working its way toward the entrance of the building. A foolproof yet unorthodox method could easily show the grade of any student walking into the doors. Freshmen greeted the gates of hell with grins and smiles. Sophomores kept a tired grin on their faces once they reached the halls. Juniors waked in with the corners of their mouth up, but the smile never reached their eyes. Seniors felt no reason for such pretentious etiquette. With their dead eyes and deadpan faces, seniors looked like extras on the latest horror movie. Some greeted Lye as they walked past, others simply wanted to get the day over with before it started.

Two figures stood outside the entrance to the

25

school. Body armor and masks greeted the students. Because of the masks, it was hard to tell if they were the same officers who watched every morning, or if they had been relinquished of their duties. Each officer gave the kids a head nod, but the students' attentions were not on the officers; it was always on the assault rifles the officers held. Politicians of old passed laws to deter any school violence; proclaiming the sight of guns would deter the prisoners in the school from bringing outside guns. As with any prison, the sight of guns didn't stop the most stubborn of students from causing havoc in the halls. Lye for the most part believed it just allowed the parents to believe their kids were being protected. Mostly it kept the students in line. Mostly.

"Good morning Lye," said one of the officers as he walked up. The air of hospitality brought Lye out of his absentminded stupor. He instinctively looked down at the officer's rifle. Unlike his partner, the officer kept his left index finger close to the trigger. Recognition dawned as Lye imagined the blond hair and crooked teeth hiding behind the mask.

"Hey Will! You still liking the job?" Will had been a senior when Lye first started school. They had become friends during their short time together. A difference in upbringing didn't allow them to continue most of their friendship outside of these brief greetings. Still, he was happy to see his old friend, no matter if there was a gun in between him.

Passing Will, Lye walked into the school and waited in line to pass the x-rays. None of the students talked as they placed their backpacks on the conveyor belt and walked through. At times Lye wondered what they were looking for in their bags, if they were actually looking for anything. He had accidentally walked in to numerous drug deals in the bathroom in the past semester.

Lye walked toward his homeroom. Twenty-four students passed through the door to their homeroom without saying a word. The same dull gray paint on the outside of the building clung to the walls of the classroom. The only difference was the three windows along the wall, giving the students a clear view to the Common Connector. There was no longer a reason to greet anyone, they saw each other five times a day. Each student took their assigned seat; waiting for their homeroom teacher to walk in. His first class was Government. The amount of useful information gained from the class made it seem more of a time for babysitting than actual learning.

"Good morning class!" yelled the obnoxiously happy Mrs. Peeves. She wore her hair in a pixie cut and had an extreme amount of energy that began in her toes and ended at her smile. The energy she had never reached her eyes. She carried the eyes of the oldest student there. Nothing would ever grow in Mrs. Peeves' barren irises.

"Good morning." echoed the class in a low murmur. Mrs. Peeves ignored the lack of enthusiasm, and for all they cared, that was okay. There were a select few that were happy to be there. But they were the exception, not the rule.

"Today is a special class, because we have to speak about a special thing. As you all are painfully aware, you are all seniors, which means in three months you will be walking across the stage into your very own lives."

Lye snorted. The sound did not go unnoticed by Mrs. Peeves. She scorned him but went on with her rehearsed speech.

You're going to hate what she says.

"As you know, you have been assessed since you entered the halls of this great school. All of your teachers have tried their hardest to figure out which job, school, and life you would best be suited for at graduation. You will learn. Many of you will be excited when you figure out the job you will have. I will admit, every graduating class has a few strays that believe that we have made a mistake. But I will assure you my students, the system never makes mistakes. While some of you may be irritated, sad, or god forbid, *confused* about the decisions that have been made, I can assure you that everyone in due time will understand. I am happy to have you as my first graduating class."

Mrs. Peeves very well could have been speaking to a room of cadavers based solely on the response he received. Many of the kids got comfortable in their seats. By now all of them could tell when she was getting ready to tell a story. If history was a witness, there was no way to stop her when she was in a storytelling mood. The classroom filled with passing glances; all students silently agreeing to allow this story to run its course.

"I remember when I was in your position. I was told I was going to be a teacher, and honestly, I couldn't believe it! In all of my classes, my grades usually kept me at the bottom of the barrel. I just couldn't stay awake! I was on the cheerleading squad, and I had a lot of friends, like a lot. But there was nothing academically about me.

When I saw I was supposed to be a teacher, it made no sense to me. I never liked class, nor learning, but there was something I had more than anyone else. I had school spirit. I was patriotic. I loved my government. When I was given my assignment, I foolishly asked my teacher why someone in the right mind would give me this job." Lye snorted as he too wondered the same thing on a few occasions. "I had realized it was me that was wrong, and not everyone else. I do hope none of you make the mistakes I made. Everyone who has worked for you has nothing more than your best interest in mind."

She looked around to the murmurs of her class. Some of the students continued to look out the window as she spoke; their brains looking for anything that didn't follow the strict sameness of their school.

"Last month you all took the Alabama Graduation Test. It is the most important test you will ever take in your life, as it helps us determine what you should do for the rest of your life. Two weeks ago, very important people finished grading those tests. I am happy to say that tomorrow you will see the results. You will get to see what type of options you have concerning your vocation, your partner, among other things. As you all know, you have been scored on your ability to retain information, apply that information, and how well you work with others." Mrs. Peeves continued, never straying from her bubbly demeanor.

The Alabama Graduation test was the standardized test all students in Alabama had to take. Each state had their own graduation test. The government must have thought it not unique enough to call the whole thing the Graduation Test. Seniors took the test in the cafeteria of each school in January. Everyone sat down at their respective desks and stared at a packet of paper for three hours. Lye wondered how anything of that nature showed how someone worked well with others, but he had long given up trying to get answers from his teachers.

A student in the front of the class raised her hand. Lye only knew her because of an incident when they were in tenth grade. Her name was Jessica, and she loved the color blue. She loved it so much in fact, she dyed her hair dark blue for a week. She would have kept it blue for a longer period if the principal hadn't scolded her for wearing her hair in such a distractive color. He berated her, telling her the male students and teachers in the school would not be able to concentrate because her bizarre hair would distract them. Lye wanted to laugh every time he thought the idea of blue hair sending him into a sexual frenzy, but he stopped the thought when he remembered Jessica running from the halls crying. Since that day she had left her hair jet black.

"You said this test will show us who should be our partner? What do you mean by that? I already have a girlfriend . . ." she trailed on, wondering if she had said too much.

Mrs. Peeves bit on her lip like she was trying to hold her breakfast in her stomach. She composed herself again before she rebutted. "I know you are young, so you may think you understand what you want, or who you love. In the nicest way I know possible, I will tell you that you are wrong. You are not an adult; you do not really know what you want. But we do. One day you will look back at the time in which you thought you didn't need the love of a man, and you will laugh. I promise we are not so sadistic not to give you time to realize this. You have until graduation to convince your friend you do not love her."

Mrs. Peeves looked around the class again. She wore a smile on her face, but there was no happiness, she was waiting to see if anyone else wanted to question her authority. Her eyes fell on Lye a few times, waiting for their little game of chess. To her dismay Lye had found something incredibly interesting on the ceiling and wouldn't make eye contact with her. After a few moments of staring, she clapped her hand in finality and resumed her lesson.

"Now, I have finished my little personal note. Everyone, turn in your assignments." She gleefully commanded.

Lye's seat stood in the back of the class, the furthest from the words coming out of the teacher's mouth. That didn't give him reason to believe he could do anything without being watched. As the thought crossed his mind, he looked toward the door to the hallway. Like a spider too stubborn to understand when he was unwanted, a camera perched in the corner above the door, its ever-blinking eye watching all the students. Of all the things in the building, the cameras were by far the most expensive and most frequently updated piece of equipment.

Lye looked out the window to a constant show of people walking toward their various destination. A patient student would see three drones zip by in order to fight the crime that *plagued* their city. Even with all the things going outside the window, only the Common Connector could catch Lye's gaze. Each time he looked at the building, he thought on how the architects had failed to achieve an imitation of ancient Greek. The inside of the school matched the gray of their uniforms. The crimson of the banners outside matched the ties the males were supposed to wear. Even if he didn't want to admit it, the banners served as flame in a dark room. The accents of the golden letters allowed anyone who wanted to stare an escape from the grayness of everything around them.

"Lye."

Lye wretched his eyes from the banner to see the class staring at him. A few seconds passed before he remembered what his teacher had said before he was sucked in to the redness outside. He reached inside his backpack and pulled out the assignment from the night before. To no one's concern, Lye's assignment was several pages longer than those of his classmates. No one else besides the teacher made notice of this. She had the disappointment of a trainer who studied the buck that wouldn't break.

"Now, I would like everyone who is willing to, to read their assignment." Mrs. Peeves walked toward the whiteboard in the front of the class. She grabbed a black marker and began writing. When she finished, the words on the board read:

Why Did America Win the Third World War?

Several students raised their hands in anticipation. She selected one of the students in the front of the glass. Somehow, said student had survived the soul sucking of the institution. She was one of the only seniors who continued to smile throughout the day. Her hair was tied in pigtails, and she bubbly waited for her turn to speak.

"Now Karen, why did we win the third World War?"

Karen looked at the teacher and looked back at the class. "We won the third World War because Lord President says we did!" she said excitedly.

The teacher clapped with glee and hugged the student. This went on for some time until Lye was one of the last students left. He slowly walked up toward the front of the class. Some of the students grew a renewed interest in what was going on as he walked past. More than a few straightened up in their chairs. Even Mrs. Peeves straightened her back as he walked up, the smile no longer on her face as the prompt escaped her pursed lips.

"Lye, why did we win the third World War?"

Lye looked at his teachers, and again at his classmates.

"First, I would like to mention, I believe the question should be '*How* did America win'. Besides that. . . we couldn't have won the war. Because there was no war to win." He said blandly.

A scream escaped someone's lips. Mrs. Peeves looked as though she was about to faint; all the blood in her face had washed away. It took her a few moments to reset her face, "And what makes you say such a terrible thing such as that?" she asked, her voice raising considerably higher than her usual teaching voice.

Lye looked at his teacher with mock innocence, but the façade melted away when he began to talk. "There are records of every war America has been in. These records go back as far as Revolutionary War. The one war where I couldn't find any information about, was World War Three. In almost every war we've been in, I could find the number of people who died, the locations of the battles, how long the war happened, and in some cases, the different races of those who fought in that particular war. But for this one, nothing. I even looked at different countries that had been in war with or alongside America. There was no information from our enemies or our allies in terms of World War Three. There has been commentary on World War three from inside our borders, but no official records. The lack of evidence for an entire war is unheard of, even by American standards."

Some of the kids put their heads down as Lye continued to speak. The camera in the corner recorded most of what happened in the room. No matter if they agreed with Lye or not, none of them wanted to be caught laughing. A Hispanic boy near the front of the room developed a bad case of coughing. He continued to cover his mouth, making sure Mrs. Peeves didn't see the wrinkles in the corner of his mouth.

"You weren't supposed to research it!" Mrs. Peeves yelled at him. Her face was as red as the banners that flew outside the window. She almost bared her teeth as she looked at Lye.

Again, mock innocence plastered itself on Lye's face. "I'm sorry Mrs. Peeves, I was confused. I thought it was a research paper, that's why I did research."

Mrs. Peeves' anger for Lye subsided for a second as she pondered her next words. She quickly smiled at her classroom as she gained control over the situation. "No. Lye I worry about you sometimes, but I understand sometimes people of your nature need a little more time to understand things. Even though it *was* a research paper, there are some things that you are supposed to *just know*. The reason there are no records of World War Three is there were too may atrocities that went on in that time. We had to do unspeakable things in order to win, but we never wanted our children to know about the sacrifices we had to make. The morals we had to break to ensure freedom for our future generations. Trust me, I am an adult. I know more than you. This time I will forgive you and give you an A. But we can't have much more of these interruptions in class, okay?"

Lye sheepishly shook his head. "I am so sorry, forgive me. May I use the restroom ma'am? I think a restroom break would help to get this foolishness out of my head."

Mrs. Peeves patted his head and kindly shooed him out of the room after she signed his hall pass. Before he made it out the door, he could hear someone else answering the prompt (Because Lord President says so!).

Lye lazily walked down the hallway, the same long hallways he walked down every day. Never changing, dull, and gray, like the majority of the school. The walls of the halls had no pictures of colorful paint. Only red banners in gold letters. These too were hard to ignore; there were far more of these in the hallway than flying on the Common Connector.

"Student stop."

Lye looked behind him to see one of the patrolling officers standing behind him. The thought occurred to Lye that if he was to sneeze right now, everything would fall on the officer. The thought tickled him; there was no reason to be this close to him before announcing himself. Most people would instinctively step back when someone was this close without reason. Lye commanded his feet to stand in the same position as he acknowledged the officer.

You're going to be arrested.

"Yes?" Lye asked.

The officer stared at him for a second and placed his hand reassuringly on the pistol on his side. He *had* expected Lye to step back. The closeness made him feel uncomfortable.

"Ar-Are you a student here?" the officer asked, shuffling his feet.

Noticing the hesitation, Lye stepped forward a little. He smiled when the police officer stepped back. Lye let out an annoyed sigh. "You started this... conversation, if you will, with the words... 'student stop'. If you want to know my name, it's Lye Davis. I'm going to the bathroom. Would you like to check my hall pass or am I free to go?"

The officer stood still for a few moments, trying to figure a way to regain control of the conversation. When he found none, he answered the question.

"You are free to go."

Lye chuckled a little as he turned around and

continued toward the restroom. As the day went on, he made sure he kept an eye on this particular officer. People of authority rarely took humiliation well.

***

"Lye, when are you going to learn to stop making people mad?"

Afternoon sun welcomed all the students while they walked outside. There was no reason to look back, he recognized the voice. An arm wrapped around his shoulder, and he looked to his right to see Bernabe cheesing at him.

Lye and Alexis Bernabe had been friends since their brains could make memories. Their mothers had known each other in high school, and they happened to give birth on the same day. It was common for Bernabe to say something along the lines of "when I was your age . . ." to speak of something he had done an hour ago.

"What are you talking about homie? Mrs. Peeves still thinks I'm just not patriotic enough. Unless Lord President himself comes to talk to me, I doubt anyone is going to mention the fact I'm constantly talking smack about him. I'm still a little salty you continue to say whatever she wants you to say."

He turned to Bernabe with a grin on his face, but Bernabe was looking toward to a space not yet there. "I don't care. As long as I get the veterinarian job, I'll be fine. Mrs. Peeves suggested I've already been selected as that, so as long as I keep my head down, I'll be good."

"And what are you going to do if you don't get the

job you want? Are you going to continue to keep your head down?" Lye asked. They've had the same conversation many times. Before he had finished the question, Lye knew the answer.

"There's nothing I can do if I don't get the job I want, so I don't see any reason in being mad about it." was his answer. Sensing he was about to get a lecture, he decided to change the subject. "Today is Tuesday, do you need a ride, or are you going to take the bike?"

In all honestly Lye would have preferred to take his bike. But his errand for the day took him out of Justice, and there was no reason to go through that exercise when there was a perfectly good friend willing to give him a ride.

"As long as I can put my bike in the bed of your truck, I'll be good. Do you remember the way, or do you need directions?"

Bernabe waved the question off. "I'll meet you in the front of the school."

With that Bernabe walked off.

Lye stood at the curb, watching the black birds go by. They flew in groups today. This wasn't unheard of, but there was usually an obvious incident tied to their movement. The five birds headed west toward one of the residential parts of Justice. Old Calera lay farther west across from the bridge, but the chances of the black birds going to Calera were slim. Lye shrugged his shoulder and daydreamed a little.

Not too much later, an antique truck rolled up to the curb beside Lye. Most of the kids that drove cars to school drove because their parents bought them the car. Bernabe had found an abandoned truck in his neighborhood. With a few detective skills, he had learned the owner had died a long time ago, and the current owners saw it as nothing more than an eyesore. For the entire summer, Bernabe took his time working under the table jobs to find parts that would make the truck work again. Bernabe and Lye had spent many nights tinkering with the truck, well into the early hours of the mornings. It was more than fifty years old, but it ran as though it was only ten. And more than anything, it belonged to Bernabe and Bernabe alone.

Lye walked up and placed his bike in the bed of the truck; gently to make sure he didn't scuff the paint. Bernabe had screamed the last time he carelessly threw his bike in the bed of his beloved truck. Lye hopped in the passenger seat and Bernabe, not without a hiccup from the engine, continued on their way.

After a few minutes of silence, Bernabe sparked conversation.

"So, who are you taking to prom?"

"Whooda taking what now?" Lye said, launching back into reality by the sound of his friend's voice.

"To prom. Taking. Who are you . . ." Bernabe trailed off. Lye stared at his oldest companion for a few moments in an attempt to dissect what the conversation was really about.

"Do not bring her up." Lye snapped.

Bernabe had known Lye long enough to know

when he was faking anger, so he continued. "I have no idea what you're talking about. I am simply asking my friend here, who isn't half-bad looking if I were to comment, on which woman he is taking to prom. I don't see any harm in that."

Bernabe stopped at a red light. Three little kids ran through the light, oblivious to the crosswalk they were supposed to be on. A small pop rang through the scene, and a rubber ball whizzed by the head of the oldest child. The three children looked up to see a drone hovering over them with smoke slowly rising out one of its torrents. They quickly slowed down, coming from a laughing sprint to a solemn walk.

"When you finally tell me who you are taking to prom, I may, probably, ask her out... again." Lye said.

"Last time I checked she didn't reject you. I mean I could understand if that had been the case."

"That was the problem. Please shut up and drive, it's a green light."

Bernabe's response was a wheezy laugh. Doubtlessly annoyed, Lye turned the radio up.

Two

Bernabe turned into a business complex. The red bricks contrasted with the green tile on the roof. The entire building looked plain, the atmosphere felt peaceful, but no one would ever be caught here without an appointment. These walls had held the psychiatric needs of Shelby county for decades, even as the name of the business changed. In response to the silence they held while he drove, Bernabe decided to talk about what he planned to do once he had his dream job.

"I doubt I would be able to get into Cornell University, but I can get into a smaller, less expensive college. And give it a few years after working under someone, I could put my own vet hospital in Justice. Once we have a vet hospital, I think more people would actually buy pets." He said. Cornell University was one of the best schools to get into for vet work. It only made sense he wanted to attend.

"And how much would you charge for such services?" Lye asked.

Bernabe parked his car. "Well you know your man has to eat. But as to not offend my social warrior companion, I would charge on an income-based level."

Lye put his hand on his chest in mock appreciation. "Aww, you would put me into consideration for your paycheck. Are you doing this to help people, or because you don't want to hear my mouth?"

Bernabe put his truck in park. "You and I know I feel like I'm the blame for the way you are to some degree. To be honest, I am happy at the way my friend has turned out. But, because it is my fault, I am doing this because I don't want to hear your mouth. I don't want any black birds over my building because you're...what's the word?"

"Protesting?"

Bernabe winced. "Yeah, that. Anywho, I can take you home as well. I don't have anywhere to be this afternoon. Don't worry about paying back for the gas, I see it as community service."

Lye climbed out of the truck and opened the door to the one-story building. The receptionist looked up from her computer and put her glasses back on her full moon face. The prescription made her eyes look bigger than they were. She looked more suited in the latest sci-fi movie than behind a desk. But she was nice, and her face rarely mattered to anyone. He had seen the same middle-aged white woman for years, the sight of her brought a little feeling of relief.

"Mr. Davis, are you here by appointment?"

"Yes ma'am." He said, walking up to the desk to sign in. He grabbed the pen and quickly signed. "Have there been a lot of people around today?"

She gave a bored sigh. "I wish, I have been watching movies on my computer all day. Which isn't a bad thing, but the others have been a little restless. Yesterday they had a hacky sack tournament because they had too much time on their hands."

"You didn't join in hacky sack?" Lye asked, intrigued at the thought.

"Now boy you know I don't need to be doing all that moving, especially if no one is paying me to do that. One wrong move and we're all going down, and I'm breaking another hip."

Lye chuckled. Once she realized there was no malice behind the laughter, she allowed herself to laugh too. It didn't take time for the door behind her to open. A short man came out. He too wore glasses, but he didn't have the prescription that enlarged his eyes. He had a small stain on his teal shirt. His brown eyes were almost completely eclipsed by his thick eyebrows. His entire demeanor oozed kindness as he looked at Lye.

"Lye, are you ready?" he asked.

"Absolutely, one hundred and ten percent."

Lye followed the kind man down the long hallway into an office space. As Lye sat in one of the chairs facing the desk, he looked around the room. It was more instinct than anything, the image was branded in his mind from years of occupying the same chair. Most of the interior of the building was painted gray. But this room was painted a dark blue. Mr. Mike closed the door and flicked off a switch near the door. While it turned no light on, the camera in the corner of the room no longer shined red.

"So, how have you been since I last saw you?"

Lye hesitated long enough to think about it. "I'm, doing better? I'm still riding my bike everywhere, and I still exercise in the morning. I try to eat every day, but sometimes I forget. And it's been about two weeks since I stayed in my bed for the entire day and I'm happy about that. So, really, I don't think I have much to talk about this week."

Mr. Mike nodded. Lye looked around the room again. There were three degrees framed on the rear facing wall. Their number equaled the same number Lye would wager counted the number of hairs on Mr. Mike's head.

"Would you say the increase of medication has helped you? How are you at making friends? Have you found more success in that part of life?" he asked.

Once again, there was a slight hesitation as Lye thought about the questions he was being asked. "I guess? I haven't had any side effects, which is good. I haven't made any new friends, but the two I have are all I really need. Better two friends than a hundred associates." He put up a tired grin as he looked at his psychiatrist.

"You have two? Are you talking about Felix? I thought you no longer talked to her. You never mentioned what made the two of you stop talking to each other. I could imagine that it would be... awkward. But you can bring that up whenever you're ready. Do you still feel as though you are constantly being watched? That there is an impending doom you are unaware of? Are you still having difficulty concentrating and focusing on one task at a time?"

Lye subconsciously looked at the camera in the corner; thinking about the irony of being asked if he feels he's being watched. "Well... those are pointed questions. Felix and I... are friends. We're just not talking at the moment, but I'm sure things will change."

"Like?"

"The apocalypse." Lye quipped without skipping a beat. "Besides the obvious fact that I am literally being watched every moment of my life, the feeling has subsided a little. And my impending doom. Those used to be deafening voices. They're still there" he pointed to his head. "But they are less forceful. They're more like the sweet nothings of a lover than a drunk college student with a hard on. I'm getting better at focusing, but I can tell a difference in the early morning and in the evening. During those times I feel like I'm playing tug of war with myself still."

Mr. Mike nodded again, a notion that slightly irritated Lye. He stared at Lye the way a scientist stared at an ongoing experiment. The word *trust* wouldn't be the first word to pop in Lye's head when he thought of Mr. Mike. He wouldn't entrust him to pick him up from school, this trust was only conditional. He trusted him to do his job. And that only went as far as what Mr. Mike did benefited his health.

"Attacks? Hallucinations? Sleep paralysis?"

"None of those." Lye lied. Admitting to those would bring forth more medication, and there was no desire to increase the doses he was already taking. Lye averted his eyes after the answer. An action he hoped the watchful eyes of Mr. Mike would ignore.

"I will have to admit you have been distant these past few weeks. I have an hour of your time, and I do not want to end this session doing what we usually do: sitting in silence. Is there anything you wish to talk about?"

Lye hesitated. Not to think of his answer, but to look at the camera in the corner again. He couldn't be sure that it was entirely off, of if that was just a show. He didn't know how much his confidentiality protected. This action did not go unawares to Mr. Mike.

"If you are worried about whether or not I turned off the camera, look me in the eye." He said. Once he had Lye's attention, he continued. "I plan to kill Lord President. I wish nothing more than to see his corpse in the trunk of my car, and there is nothing that anyone could do about it. But before I kill him, I will kill the mayor of Justice, Alabama. I plan on killing Mayor Cambridge Friday evening, to be exact."

Lye felt no shock by the words. He saw the motive behind the words almost as soon as they were heard. There was no doubt in Lye's mind his therapist had no plans on doing that. But if the camera was on, there would be police en route as they spoke. To speak ill of any public official was a felony. To joke about murdering Lord President was an act a treason and would be punished by death.

"Is it wrong for me to admit I'm worried about graduating? I still don't know what areas they will put me in." Lye said. "I'm not worried about my score. I'm sure I made a good score, that I'm not worried about that." He thought a little bit, realizing his grammar in the last sentence was subpar. "But I want to know what they think I want to do. Why doesn't anyone care about this? Why are we so content in receiving what everyone else wants us to do? Why can't I decide what I want to do in my life?"

Mr. Mike smiled again. "I wish I could help you-"

"Isn't that your job description? Aren't my parents paying you to help me?" Lye interrupted. Anger rose from the back of his throat. He knew the words that would come out of Mr. Mike's mouth.

"I wish I could help you. All that I can tell you is this: you will grow out of these feelings. You are young Lye. You still have the idea you are in control of your life. Soon enough you will not burden yourself with that responsibility, and you will feel better for it. Give it a few years and you will see how insane that responsibility is. It's a responsibility most adults don't want over their lives. I can only imagine the turmoil this responsibility would cause a teenager."

"I would rather die than let someone control every aspect of my life." Lye said.

Mr. Mike raised his hands in defeat. "Well that is our time. We will meet next week at the same time. I do hope you can get rid of these feelings sooner."

Lye stood up and walked out of the door, not waiting for Mr. Mike to open the door for him. With his mind racing, he gave the receptionist the money his mother gave him to cover the copay and walked out the door.

He climbed into the passenger seat of Bernabe's truck and slammed the door. "Sorry,"

"You're good. If there's a day when you come out of that place and didn't slam my door, I would assume Mr. Mike didn't come to work. Am I taking you home?"

Lye nodded, determined to look out the window for the entire drive. Eye contact would prompt Bernabe to start conversation, and conversation wasn't something Lye wanted to have for the time being.

Bernabe parked his truck on the curb of the house, the usually unoccupied parking spot was taken by a gray SUV.

"Are you coming in?" Lye asked.

"I would, but my mom wants me to be home soon. She said she has news she has to give me. I don't think it's good news; if it was she wouldn't have warned me she needed to talk. I'll see you tomorrow."

They hugged. Lye grabbed his backpack, putting effort to carefully close the passenger door, and walked into his house.

His father sat at the dinner table. He was a tall man, a figure that demanded attention and respect. His father looked up at the tablet he was reading and gave his son a warm smile.

"How was therapy?" he asked. His voice was

deeper than anything Lye could hope for. It always washed over him like a lullaby.

"It was the usual. I don't have to worry about my meds getting increased for a while, so that's a good thing."

Lye's phone vibrated in his pocket. He pulled it out to see that he Bernabe had texted him.

"I put your bike on the side of the house. See you tomorrow. Love ya."

He looked up from his phone. "I'm sorry dad, what did you say?" Before his father had a chance to open his mouth, Lye texted Bernabe. "Thanks man, see you tomorrow. Love ya too."

His father simply smiled. Having a son like Lye taught a person patience above everything else.

"I didn't say anything, but I am happy to know it went well."

Lye placed his bag at the front door and walked over to hug his father. After which he sat down next to him, a puzzled look on his face.

"Did you shave?" Lye asked.

His father usually wore a trimmed beard. As one of the neurosurgeons at the Birmingham hospital, he was not allowed to grow his facial hair out too much. But a clean jaw greeted Lye when he sat down. After years of not seeing his father's chin, the sight was unsettling. His father was an attractive man, and a change in his appearance only solidified the fact. To Lye, it reminded him of his younger days when he saw a team mascot take off their helmet at the end of a football game.

"I shaved this morning. I'm surprised you noticed. I think it was time for a change."

A mischievous grin crept on Lye's face. His father sighed, as he had seen the same grin for years on his wife's face, and on the face of each of their children. "What does mom say about that?"

Mr. Davis straightened his posture, fully captivating his overwhelming height before he spoke. "Your mother doesn't tell me what to do. I am king of this castle, and I will do what I please."

"Is that so?" a voice came from behind them.

Lye's father jumped at the sound of his wife's voice. He looked back at her to see the identical mischievous grin coming from his wife. At her hip stood Courtney, covering her mouth to hide her laughter.

Mr. Davis threw an accusing glance at his son. "You knew she was behind me, didn't you?" his voice sounded hurt. In the time he noticed his wife, he went back to his previous slouch over his tablet.

Lye made no attempt to hide his laughter. "Yeah, I asked the question when I realized you didn't notice her."

But Mrs. Davis wasn't done.

"Lye, do you remember what I asked you to do tomorrow?"

It was now Lye's turn to deflate. The question choked the laughter from his throat as Lye tried to remember his appointed task. Mr. Davis reached inside his pocket and pulled out a dollar, placing it into his wife's outreached hand. It was Lye's turn to throw an accusing look.

"You make bets on my memory? What kind of parents are you?"

Mrs. Davis put the dollar in her pocket. "The kind of parent that knows what bets she's gonna win. I pushed you out, big head and all, the least you can do is help me win a few bets. Are you staying for dinner?"

Lye nodded. "I have to relieve myself and put my things up, but after that I will be back down." He got up, hugged his sister and mother, and went to the front door to grab his backpack. The tension of his next move was known to none but Lye. He tried to keep his face composed and carefree as he went upstairs to commit his premeditated felony. The cameras in the hallways and stairwell watched him as they always did. With great effort he kept his eyes away from them. They had always been there, any unnecessary attention to them would show whoever was watching Lye was doing something he didn't need to do.

They know what you're doing. Stop it now.

With that knowledge, each step brought the idea someone was going to burst the door down and arrest him. It was only a few feet from his destination. However, the weight of his backpack, and his anxiety, made the walk feel like an eternity.

Lye carried the backpack into the bathroom. After his third silent inspection of the bathroom door and lock, he brought the toilet lid down and sat. There were no cameras in private bathrooms, it was one of the few places his felonies could go on without eyes. After glancing at the door to check the lock for the fourth time, he brought his backpack closer to him and reached deep inside the biggest pocket. He pulled out a lead box he had found playing with Bernabe one day. It was the best size. It could fit into his backpack without bringing any attention, and the x-rays at school couldn't look in to see its contents.

Lye brought the box to his knees and opened it, revealing a rectangular object. No matter where he looked, he couldn't find a word for the object. The mystery behind the name only seemed to allure him more. He brushed some of the more stubborn dust off the cover in order to read the front.

"Hamlet. William Shakespeare." He said to no one in particular. He didn't know who Shakespeare was, but he did know Shakespeare created beautiful pieces of contraband. Unlike a tablet, in which turning the page was done with a flick of the finger, the pages on this thing had to be turned with effort. Lye enjoyed the effort in turning the page, it allowed him a few milliseconds of wondering what the next one held. The smell of old wood and paper made him smile. He sat and read, consuming the long-forgotten format of words. After thirty minutes he got up and placed the object deep inside his backpack.

"One thing for sure, at least my life ain't as bad as yours." He said to the protagonist of the book. He washed his hands and flushed the toilet, and placed his treat back into the lead box, and the box back into his backpack.

He threw his backpack into his room as he passed

the open door and walked down to see his family sitting at the dinner table. The food sat untouched in the middle of the table. It was a damning offensive gesture to begin eating without the entire party present at the table. Lye quickly put on a smile and joined in on the conversation.

"Tomorrow you get your results for your test, are you nervous?" Courtney asked.

"Nah," Lye lied. "I'm sure I did well. I just hope they choose the right job for me."

I just hope they choose the right job for me. Even as he said the words, his anger threatened to reach his lips. There was hatred at the thought. Everyone at the table complacently shrugged at his words. Their acceptance threatened his anger even more.

"Would you want to be a surgeon like me, or . . ."

"You could be a CFO like me." Mrs. Davis said. She had received the highest score in the state when she took her test. She never talked about it; she wasn't one to rub things of that matter in people's face. Lye knew it happened because he found her results one day a few years ago in the attic. The test had twenty-two hundred possible points. She had scored a hundred shy of a perfect score. "It's a fun job, and since robots take care of a lot of work, I have a lot of free time to create more bets on my children."

"I do have a question. Mrs. Peeves said they choose our partners as well. How true is that? Will they choose from just the kids in Justice, or will I be partnered with some unknown woman in Wisconsin?"

His parents looked at him, then looked at one another, having an unspoken conversation on which parent was to answer. Mr. Davis coughed in a sign of defiance, which prompted his mother to speak.

"From what I know, they try to keep the kids paired with people from their hometown. That way they live with people they've known most of their life. Your father and I went to school together. I was one of the few people who married the person I wanted to marry. A vast majority of kids don't get to be that lucky as your father. We would probably have to go all the way to Wisconsin to find a woman for you, but it's in extremely rare cases they have to search that far for partners."

Courtney, who had only been listening to the conversation until that point, had a burning question. "So... what are the chances that Lye will be paired with-"

"Do. Not. Say her name." Lye growled.

Courtney rolled her eyes at the authority Lye fantasied he had over her. "It's not my fault she's a constant in your life. I'm best friends with her little sister. And I didn't say her name, I just think it would be funny."

Lye's parents had grown silent. After ignoring Courtney, he looked over to see they were both on their phones.

"For the love of God, please tell me you're not making bets." He asked.

"It is a sin to lie my son." Mr. Davis said, "Alexis is

twenty for, and Mrs. Bernabe is twenty against."

"You brought the Bernabes into this?" Courtney asked with glee. None of the children had seen their parents making their bets. All they've seen was the exchange of funds after the bet was already over.

"Yeah... " Mrs. Davis commented, keeping her eyes on her phone. "Mom is putting ten for, and sissy is putting fifteen against."

"YOU BROUGHT GRANDMA INTO THIS?!" Lye exclaimed. Courtney nearly fell from her seat in her fit of laughter.

Mrs. Davis tried to look innocent, but remembering she had nothing to fear from Lye being angry, she responded "Boy we've been betting on whether or not you would marry a white girl since the first time you brought her home. Okay, phones are off for now."

After the embarrassment session, they continued to eat with mutual laughter and love. Lye couldn't complain about being ganged up on by his family. This was one of their favorite pastimes. It wasn't about teasing a family member, but simply making the best quip. Tonight just happened to be Lye's turn in the hot seat. After dinner Lye and his father wrapped up by washing the dishes, still laughing at the conversation they had at dinner.

Lye walked into his room with his belly full of food and his heart full of laughter. He grabbed the pill bottle on the furthest right and took a pill. He was grateful the past few hours had been filled with laughter. He laid on his bed with a smile. The moment his head hit the pillow, the happiness he had been feeling drained away from him without warning.

You will never find a good job.

The insecurity of his job came over him in waves. There was no escaping them, as he had no information that could ease his racing mind. Lye had no real evidence he would receive a well-paying job; for all he knew he could wind up homeless. His heart threatened to race, but the effects of the drug escorted him into sleep before any damage could begin.

Lye woke in a start; a boulder in his stomach. He looked at his clock and quietly cursed at himself for sleeping past his alarm for his morning bike run. He had naturally woken in time to get ready for school. Lye walked with lead in his shoes the entire way into the kitchen, stopping at the refrigerator and pulling out some milk.

"Are you okay? If I wasn't completely sure we didn't have a dog I would swear your dog died."

Lye closed the door and turned to see his mother, walking as silent as ever. "Have you ever wondered why the death of a dog is the biggest epitome of sadness? Like, even for people who have never owned a dog in their life, that's always the first thing that comes to mind." Lye asked, trying to avoid the conversation in vain.

His mother took him in for a minute before she spoke, carefully choosing her words. "I know today is going to be a big day for you. You feel like everything is going to go wrong. But I think you're forgetting something: you already did the work. Today is just the day you see the fruits of your labor. So, no matter what happens today, you already put in the work. You already did what you were supposed to do. And remember this, no matter what career you get, you will always be welcome here. We will always love you. If it would make you feel better, you can wait until you get come home to open the packet. That way we can share the burden."

"Really?" he pleaded. Lye had thought the best course of action was to ignore how he was feeling. But he had to admit his mother's option sounded better.

Maybe it was the plea in his voice, maybe it was the tears threatening to swell in his eyes, or maybe it was just motherly instinct causing her to walk over and hug her son. Lye gripped his mother tightly and let out a few sobs in her care.

"Mom, I'm scared." He said between his chocked sobs.

"I know, son. I know." She held him until his sobs stopped. After he signaled he was okay she held him at arm's length. "But if there is one thing that describes you, it is intelligent. Intelligent black men are a virtue. I know you are scared, but with that brain of yours, you need to know that you will make a difference no matter what you do with your life. Do you understand me?"

He sniffed a little as he cleaned wiped his nose with the back of his sleeve.

"With that being said, go upstairs and clean your face. Get on the bike and go to school. The last thing you need is to face the day with tears running down your face."

He nodded and followed her instructions. The

closer he got to school, the better he felt. Then again, most of his relief came from his mother's words. It was easier to reflect on them as he rode to school. She was right, Lye had already taken the test. And learning what type of jobs he would have to endure could prepare him for the months to come. Also, with graduation to come, release from this prison would be solidified.

Unfortunately- or thankfully- he was not the only student who felt tension. As Lye walked into his homeroom it was obvious no senior in the school seemed able to hold eye contact longer than two seconds. They sat in their seats in silence, staring at the stack of files on Mrs. Peeves' desk. When the final bell rang, Mrs. Peeves stood from her desk and picked up the stacks. She was the only one who seemed unaffected by the tension in the air.

"Who would like to hand out the packets?" she asked.

"I'll do it." Came a familiar voice from across the room.

"Ah, Alexis, are you that excited to figure out what job you have been given?"

Bernabe stood up from his desk and walked over to Mrs. Peeves. His back was toward Lye, but the smile in his voice was evident. "Not exactly, I really want to know if I'm getting twenty bucks today. At this point knowing my results is just icing on the cake."

Bernabe turned around to smile at Lye. Lye threw an offensive gesture at his friend. He passed the packets out with anticipation. So much anticipation, in fact, Lye had to laugh as he watched him move around the room.

He was as impatient as someone waiting in line for the atm. It wasn't his own results Bernabe was waiting for; he could have opened those as soon as he received the pile. As Bernabe passed Lye his results, he stood over his desk, waiting for Lye to open the packet.

"I'm sorry, but I told my mom I wouldn't open it until I got home tonight." Lye replied, grateful tenfold his mother gave him the idea. Students who had made no promise ripped open the seal to their future the second they received them. Some exclaimed with joy, realizing they had a chance at getting the jobs they yearned for. Others simply cried at the lists of jobs they would have; they couldn't see themselves enjoying their lives anymore.

The results of others mattered not to Bernabe. He stood over Lye's desk, oblivious to the sounds of joy and agony going on behind him. Bernabe stared, trying to bore into Lye's cavalier façade. Lye yawned. "That's fine by me, there are other ways to figure out if I'm getting paid, my brother."

Bernabe shuffled through the stack until he found the packet he was looking for. With a grin he walked over to a girl who sat four rows away from Lye. The girl had not said anything the entire period. They were four rows away, but the tension in the voice had created an abyss of sound as everyone held their breath. Lye could hear easily.

"What do you want Alexis?" she asked, none so gently.

Bernabe, for all his talk, seemed genuinely taken aback. "Felix. Why so hostile? We're friends, aren't we?" He said in complete innocence. A few of the students exclaimed their frustrations at Bernabe. He held up their future for what seemed to be idle chat. He stood at her desk the same way he stood at Lye's waiting for her to open it. He held the file in front of her, making no attempt to hide he wanted to see what it read. She was stubborn enough to wait the entire period to open the file, but her curiosity was quickly eating at her. She yanked the file from his hand and ripped it open, opening the file and staring at it.

"My occupations could be a lawyer, politician, and a teacher, are you happy?"

Bernabe continued to smile. Some of the students found the will to groan as they watched him stand. "The first two make sense, given your family." He took a step back after seeing the look on her face. "By no means am I implying your daddy pulled strings, I'm just saying you know your way around the system. Now what we're all waiting for is that line that says *partner*. C'mon partner, I have money riding on this answer."

She sighed. "My designated partner will be- Lye Aesop Davis."

"Fuck yes," then, realizing where he was, he apologized and finished handing out the files. Lye couldn't help but notice he took his time handing the files to those he was sure groaned during his conversation.

"Who in the world is Alexis Bernabe?" asked a female student sitting in the front row.

Without missing a beat, nor looking from his appointed task, Bernabe replied "Who's looking for their future baby daddy?"

"Bernabe, I will cut you." replied Lye from across the room.

"You got your own problems to worry about." Bernabe quipped, looking over his shoulder at Lye.

The smile slowly left Mrs. Peeves' face. Soon she would lose control over her class if the tension in the room was not taken care of. "Well, given the obvious tension in the room. I believe we should take the time to get to know your partners. Elsa, take Bernabe and stay with Lye for the rest of the period, please. I'm not sure what the mayor will say about this."

"Of course." Elsa's back was to Lye; he had no way in seeing who the voice belonged to.

The class separated into a noisy rumble of students trying to move desks and find their partner. Some voted to stand in the corner, as their partners weren't in the room. Still, the sounds of cheers and groans from realizing who they were destined to marry filled the room. Mrs. Peeves' smile had returned as she watched the foursome head to the back of the class. Bernabe grabbed a desk and, very nosily, dragged it into Lye's personal space. Felix had taken the seat directly at his right. Elsa, who had brought a chair, sat between Felix and Bernabe.

"A simple hi would be nice."

Lye picked up his head and looked at Felix. They both knew the path of least resistance was the path in which Bernabe didn't have center stage. She was a few steps ahead of him, as the only way to make sure that happened was to puncture the tension before Bernabe had a chance to talk.

"Hello," Lye said, a frown deepened on his forehead while he thought of what to say next. "My family has placed bets on whether or not I would be your partner."

They both looked at Bernabe. While he had said nothing, the smug grin on his face was damn near contagious. "*Of course* I placed a bet on it. Blood or not, I am his family."

"Did Courtney bet for or against?" Felix asked. Courtney had always been Switzerland for them for the past two years. The sounds of conversation across the room only grew louder.

"She bet for... I believe. Numb nuts over there also bet for. Which is why he's staring at us and NOT TRYING TO GET TO KNOW HIS PARTNER."

Elsa, who surprisingly had not said anything since she figured out who Bernabe was, finally pitched in. "Actually, I want to see how this plays out. Not every day you get a view into the life that was the Tragic Duo."

Lye and Felix threw glares at Bernabe. Bernabe shot his hands up in a submissive gesture.

"Look man, not everything is my fault. I even had a relationship name for y'all: Felye. Like feline but without the- I see you understand where I got it from. People didn't start calling you the tragic duo until you two split." He threw an insulted look at Felix. "The boy cried when you didn't go to school for a month after the breakup, I was not about to rub it into his face."

"Fine." Lye and Felix said in unison. The preemptive

notion to keep Bernabe from the spotlight had been washed away, so Felix decided to change subjects.

"So, Elsa, what's your occupation choices?" Felix asked, awaiting a snort from Lye. The snort never came.

Elsa jumped for a second. She had forgotten the entire point of the exercise, instead getting caught up on what was going on in front of her. "Oh, I got teacher, nurse, and phlebotomist? Does that have to do with plants?" she asked, looking at the three.

"No, that's the person who draws blood at the hospitals. They pay good money I believe, so you're in luck." Lye responded. "Bernabe?"

"They only gave your boy one option: veterinarian." Bernabe said with pride. Even with the prior conversation, it brought joy to Lye's heart to see Bernabe so happy.

"Are you going to open your packet Lye?" Felix asked him. They all glanced at the unopened packet sitting on his desk. Lye shook his head.

"I told my mom I wouldn't open it until I got home." He repeated. To be frank, he *wanted* to open it then and there, but each motion toward the packet brought fear to his throat. He couldn't open it in front of them no matter how much he wanted. For the first time in his education, he was happy when he heard Mrs. Peeves voice silence the conversation across the room.

"Okay class, I hope you're having fun with your future partners. For those whose partner isn't in your homeroom, I thank you for your patience. I want you to remember: your ties to this person doesn't start until after you graduate. With that being said, you have more than enough time to end the relationships you're already in." Mrs. Peeves had the grace to toss a look of disgust towards Jessica before she continued. "For your homework I would like you to spend some time with your partner tonight. Whether it is a minute or a few hours, get to know them. Your homework assignment will also be two essays. You will have to write a five-hundred-word essay about your partner's past. This is due tomorrow. You will also have to write an essay on "What Makes America Great. This will be due in two weeks. Class has been dismissed."

Everyone stood up to leave the class. Lye felt a hand on his shoulder before he had the opportunity to stand. There was no need to look back; he knew it was Bernabe. Yet when he looked at his oldest friend, he was taken by the lack of smiling on his friend's face. It seemed unholy, unnatural; Lye raised his eyebrow in question.

"I have to talk to you about something. I would appreciate it if we didn't mention it until we got to the bathroom."

Lye simply nodded. The times Bernabe said something like this in such a serious manner were few and far in between, so each occurrence was treated with the utmost sincerity. The hallways were filled with seniors talking to their partners. Whether they were enjoying it or not was on an individual basis. Some smiled with glee as they were partnered with their secret crush. There were some who fumed with mutual dislike. Many of the underclassmen tried their hardest to get out of the way of the parade of seniors, worried they would get trampled by the stampede of angry teenagers.

Lye and Bernabe walked toward the closet bathroom. They too had to watch out for the stampede of their fellow seniors; thankfully most of the underclassmen recognized them as seniors and did their best to stay out of their way.

Before Lye had a chance to ask Bernabe what was going on, Bernabe started. "Look, two years ago when you two broke up. You never told me what happened. And I respected that. But given the fact you will have to marry this girl whether you want to or not, I would appreciate it if you told me what happened. I know it was bad."

Bernabe sighed at the signs of provocation smeared on Lye's face. He put his hand up to stop Lye from talking. "I know it was bad. She left school for a month. *School.* You don't have to tell me now, but I would appreciate if it you allowed me to carry some of the burden before I'm your best man trying to figure out why the mayor is giving both of us a death glare."

Instinct caused Lye to look around to see if there was anyone watching, though there was no one in the bathroom. "Fine. I'll tell you. I have to be at the mayor's manor tonight, so it'll have to wait until tomorrow. I'll meet you at your house."

Bernabe swallowed while he collected his thoughts. "So you're telling me... it wasn't like she caught you giving attention to other girls."

The final bell rang, announcing to the partners in crime they were late to their next class.

Though it was unintended, the insult made Lye take a step back. "Why in the world would you think that?"

Bernabe shrugged. "I don't know if you noticed, but most of the girls here watch you when you walk by. A lot of the guys here don't like you for that reason alone. I guess it doesn't matter much now, but it did ever since we were in freshmen year. While you were busy being you, they were busy wondering why their girlfriends watched you walk pass all the time. Anywho, I will see you tomorrow night."

Bernabe made a move toward the bathroom door but stopped when the door opened before he had a chance. A police officer walked in to the bathroom and noticed the two students. Tardiness was usually dealt with using the trusty baton, but the officer in question made no move toward his weapon. He reached up and pulled his helmet off his head. He shaggy hair was matted after many hours in a sweaty helmet. He smiled at his old peers for a minute.

"Lye, Alexis, you know you're late, right?" Will said. He leaned against the wall, waiting for them to admit their crimes.

"Yeah Will, I'm sorry. We were just talking about our results." Lye said.

Will laughed. It was an odd image to see someone in a police uniform laugh. He came over and hugged each of the boys. Before he met Lye, there wasn't anything in the world that would make him hug another person, let alone another man. But there was something about Lye that caused even the hardest of hearts to show emotion.

"I get it. Today is one of the busiest days for us here. There's always a pack of seniors in the bathrooms and hallways crying over their results. I had to get Officer Parker to walk into the women's restroom. There was a girl in there exclaiming how she was paired with the only attractive Mexican in her class." He scowled when he repeated the statement.

"What was her name?" Bernabe asked. His free nature was missing in the question. He was more than annoyed.

"Uh..." By all accords, Will didn't take much notice to the finer details. There was a problem, and he simply sent someone to fix it. "Alice? No, Elisa? Wait, I think it was Elsa. I take it you know her?"

"Yess . . ." he growled. "I think I need to explain to her I'm not fucking for equality. *The only attractive Mexican.* I'm not even Mexican; my family's from Ecuador!" he stormed out with anger.

Lye and Bernabe went to leave, but Will put his hand out to stop Lye. Once the door was closed; he spoke again, this time in a low whisper.

"That lead box in your bag. Does it contain drugs?" he asked. Lye had spent a good deal of his high school career convinced he was outsmarting the cops. To have someone blatantly ask about his contraband almost sent him running. Running would only prove guilt, so he stayed where he was.

"No. You know my mother, there is no way I would

make it to school alive if she even thought I was doing drugs." He smirked. But his friend would not return his smile.

"Lye...I know you're *different*," he said, keeping his voice in a whisper. "But others have noticed as well. Do not tell me what *is* in the box, but I would advise you to leave it home for the time being. I'm risking my ass telling you this, so please take my warning."

With that he patted Lye's shoulder and walked out the bathroom. Relief and fear rose in the back of Lye's mind. He had spent so much time making sure everything seemed okay. But apparently, he had gotten sloppy. He silently thanked Will for the warning and continued on with his day.

The tension of the morning evaporated across the school with the final bell of the day. While there were many people who weren't happy with the results they received; they still knew what they were supposed to do. Lye laughed to himself as he saw Bernabe talking to his new partner. Bernabe had lost his anger from earlier, but from where he stood Lye was sure he heard the word *Mexican* leave his friend's lips.

THREE

"A re you nervous?" Mrs. Davis asked. The entire family sat at the dinner table, all staring at the envelope that contained his future.

"A little bit." Lye said as he grabbed the envelope and opened it. He pulled out the paper. It was made of expensive stock; solidifying the importance of the details.

The tension of the morning had resurfaced. He looked at his score, and his heart leapt to his throat.

"I... I got a perfect score."

"What?" his parents said in unison. Their surprise had nothing to do on their expectations of Lye. They knew of his intellectual prowess. It was the probability of *anyone* making a perfect score that baffled them. Proctors let everyone know in every session of the graduation test that getting a perfect score was unheard of. Only Courtney, the only member who hadn't taken the test yet, seemed unmoved by the information.

"What does it say your skills are?" his mother asked.

He read more of the paper before answering. "Leadership, communication, problem solving, analytical, persuasion. Math. Weird, I never though math was one of my strong points."

"Alexis told us who your partner was, he wasted no time to tell us he won twenty bucks." Mr. Davis said, smiling at the realization his son had made a perfect score. He made a mental note to tell everyone in the hospital about it; smiling at the idea of proclaiming it on the intercom.

Lye searched for his occupation. There were usually two to three 'options' on the paper. The word option was used loosely, the student in question never had the choice. Either of these three could be the occupation the government decides to give them. The option was based upon the need of the locals, the skills of the student, and whether they could improve the workforce. Whether or not the student would enjoy the job had nothing to do with their decision.

Lye choked as he found what he was looking for. He stared at the paper for a few moments, forgetting he had three people waiting on his response.

"I don't have anything." He said in a timid voice. He looked at his parents for guidance. Shame and worry threatened to rise along with tears as he stared at the piece of paper. The tension of the morning swooped upon his shoulders as he stared at the blank space.

"Well, think of it this way. You are the first person

to have a perfect score in God knows how long." Mr. Davis began, trying to find the right words to help Lye's heart. "Which means, the protocol for a perfect score may have been forgotten. You are a source of infinite potential, and they don't want to waste that potential on a mundane job. So, don't think of it as a bad thing, it doesn't mean you don't deserve a job. This just means you exceeded the expectations of the government. Enjoy it." He said.

They were simple words, but the smile on Lye's face told Mr. Davis his words had worked. Mrs. Davis smiled a smile of pity at her son. Lye clapped his hands and brought his attention to Courtney.

"I'm going to get ready for the party. Tell me when you're ready to go."

She nodded and left. Lye hugged his parents and went to his room. He sat on the edge of his bed and stared at the results of the paper. Even with his father's words, the blank space where his occupations were supposed to be mocked him in its whiteness. He wished for a moment he could figure out what was being planned. Even those who scored lower than him received an idea of where they would be going at least. He chuckled to relieve some of his stress. *Everyone* had received a lower score than him.

He went to his dresser and pulled out a simple Justice High school shirt and went to his closest to pick a comfortable pair of jeans. Lye was simply a chaperone. He was quite fond of Michelle, but no one going to this party would be worried about what *he* was wearing, especially since it was daddy's little girl's birthday. Everyone's attention would be on her, and maybe Courtney. After he put on his desired clothes and grabbed a gray hoodie, he walked downstairs to wait on his sister.

"The keys are on the table," his mother said. She too had gone to change. She wore a simple red knee-long dress. Lye wasn't used to her wearing make-up. She notoriously went to work without it on. Tonight, she had drawn cat eyes with her mascara, and followed with a shade of deep red lipstick to match her dress. His father had put on a black tux. His shaven face suited what they were wearing.

"How long was I upstairs? Where are you going?" Lye asked.

His mother looked at him and smiled. She wrapped her arms around his father. "We've had years of practice in getting dressed quickly. Don't make that look, I didn't mean it like that. But we're going on a date. I like dates, and the kids are going to be gone for a few hours. Maybe we'll try to make another genius tonight."

"How dare you tarnish my innocence with such a nasty thought?" he asked to his parent's laughter.

Lye was grateful Courtney came downstairs before they had a chance to respond. Of all the outfits worn by his family, hers seemed the most out of place. She wore camouflaged pants, a black tank top, and combat boots. On her hip sat Lye's paintball pistol he had lost a few days prior. She still had her hair in French braids.

Lye took in the scene for the moment and grabbed the keys. If Courtney wanted to explain what she was wearing, she would do it in her own time. A joke rested on his lips, but he quickly put it away as he couldn't remember if the pistol was loaded.

"We're playing war games tonight for Michelle's birthday party. It was my idea. Dr. Cambridge had set up a paintball field in the backyard. Don't worry, I'll have more armor once the game actually starts." She stated, seeing the confusion on her brother's face.

"Is your boyfriend going to be there?" Lye asked.

She laughed, "No, but I'm sure Felix is missing you. Michelle keeps telling me Felix can't buh-*lieve* you are at the top of the class and not her." Her pigtails fell off her shoulders as she bent her head in deep thought. "What is it she called you?"

Lye perked up. *"Was it sexy?"*

"How *dare* you tarnish my innocence with such a nasty thought?" Mrs. Davis asked, her voice slick with sarcasm.

Courtney snickered. "I'm sure it was goof."

"I do love nicknames." Lye solemnly confessed.

Courtney put her hands up to protest the upcoming battle of wits. "Please shut up, I don't want to hear another lecture on dating. Not today."

Courtney and Lye stole a glance at their parents. Both of them shrugged, in their eyes, it was their duty to give unwarranted dating advice to their children.

"Cool. Cool." He noted. They walked their way to the front door before Mrs. Davis called after them.

"Remember to put your seatbelts on before the car goes off or it will stop in the middle of the road. Also, did you buy a gift for Michelle?"

Lye made a face somewhere between a smile and a grimace. "I forgot."

Their dear mother picked a bag off the floor with "Happy Birthday" decorated on the side of it. Lye reached for the bag, but she gave it to Courtney and muttered something under her breath.

"Remember to pull out your license when you reach the gate, you should be able to use it to get inside the manor. Courtney, make sure he stays out of trouble."

"I- I never get into trouble!" Lye felt a little hurt. Of course he caused trouble, but the times he got caught were few and far in between. Denying him his props for concealing his crimes was an insult.

Courtney grabbed Lye's wrist to lead him out the door, but not before he yelled something to his mother. "I have stayed out of trouble for two years now! I do not need to be handled by a pre-teen babysitter."

Mrs. Davis laughed, "Courtney, I will give you fifty dollars if I get not one complaint about my son tonight."

"Deal." She replied. She looked at Lye like a trainer in the presence of a new animal to her carnival. Lye began to sweat as he thought he could tell she was salivating at the idea of keeping him in check. Lye looked wearingly at the paintball gun on her hip. Only after they had walked outside of the red door did he realize what his mother had said under her breath:

"I bet you remember Felix's birthday."

Lye headed toward the mayor's manor. By this time in their lives it would have been an insult to ask if he knew the way. While houses rolled by, Courtney looked over to start conversation.

"Why don't you wear your armband anymore?"

He thought about the question as he turned out of the suburb. "I don't believe in that stuff, and so I won't wear them."

"But, it's the law-"

"Until an officer comes to my house asking me why I'm not wearing an armband. I will treat it as an unwritten law."

He looked over her way; she started the conversation, but he felt it was a good time for a lesson.

"Do you know why you wear the armband?" Lye asked.

Courtney looked at her arm and shrugged her shoulders. "I'm pretty sure Mom told me before, but I forgot. You mind telling me?"

"Sure thing, stank butt," he laughed as she squirmed from hearing her nickname "It allows people to know what religion you ally with. That's why you only wear it when you're in public. Red is for any religion that has ties with Christianity-though Catholicism is pink. They have to stand out. Green is for...I believe Islamic ties. Blue is for Judaism, and Purple is for Buddhism. I know there are a few more but I can't remember them off the top."

Courtney stayed silent a few moments as the gears

in her head turned. "I hear you, but I have only seen red armbands."

"Yeah... but you gotta realize we live in the Bible Belt. That's why you will rarely see anything other than red in this part of the state. But there are more, I have seen pictures of them in the memorial. It is a nice place to learn things you aren't learning in school."

"But do you think Lord President would like that?" Courtney asked.

"I really don't care what he thinks." It wasn't the smartest time to make that statement given the fact they were in a newer car. A car that came with microphones so the conversations would be recorded.

The sameness of the residential parts of town began to fade away to show the market and malls. There were lights everywhere, as many people who had free time came to this point in order to forget about their worries. Anything a man or woman could want could be found in the stores, even if what they wanted was a man or a woman. Lye had accidentally walked into a hidden brothel on more than one occasion. Video game stores and theaters littered the horizon. Even though he wasn't big into material things, the sight was spectacular. Music could be heard leaking out of the clubs blocks away. But that too faded away as they began driving toward a manor on a hill.

The car stopped at the gate. Courtney reached inside the console to get mom's ID card.

"Identification."

The automated voice came from a small robot perched near the entrance of the gate. It rolled around on four wheels, and its silver body gleamed in the low sunlight. Of all the words to describe it, 'cute' was the first that popped in Lye's mind. Lye put the car in park and pulled out his driver's license. The robot wheeled itself closer to the car and scanned. After a series of affirmative beeps, it wheeled back to its original position.

"Welcome, Davis Family."

The gates open and the car headed toward the entrance. The manor couldn't be more than seventy years old, but it was tailored to look from a much older time. The manor was made of stone, a nice six-thousand square foot house for those pompous enough to enjoy the life as a politician. An American flag flew in the front yard. Under the American flag flew another one, a red flag with gold letters stitched unto it. Golden letters that spelled the words 'America is Great'.

Lye parked the car and went to open the door for his little sister. With the sixth sense only friends had, Michelle opened the front door. Lye had noticed the paintball gun before Courtney did. In the time it took Michelle to aim and fire; Lye had opened the passenger door, grabbed his little sister, and ducked under cover. Five thuds hit the other side of the door while he sat under cover.

"You mother-" Courtney cursed, rising to send eight paintballs in the direction of front door. They both heard the yell of pain and stood up from behind the cover. Courtney had hit Michelle in the right shoulder. As they walked up, Michelle kept her hand on her shoulder, the other hand on the trigger of her new toy.

"That was unfair. We were not prepared, and the game doesn't start until everyone is here." Courtney said. Only her slightly raised tone of voice betrayed her satisfaction in hitting her mark.

Michelle smiled through her grimace. "You were the last person to get here girl. We were waiting on you." She took her attention off her best friend to look at the brooding teen in front of her. "Is Lye going to play?"

"Lye is going to sit himself down somewhere he doesn't have to worry about getting shot." He said smartly. Still he embraced the birthday girl, gently because of the welt growing on her shoulder. He made a notion not to make Courtney mad any time soon. It was a well-placed shot.

Michelle was one of the smartest children in her grade. Lye listened to Courtney talking about her before, and she mentioned on numerous accounts Michelle was almost always one point ahead of her in anything. She liked the rivalry that took a place in her friendship; it was important for the both of them.

"Shame. You're just like Felix. Still, thank you for coming Lye." Michelle beamed.

"I wouldn't miss it for the world." Lye said, disregarding the fact he had completely forgotten her birthday earlier this week.

The cry of pain had reached the ears of those inside, and a pool of middle schoolers stood at the door. Seeing Michelle's dyed shoulder, and the one holding the pistol. Lye could see them trying to decide who should be on Courtney's team. On the ride over, Courtney had mentioned there would be sixteen of them in all. The idea of all of them with weapons didn't sit well with Lye, but he shrugged his shoulders at the thought. He was only to worry about one solider in this battle, and he could do more than bet she would be able to hold her on.

"At any time, you can come in, we don't bite." Felix said as she walked toward the door.

Michelle and Courtney grabbed hands and ran inside the house, leaving Lye with Felix.

"I'm glad you didn't opt in for the whole Dorito look. Thought I'd mention that." He said.

She titled her head "I could've heard that last year, when it was an option. You know before-"

"Is that Lye?"

Dr. Cambridge stood behind his daughter. For the first time since Lye had met him, he was happy the mayor was interrupting a conversation.

"I'm happy your mother told you I wanted you to be here." His mother had failed to mention anything that resembled Dr. Cambridge's desire for him to be there, but Lye didn't have the heart to tell him that. "I have been meaning to talk to you for some time. If you would mind, could you meet me in the study? I'm sure you remember the way around this manor." He said smugly. Lye stole a glance at Felix, but she had become preoccupied with something on her shirt.

Dr. Cambridge wore a simple t-shirt and cargo shorts. He used to play football in college, but it was apparent his desk job had taken a toll on his physique. A body once laced with muscles showed little of its former glory. A belly had taken a place of abs, and his face showed more meat than it had since the last time Lye saw him in person. Unlike his daughters, Dr. Cambridge had chosen to go with the orange tint that went along with this regime. His hair had begun to get gray around the edges, and his stubble was almost all gray.

Felix moved out of the way as he walked past, making sure not to make eye contact. While passing Dr. Cambridge Lye caught a glimpse of Mrs. Cambridge. She made brief eye contact with him and hurried off before he had a chance to start conversation. This had always been their exchange, and he was sure it was on someone's request he never have a conversation with Felix's mother. Exactly who, Lye wasn't sure.

His trainer had already disappeared to enjoy the festivities. There was no reason for him to worry, he knew she would be the safest kid out there, and she could use the fifty bucks.

The study resided on the second floor of the manor. In order to get to it one had to walk past a mahogany staircase, three oil paintings of the family, a vase older than the state of Alabama, and a Persian carpet whose authenticity escaped him every time he had walked past it in the past. Dr. Cambridge's study looked exactly what anyone would expect from a misuse of taxpayers' money. The wooden desk, the mahogany wet bar, and chairs all came from the finest places.

Dr. Cambridge walked into his study with a mission.

"Lye, I've missed you, how have you been?" he asked, pouring two glasses of the liquid that had been the muse of Lye's temptation years prior. The mayor handed Lye a glass, which Lye accepted with a raised eyebrow.

Alarms went off in Lye's head. The idea of the mayor showing him any affection was as absurd as a germaphobe laying on a bed made of black mold. He eyed the mayor. The image was, like most things in his life, ironically laughable. If anyone of the girls at his school did drool over Lye like Bernabe said, they would look like the mayor's current state. His eyes were wide in expectation, and he leaned over his desk a little to close the distance between him and Lye. From the sound of tapping under his desk, Lye could tell the mayor couldn't keep his leg still.

"I severely doubt you've missed me. But I've been good. Is there any reason you wanted to talk to me? From the looks of it, you're waiting to ask me out on a date." He looked at the glass of whiskey in his hand, "Speaking of date, you should really take me on a date first before you offer me this. And at least wait a few years." He said.

"Lye don't be that way. I *have* missed you. You are such an intelligent... anomaly. I hear there is word you might become Valedictorian at your school. And you received a perfect score on your graduation test. To think such a man is so close to me."

Lye was convinced he was dreaming. Never had he thought the relationship between him and the mayor as 'close'. "You never answered my question. What do you want?"

"I've been meaning to talk to you for quite some time now Lye. Do you drink?"

Dr. Cambridge held out a glass of whiskey for a toast. The silence that followed was amplified by his lack of desire to put the glass down.

"Don't worry, there are no cameras in this house, but you would know-"

"Dr. Cambridge, if there is something you would like to talk about, I ask you do it like an adult." Lye interrupted. "All this beating around the bush is not helping your case. Felix and I haven't been an item in over two years."

Dr. Cambridge held up a hand before he started. "You are right, that was a little rude of me. Thankfully, I'm not here on a personal note, I am here strictly for business."

Dr. Cambridge sat down in his high-backed chair and signaled for Lye to sit. While Lye sat the mayor finished the rest of his glass.

"I have been hearing talks about you at your school. Did you know you would be the first person of color to be Valedictorian at Justice High school?"

Lye swished the whiskey around in his cup. "I would say it's more of a show of my parents' salary than a show of my race's intelligence. I'm quite sure not a lot of people who look like me can afford going to that school. But continue, I am the first black valedictorian at this school, does it tarnish the name?"

Dr. Cambridge continued to study Lye. If Lye had any doubt the mayor didn't completely love his wife, the doubt would have come from the assumption he planned to court Lye at that moment.

"You have kept perfect grades your entire time at this school. Like I said, we have noticed," Dr. Cambridge refilled his drink and sat upright, appearing somewhat taller now that he had corrected his posture. "The next election for mayor will not be for another ten years, and I'm obviously not getting any younger. How would you like to run Justice? You could have all of this..." he leaned back in his chair and opened his arms wide. Lye's eyebrow went even higher, he couldn't disprove his assumption Dr. Cambridge had rehearsed this speech.

"Because the election is in ten years, I will be announcing my choice for my replacement soon. I want that to be you. Many of the people in my team want it to be you as well. You are, I shall say, the perfect specimen. And with your looks, Justice will have the love of-"

"Nah," Lye interrupted.

Like an actor who was interrupted during one of his sets, Dr. Cambridge was stuck. He simply stared. "I'm confused. You would be mayor, on his way to governor. In fifteen years, you could be running the state. Don't you see the glamour and glory in this?"

Lye abruptly put down the glass.

"Well, this could be an assignment of a few things. Either you could want me to run for mayor as a token black guy, so a community of black people will believe they should listen to the words the government is saying. Or you could actually want me to be a part of this sick twisted thing we got going on around here, which, in my opinion, is actually worse than becoming a figurehead in this country."

The man in front of Lye deflated. There was something about the conversation that didn't seem right. Lye shouldn't have any say in what his job was. The entire process of the graduation test told him he had no choice in the matter. Yet here he was, with the representor of his city *asking*, not telling, him about this job.

"And what do you think you will do as a job? You are aware I am one of the members who decides what you do for the rest of your life? How about you think it over? That way you can realize what exactly you could be doing for your occupation? I think you're an amazing person."

Lye looked at the glass of alcohol and picked it up. He didn't have the nerves for whatever conversation they were going to have. The drink, even though it was chilled, burned as it went down his throat. "This is coming from the same man who told his daughter he would rather her die an old hag than date a boy like me. What changed your mind? Two years ago, you threatened me in this same room."

A snarl crept on to the mayor's face. He quickly covered it up with his smile again. "I was wrong. I didn't see the... the benefits of the relationship, and for that I apologize. If you would allow me to make up for that, I will do anything. I actually, have done something, as a token of my apology."

Lye put his glass back on the desk and sat back in

the chair. The drink had warmed him up, and he placed his hands behind his head, interlocking his fingers. "I'm guessing you pulled some strings to make sure I'd be marrying your daughter. I think this is the closest thing I will ever have to getting your blessings. But if you remember, she and I haven't spoken in almost two years. I would be remiss if I didn't mention the reason; I stopped talking to your daughter because of your wishes. Didn't you think that would have an effect on how we acted toward one another? I haven't had a conversation with her until today." He said.

Which was true, but that didn't mean it had been easy. Lye secretly wished he could go back to those days. But admitting that would give away his only point of debate.

"I'm aware. But I figured we should tie our two families together when we could." Dr. Cambridge said. He rapped his fingers on his desk. The conversation wasn't going the way he had wished it would, and his frustration was starting to leak. Lye, however, wasn't done making his point.

"I was hoping I would be chosen to become a neurosurgeon like my father. That way I can help people with their problems, no matter how privatized those problems may be. I have excellent grades in all of my classes, but I have always shown a little more enthusiasm for biology and anatomy and the like."

Lye could tell his words left a sour taste in the mayor's mouth. The scrunched brows and flared nose of the older man made that apparent. Lye's need to laugh was getting incredibly harder to ignore. In a government that spent most of its time telling citizens exactly what they were supposed to do, the idea of a grown man being told what to do by a high school kid was amazing.

Dr. Cambridge massaged his temples as he thought of the next thing to say "I will tell you this, if you are as smart as everyone is telling me, then I am sure you will make the right choice. I'm sure you wouldn't want anything bad to come of this." He stated. Even through his persistence, there was a burning question in the back of Lye's throat.

"Why isn't Felix an option? She is second in her class; she has literally grown up around politicians and knows the ins and outs of this place. She is very intelligent, multilingual, and has class. Her only disadvantage is that she's your daughter, and even that is an advantage, as I had stated earlier."

The mayor chuckled a bit. "We all know that women are too emotional to be in politics. Simple biology shows that."

Lye choked on several responses before he composed himself again. "Didn't you- I'm sure you *just* punched a member of the Senate last month because he voted against the bill you were trying to get passed. I'm quite sure I remember having a conversation with someone who watched that altercation go down."

The mayor quickly looked up, offended. "How did you know that? You just stated you and Felix don't talk the way you're used to."

A groan escaped Lye's throat before he had time to register it. "You *literally* had my sister in your presence.

That was the day you went shopping with her and Michelle? We had small talk when I came to pick her up that day?"

"Well, even if I had forgotten about that. It proves nothing."

There was a knock on the door. Both men ignored it as they sat in silence, each waiting for the other to answer the knock.

"I know you're not doing this for me. Are you doing this for her or for you?" Lye asked. The only answer was the knocking on the door.

"Come in." the mayor said, annoyance thick in his voice. His face softened when he realized the topic of their conversation was the one knocking. Her hair was wrapped in a towel, and she had on her old pink robe on. It was obvious this was the last thing on her pallet before she went to bed.

"I've come to get Lye. Mother said I should get a head start on my wifely duties." She said timidly. Both males snapped their heads at the words. The mayor was the first to recover, he simply smiled and waved for her to continue. Felix walked in and grabbed Lye's hand, leading him out the room. Once again, he was being led to a destination no one talked to him about. She led him upstairs to a balcony. After making sure no one could hear them, she turned her attention to Lye.

"Wifely duties?" Lye asked.

"I needed something my father would swallow to get you out of the room. I figured wifely duties would work better than just telling him I want to talk to you. I don't know what his thing is. When I told him my results, he damn near leaped with joy on the fact that you and I were paired."

Lye felt more at ease than he had in a while. It had nothing to do with the drink the mayor had given him, but the realization Felix was just as confused as him.

She's in on it.

"What did my father talk to you about?" she asked.

Lye threw the thought out of his mind. "He did everything except blatantly tell me he pulled strings to make sure we were paired. Before you ask, he didn't tell me exactly why. Apparently, he knew I made a good score."

"So, what did you offer him, a flock of sheep and some land for my hand in marriage? My father is breaking laws just because you make a good score on a test?" She asked. Like her father minutes prior, she looked at Lye with flared nostrils and lines of frustration on her face. Only this time, Lye didn't see it as a laughing matter.

"Felix, if you're being offered like sheep. I'm being auctioned. I had no idea this was going on. He wants me to become mayor in ten years, and then governor, I guess."

"And are you going to take that?" Felix asked.

Once again, alarms went off in Lye's head. None of this made sense; everything he had learned went against everything that was going on today. "What little individuality we have as people is going to die from starvation by the time we're twenty-five. I'm not exactly gung ho with the idea of giving that away before they take it. How's the party though? Has my sister started to miss me yet?"

She grabbed his arm.

"You really don't have to show me the way. I remember it."

The living room was filled with the laughter and shrieks that accompany any preteen party. The paintball game lasted a lot longer than anyone had planned. Lye's leash wasn't taking him into the living room, however. A sharp turn to the left took them away from the laughter and toward the kitchen. The mahogany staircase still gleamed a little in the moonlight creeping out from the windows. Rugs and animal skins lined the stone floor whose cold touch was indiscriminate. Lye kept looking around and confirmed the fact that there were no cameras in this house. He didn't realize how long he had been with the mayor until he looked at the moonlight.

"No, seriously," he started "You don't have to show me the kitchen, I know the way. Also, I think your dad is still mad at me about some internal things he's not telling his therapist, so-"

"Please shut up for a moment."

The lack of emotion startled him for a second. It was always hard to determine which emotion she felt. But there was no second guessing the authority she held in her voice.

"So we're being serious. What's wrong?"

Felix took a look behind her back and crossed her arms.

"Look, I don't know all the details, but I'm pretty sure father told you it was not only his decision to make. Of course, I couldn't be the decision, given my *disadvantage.*" There was a look of disgust at that word, the word many politicians used to describe the female reproductive system. "But you are the best candidate. And I don't mean that in a nice way. I have had to speak to five different people asking about how well I knew you."

Lye shrugged at the information. "So they know about us being an item before?"

She glared at him. Lye had seen her father do it before. He could promise the remake was better than the original. "Technically we're still an item, but I implore you. Oh wise Lye, do think of a second. I am not here speaking to you because I am mad at my asshole of a boyfriend. They weren't asking me how great of a kisser you are. Everything from your favorite color to why you spend so much time out of town every week. They had me tied to a damned lie detector test. What have you done to alert all this attention? I have seen more handshakes in this house after conversations concerning you than at his damn inauguration."

A weak smile crept across his face. "Thank you for caring, so I have a target on my back. Nothing new. I am not going to become mayor of this town though; I can tell you that. They'll have to kill me before that happens. I'm sure I can talk to your father again, find someone that can fill in my place. Thomas Shillington, they would love him. He's intelligent and white just like they like." He casts his eyes down, knowing what was coming next.

"For someone who talks about how his race needs to be represented more, I don't understand the hesitation..."

"My credibility for racial progress was confronted by naysayers the day I put a picture of me dating a Caucasian woman on social media." He shrugged off the look he was getting. "I'm not saying I regret either of those decisions, I was simply stating facts. And I do want those things, I just I don't want to be mayor. You and I both know someone higher up would try to use both of those agendas for their own. I would be nothing more than a guinea pig."

"You still don't get it." No longer did she keep the anger out her voice. "*He* was here Lye. Talking about you."

Lye didn't have to ask who she was referring to. The conditioned reverence in her voice gave that away. The man in the picture in every bedroom. The man who they saw on the television so many times it was only human nature to feel a sense of familiarity on his features. The man everyone was too afraid to talk bad about. At least, almost everyone.

"Lord President came here to ask about me?" He asked redundantly.

"Yes!" She almost yelled.

The laughter and shrieks had stopped a few minutes ago. There were a few giggles coming from the hallway and staircase, but other than that all was silent. A few members of the party could have gone to explore this house, or they could have been looking for a few missing members.

"Do you honestly think this is just about you?" Felix asked.

"I think this is just about money if you want me to be completely honest. If this was about getting more people of color around this town, then yeah, I would listen. But I doubt this is coming from anyone's heart. How much does your father make? Is it still three hundred thousand... or did that pay raise finally come through?"

"He actually got a pay cut because his eldest daughter was found with contraband her boyfriend gave her. Not that that changed anything about the way he sees me. He's had a stick up his butt ever since my blond hair turned brown."

The giggles started to get closer; there were several in the kitchen by this point.

Lye kept eye contact with Felix for a few moments and cast his eyes away "You're right. I'm sorry."

Her mouth clamped up as a look of surprise washed over her. A few feet away from the duo, an audible gasp could be heard. Lye turned his head in the direction of the gasp, already sure who the culprit was.

The culprit jumped to her feet and started at her older brother. She wore mascara across her face to match old-timey war paint, with a bandana around her hair. She still held his paintball gun in her hands, waving it around in the air as she yelled.

"I HAVE NEVER, IN THE HISTORY OF THIS THING WE GOT GOING ON HERE, HEARD YOU EVER SAY, THAT YOU WERE WRONG. WHY HAVENT YOU TOLD ME THAT?"

"First of all, why are we yelling? How much of that did you hear?" was the only response Lye offered.

Courtney pouted a little. "I heard enough to be out of fifty dollars when we get home, I know that much." Her pigtails whipped around her neck as she turned to look over her shoulder. "Y'all ready to move out? We're about to make a move on the mayor."

With those words seven boys and girls stood up, all wearing the same uniform and carrying fake guns. Courtney grabbed a walkie and started ringing "This is Jiffy to Bday, Jiffy to Bday, we have found the M.I.A soldiers. They seem to be in conversation, should we allow this to continue, or should we break it up? Over."

Lye raised my hands in the air in surrender. "Please tell Bday I am ready to come back to the station. I believe it would be best if I had an escort, that way I know I will get home safely."

The little army of children surrounded him, keeping their guns in sight for any enemy of their shared imagination. Courtney led this rescue party, constantly checking the corners and stopping the convoy. When Lye finally reached the living room (where Lye should have been in the first place) he saw the birthday girl.

Michelle wore a simple white dress, sitting on a throne that almost demanded everyone to bow. She wore a simple crown and carried herself in a way a fairytale wouldn't do justice. There were several welts on her shoulders and arms from stray paintballs.

"My lovely captain, I see you have found the deserter. I want to thank you for your courage, your grace, and your ability to pull him away from my sister."

"First of all-"

A sharp pain shot through Lye's ribs where Courtney had elbowed him. "Don't speak while the princess is speaking, your job is to do what she asks of you, not speak."

Lye rubbed his ribs. "I really think we're getting a little too into character here. I am sorry my princess, I ask that you forgive me for my ignorance. Allow me passage, so I may take our captain back to her home."

She placed her hand on her chin in a playful exaggeration of someone thinking. "I guess that's okay with me. You are allowed passage."

Not exactly waiting for his sister, Lye headed toward the door. Once they were headed toward the car, Lye brought his foot up and kicked Courtney in the backside.

"OW! YOU KICKED ME!"

"And you bruised me. Gotta love an eye for an eye, ammirite?"

They hopped in the car, and Lye headed toward their house. Lye made a mental note to figure a way best to explain the paint on the passenger door.

"Can I ask you a question?" Courtney asked.

"Are you going to ask me about what you heard from Felix and me talking?" he asked.

"Yes."

"Then no," Lye said abruptly. He realized his mistake and softened his voice. "I'm sorry sis, but I have a lot on my mind. And I can't answer any questions until I sort it out for myself. But when that happens, you will be the first to know."

Four

School was as mundane as ever. So much in fact Lye had registered nothing but the homeroom class, as Mrs. Peeves was bubbling again about graduation. The blue skies welcomed him as he walked out of school; the black birds still watching ever closely. Bernabe had offered to give him a ride to his house, but Lye had denied. He had to make a few stops before he got to Bernabe's house, and there was no real reason for Bernabe to tag along for this route.

He unchained his bike and wrapped the chain around his forearm. The black birds of Justice rarely went into Calera, as there was not as many people they thought mattered. The lack of black birds gave way to more crimes. It was always smart to have a weapon just in case things got out of hand.

The road to Calera was a straight away from Justice High School. The freshly paved roads and material attractions ceased as Lye passed over Calera bridge. Residents of Calera used to complain about this very bridge decades ago, before the size of Calera was cut in half. The right side of Calera had been combined with Saginaw and Alabaster to create Justice. The Alabama government couldn't find any profit in the left side of Calera, and so it was left as is. The complete disregard of this part of the city was evident as soon as Lye crossed the bridge. The roads hadn't been paved since Obama was in office. The scenery was calming though, there were more trees than buildings, and it made the cool air refreshing.

Lye continued to ride on his bike, thinking about what had gone on in his life in the past two days. The idea of him becoming mayor of the neighboring city disgusted him. His distrust in the mayor only caused more distrust in whatever circles they were causing him to jump through. There was a glimpse of hope, maybe he could make change in his city. Maybe if he was mayor, things could change for the better.

Or maybe you will become one of them

"Shut up." He said to the darker thoughts of his mind, pedaling faster. He hopped the acceleration would leave the thoughts behind.

Mayor Davis. A voice of the people. As corrupt as the people he hated. God bless America.

"I said shut up!" he yelled. He looked around to make sure there was no one on the road that would have seen him talking to himself. There was no one, and he was grateful. He didn't want to have to explain the situation. The first time he explained resulted in weekly therapy sessions.

The winding road finally gave way to buildings. But the buildings had nothing on the city he lived in. Calera looked as though someone placed it in a cracked time capsule. It was a sheltered kid whose parent thought they would be tarnished by the things they learned in public school. It was a small town, but it was nice. It was no ghetto, but it was evident that whatever taxes came to Calera was not used on the betterment of its people. Abandoned schools and stores littered the area. While Justice towered over Calera in its school system, its capitalism, and its small crime rate; Calera towered over Justice in one thing: sameness. No matter the race of its citizens, everyone in Calera treated everyone with respect. Black and white people, Christians and Muslims, they all treated each other with respect. The reason itself was simple: everyone here was poor.

Poverty didn't care of color or creed. Poverty wasn't sexist or racist; it took what it wanted no matter what dreams you had. No matter who you voted for, which god you prayed to, poverty was there to stay. To sleep in the bedroom without power, to prey in the cupboard without food. Poverty was there. The only way to live in poverty was to trust your neighbor, no matter what they looked like. Lye wondered at what point of a person's income did they stop caring about the people beside them. All that he could figure was it happened a few steps above the Alabama poverty line.

He parked his bike at a mom and pop store. It was a two-story building that took up half a block. The owners of the store stayed in the apartment above the store. In the center of the façade of the building lay a freemasons sign. The brick had been painted baby blue, which had becoming even lighter as the years went by. Of all the buildings in the town, this was one that did not listen to time's authority it must run down with the passing years.

Lye chained his bike and walk in.

There was one person in the store sat on a stool behind the counter. Lye smiled at her until he noticed that her eyes were red from crying.

"Mrs. Pike, are you okay?" he asked.

Through her sorrow, she hadn't noticed the new customer. Not that Lye was new, he made it a point to stop in whenever he came to this part of Calera. Over the years he had learned she was a widow with one son, but that didn't stop her from smiling and telling dirty jokes whenever he came in to the store.

She looked up at the familiar face and smiled. The smile was the summary of years of southern hospitality. It had no reflection on her current emotions.

"How are you doing Lye? I'm not doing well. I actually just received some bad news."

He dropped his backpack and went behind the counter to hug the old woman. No matter what was going on in the outside world, she always managed to put a smile on his face. Without her smile, the years she had seen wore on her. To describe her in any way was not pain, just tired. Her very soul was tired.

"If I may ask, what happened?"

She looked at him to check the sincerity in his face and broke out in tears again. "My son. I just got a call tellin' me my baby boy died. He was messin' with the blue crystal and his heart couldn't take the pressure. He died before the ambulance could get to him. I'm going to have to go to the coroner to identify the body." She said between sobs.

Three things were known for certain. People will die, people will get taxed, and people can find meth in Calera if they looked hard enough. The sounds of sirens were heard at all hours of the night in Calera, trying to save the latest victim of an overdose. There had been five overdoses in the past week. Lye always found sympathy for addicts. Even he wished he could run away from the grip of reality for a little bit. He knew addiction was more of an escape from pain than a run to pleasure. And like most people, Lye never thought he would be affected by someone's overdose. The reality of this unnecessary death never hit people until the tears of the living landed on their shoulders.

"I'm so sorry, is there anything I could help with? Do you need a ride to the coroner?" he asked, wishing to do anything that might ebb the flow of her tears.

"No. no, my granddaughter is going to take me to the coroner. I don't understand why the Lord has allowed me to outlive everyone. It's not right. Parents aren't supposed to bury their children; it's supposed to be the other way around. He didn't even get a good death."

A good death. Lye had read the concept of a good death in a textbook about the Civil War. A good death was the concept of a death with respect and dignity. A death full of last words and love. He wondered how many overdoses in Calera would be considered a good death. But that wasn't a conversation he could have with Mrs. Pike, not now.

After a few minutes of sobbing, she tapped the small of his back to let him know he could let go. "Bless your heart Lye. I don't know how many people would allow me to cry on them. Most people know me as the old lady who tells dirty jokes."

Through all the heartbreak he could feel coming from her, he couldn't help but grin. "But. . . you are the old lady who tells dirty jokes."

She reached up and pinched his cheeks. "And don't you let nobody tell you otherwise." She smiled again. This time of relief. "Did you need something, or were you just coming here to check in?"

"I always come in to check in with you when I'm in this part of town."

Lye regretted the words he said, as tears cascaded down her face once again. "You are such a good-hearted boy! Why couldn't my boy be more like you?"

Lye tried his best to show Mrs. Pike he felt sorry for her burden, but he couldn't muster the emotion. The facial expressions, the embrace... that he could do. But death by overdose was so common in this part of town, he couldn't muster the feelings to grieve along with her. To him, hearing someone overdosed gave way to the same emotion if someone told him they'd gotten a flat tire on the way to work.

"I'll be okay honey, do you need anything?" she asked again. He shook his head no, and after making sure she was okay once more, he left. He hopped on his bike and turned right, passing the abandoned Calera middle school. The space was currently being used by people who could no longer afford to live in their family homes. That meant there was an unusual number of police cars patrolling this area at nighttime. The Calera police department was one of the only things that received the taxpayers' money.

He pedaled even more as he came closer to his destination. An antique football field greeted him first. Besides the field stood another abandoned building. The lack of black birds allowed sneaking into a place in Calera relatively easy. The words Roy Down Memorial stared out from the front of the building. There was once another word, a fourth word behind Memorial. Someone had taken it down decades ago, long enough that the only evidence was the outline of an L where the word began.

Lye brought his bike around the back of the Memorial. After Lye opened the door, the familiar smell of paper and dust flew into his nostrils. He pulled out a flashlight from his back to look around at the rows of contraband sitting on shelves. He had looked at the spines of everyone here. Most of the shelves were filled with different contraband on different subjects. There were only two that were missing. It was always the same two: whichever one he carried in his backpack, and The Sonnets of William Shakespeare. He had no idea where the latter was, but by now he was sure it had been destroyed.

He pulled out the lead box from his backpack and opened it, pulling out his copy of Hamlet. Lye wasn't sure he could call it his copy, but everyone else was afraid to go near it. It had been condemned. The fact it had the word Memorial on it was the only reason Lye could fathom why it stood. He placed the contraband back on the shelf. When he turned to walk out, his heart drop as he was frozen in fear.

A dark figure stood outside the door, peering in to see what he was doing.

Lye thought of a way to run without his face being seen. The light from his flashlight was shining away from him, but there was still a good chance the perpetrator got a good look at his face. Before he had a notion on what he should do, the person on the other side of the glass door disappeared. Lye heard the familiar sound of the back door opening; the footsteps of someone walking toward him. His heart was ready to burst when the door to the sanctuary opened and he stared at the grin in front of him.

"I figured I would find you in here." Bernabe said.

"What are you doing? You can get arrested if you're caught." Lye yelled in a hushed tone.

Bernabe stared at his best friend; allowing the irony of the situation to simmer.

"Right. I could also get arrested if I'm caught. But only one of us cares about it." Lye grabbed his put the lead box in his backpack and walked out. Lye grabbed his bike and they crossed the street toward the more residential place of the town. Bernabe's house lay on the other side of the train tracks that went through the town. His house was surrounded by trees. That, along with the absence of black birds, made his place the perfect spot in order to discuss things without worrying about hidden ears.

Before they got to the door, however, Bernabe put his hand on Lye's shoulder to stop him from moving.

"Mom's not doing well. It would be best if we talked outside."

Lye looked back at the door and agreed with his friend. He parked his bike on the side of the house and motioned Bernabe to lead the way. They continued to walk down a county road leading to nowhere. They passed a few houses on the way, but no one seemed to be interested in what the two seniors were doing. Once they were away from the houses, they began to talk.

"So... you and Felix. What happened?"

Lye looked at his best friend. He knew once he told him what had happened, Bernabe would tell him that people make mistakes, that he couldn't have known what was going to happen when it did. Bernabe would make a joke and ask how he had been so hard on himself these past two years.

But Bernabe didn't know what it felt like to mess up the way he did. They continued down the road aimlessly. There was enough sunlight left in the sky for them to walk safely.

"Okay, so two years ago, when we were a thing, I wanted to give her something special. Something I know no boy could ever have given her before. And one day, I was reading, and I came across an article of contraband written by some dude name William Shakespeare. There was a lot of things about love in it, so I thought she would like it-" Lye looked over at Bernabe. A part of him wished Bernabe would stop him, to correctly guess what happened so Lye wouldn't have to say it for himself. But Bernabe did no such thing. He simply continued to listen while his friend relived his guilt. "She loved it. But she got caught. At the time I didn't know she got caught reading it. But the mayor had a hissy fit. Even though he knew it was me, there was no evidence *I* had done it. And she wouldn't give me up, so she got the punishment for it."

"So, she's been mad at you all this time?" Bernabe asked. There was no traffic on the broken road before them, but it was possible the two of them may have been the first people to use this road for the past few weeks. The view carried on for miles. There was an old junkyard, filled with cars whose owners had long expired. Not even Lye's curiosity would allow him to enter.

"No. She just went on with her life. She never talked about where she was for the month she was out of school, nor what happened to her. If you remember, one day she was gone, and then a month later she was back without missing a beat. And there was no evidence to show that she had gone through anything." Lye said.

"Well, you're a piece of shit." Bernabe finally answered.

"Hol' up, what did you say?" Lye asked. This was not what Lye expected from Bernabe. He stopped moving for a second to take in the words he heard. "You're right. I never should have given her that book."

"That's not why I'm saying you're a piece of shit. Don't get me wrong, that does make you a piece of shit. But the reason why I'm claiming you to be a piece of shit isn't that. It has been two years since that situation happened. And you have no idea what happened to the woman you've been paired with? You don't know the consequences of your actions? The great Lye Davis, who speaks on all the injustices in the nation, but he can't see when he does something wrong. And if he does, he ignores the damage. Lye, she was gone for an entire month, of course she went through something. But you never bothered to ask what happened. That is what makes you a piece of shit."

There was no cloud in the afternoon sky. The walk would have been enjoyable if not for Bernabe's words.

"So, what is going on with your mother?" Lye asked. Bernabe was right. The wrongs of his government were easy to see. Easier still to talk about. The wrongs of his own nature were a more difficult conversation.

"We're going to talk about that in a minute, but we're not changing the subject. This is a two-year fuck up, but you spend so much time speaking on national problems; you never once thought to look inside yourself and see that maybe you weren't doing it in the best of manners? Lye, you're better than that. Yes, you hurt her, yes, you did a terrible and inexcusable thing, but you gotta man up and talk about it. I'm not going to be at your wedding if you don't."

They continued to walk as Lye digested his words. Without missing a beat, he explained the situation a little more.

"Dr. Cambridge admitted to me he pulled some strings to make sure the two of us are paired together. I don't know why, but he told me last night."

"I'll let you off the hook long enough for you to explain to me what happened." Bernabe answered. They slowed their pace a bit. If they continued much longer, they would arrive at the old Calera City Hall.

Lye told him everything: about going to the party, about the weird way the mayor was treating him, even about the wifely duties joke. He left nothing out.

They had stopped walking; Bernabe and Lye looked at each other while Bernabe took it in. Suddenly a look of intense aggression swept over Bernabe's face as he raised his hand.

"Why. In. The. World. Would. You. Do. Something. So. STUPID." Bernabe said, bringing his hand down with each word. Lye easily swatted most of the blows away, if nothing more he was rather annoyed with his persistence.

"Look, I know you're mad. But you gotta remember, some of this stuff was out of my command. It's not like I went to Dr. Cambridge and said 'hey man, I know you hate my guts but I was wondering if I could be your lapdog in exchange for your daughter's hand in marriage'" he stopped himself as he thought of his own analogy. "Wow that was a long example- anyway, I didn't do most of this. I'm sorry if-"

Lye stopped talking. There was a familiar sound in the background. The ear-splitting sound of sirens. Both boys looked around, wondering if they would see blue lights or red. But Calera was pretty small; there was a good chance whatever was the cause of the sirens wasn't on this road.

"You need to figure out something." Bernabe said.

"Oh yeah? I was just thinking; we could maybe

have a riot? Would that be good for you? A riot?" Lye asked none too kindly. While he had blocked most of the blows Bernabe threw his way, a couple had reached their mark, and it didn't feel nice.

The sirens were getting louder; Bernabe and Lye looked toward the way of the sound to see two police cars coming in their direction.

"What do you think happened?" Lye asked. The two boys ran over to the other side of the road; making sure they would not be in the way once the cars past by them. The cars were a little over half a mile away from them, and they were closing in quickly.

"Someone might have snuck in that old school again. It's been colder at night around here, so it would make sense someone has been seeking shelter. Honestly, it's becoming a fire hazard."

Lye nodded his head in agreement. The middle school usually housed homeless people, but the antiquated Calera High was beginning to get its own following. The cop cars didn't speed by them. As they approached, they slowed down and parked. The sirens and lights still blared and flared, and two cops came out of their respective cars.

The one closest to them began to walk toward them. "Excuse me, we heard there was a disturbance around here? A lady called and said two suspicious looking men were seen walking down the road."

"I'm sorry officer," Bernabe said. Bernabe, for the most part, always showed respect to authority figures. "We've been walking for a few minutes now, and we haven't seen anything." Which was true. Throughout their entire walk, they saw no suspicious looking people, or people for that matter.

Lye gritted his teeth with the realization. "I think he's trying to say *we're* supposed to be the disturbance. May I ask what we were accused of doing?"

The second officer made his way to the boys. "We're just doing a check-up; an elderly lady was worried about what was going on in her neighborhood."

"Right. All the drugs that go on in here, but God forbid two teenagers go on a walk in the afternoon. Even if we had a curfew, it wouldn't be anywhere near the time for it to be enforced."

Bernabe looked over at Lye. "I don't think it would smart to make 'em mad. I don't want five warning shots in my back because you can't shut your mouth."

The officer looked the boys over and asked for their names. After they gave them, they also asked what part of Calera they lived in. Bernabe pointed over his shoulder with his thumb.

"I don't live in Calera. I live in Justice." Lye answered nonchalantly.

The officers chuckled.

"You know it's a felony to lie to an officer, right? Seriously, where do you live?"

Maybe it was the way the officer said it. Maybe it was the fact Lye still couldn't digest what happened to him the past few days. But Lye opened his mouth and disregarded everything Bernabe said about warning shots.

"Firstly, it's only a felony to lie if I have warrants, in which I don't. Secondly, I can't think of any reason why I couldn't live in Justice? Can you explain? If you're saying that based on how I look I doubt you really don't want me to run with that."

The smile on the officer's face disappeared as quickly as it grew. "Alright, put your hands behind your back, both of you. I'm getting tired of listening."

"What the hell did Bernabe do?" Lye asked.

"I would also like to know what the hell Bernabe did." Bernabe said, casting a dirty look at Lye.

But the officers didn't listen. They handcuffed the boys and threw them in the back of the cop cars. If stares had power, the look Bernabe was giving Lye could spoil chocolate milk.

"I could kill you right now, you know that?" Bernabe threatened.

"Okay, your breaking point was five warning shots in your back. While your hands are behind your back, you are very much alive and well." A small jabbing sensation startled Lye as he realized that Bernabe's elbow was resting on his ribs. "Hey, could you move your elbow a little? It kinda hurts."

"Does it hurt?" Bernabe asked, feigning concern.

"Now that you mention it, it does hurt a little." Lye said, not noticing the lack of sincerity in his friend's voice.

"Then no. I won't move it, you piece of shit."

"You know you love me."

"While that is very true, it does not negate the fact that my best man is a piece of shit."

They sat in silence for a few moments before Lye broke it. "How are we going to get out of this?"

The officer finally returned to his car after talking to his partner. He put the car in gear in started driving toward the police station.

"Well, lucky for us, we do have someone who is acquainted with laws and the such, and I'm sure you have her number memorized." Bernabe said, giving Lye a look that explained more than he ever wanted to hear.

Lye looked out of the window. Calling Felix never occurred to him. Giving in to the stereotype of calling his girlfriend to bail him out of jail left bile in his mouth. Still, calling his mother to bail him out of jail would be a death sentence to both boys.

"I don't remember her number." He lied, he continued to look out the car window.

"I'll make a bet. If you don't have her number memorized, I will kindly ask the cop driving us to give me those warning shots."

The boys sat in silence on the way to the station. They didn't say much until Lye got his phone call.

"What did you do Lye?" Felix said over the phone.

"How did you-"

"I got a collect call from the Calera police station. I don't think Alexis has my number. So, what are you being charged with?"

"I-I don't know."

She cursed over the phone. "You don't know what they're charging you with? I'm at the mall right now, once I'm done, I'll come and get you."

"You're at the mall?" Lye asked. It wasn't a rare occurrence he would become sidetracked by new information, even during the most serious of times.

"Yes. I'm at the mall, we all have things we like to do after school. Not of all us go home and brood."

"I feel you're mad."

There was a long pause on the other end of the phone.

"I'll answer that question when I get there and have all the information. Tell Alexis I'll be there within an hour."

"How do you know he's with me?"

"You're at the Calera police station. I'd be more surprised if he wasn't there with you."

She hung up the phone, and Lye was brought back to his cell.

"Is she bringing her Dad here?" Bernabe asked.

"I don't know. To be real I don't think I want to see him for a few years."

"You realize-"

Lye ran over and placed his hand over Bernabe's mouth. "Yes, I realized what this looks like. No need to bring it up."

An hour passed before an officer came back to their cell. He came around with a sheepish look on his face. He tried his best not to make eye contact with the boys.

"Davis, Bernabe, you're free to go."

That was it. The three of them walked in silence as he took them to the front of the police station. Once the boys walked through the final door, they saw Felix waiting for them. She sat in the waiting room, wearing a cream floral dress. A shopping bag sat next to her on the floor as she waited for them.

"Boys." She said without looking up from her phone.

"Hello Felix," they said in unison. Neither could figure out what had happened, so they stood idly, waiting for Felix to continue. After a few minutes she put her phone up and looked up at the boys. She intertwined her hands, covering her lips with her index fingers as she took the two in. She picked up the bag and held it out with her hand.

"Lye, take this, go in the bathroom, and change. We have a date today."

"Why- yes ma'am."

Lye grabbed the bag and went to the bathroom.

Bernabe looked at Felix with admiration, but reverence stopped him from saying anything too foolish. Felix looked at him and smiled. "It's been awhile since I've seen you out of school Alexis. C'mon, chat with me." She smiled as she patted the seat next to her.

For a moment he thought about it. Another glance toward the bathroom, and he hesitantly sat down.

"What did you do?" he asked. While he was happy, he was outside of the cell, the lack of information made it appear that she had done magic.

"Lye called me. I came here to see what the charges were. Thankfully for the two of you, being a smartass isn't exactly a crime. I berated the officer to see what they were holding you for, and when they came up with nothing, I told them to let you go."

Bernabe sat next to Felix; his eyes wide like a child sitting next to a superhero. "And they just listened to you?"

Felix blushed a little. "I really didn't give them a choice. We may treat Calera like a different city, but it's really a subdivision of Justice. I reminded them of that small detail. A reassortment of citizen's taxes wouldn't do this department well."

"You threatened their pay?" Bernabe looked around. None of the officers wanted to make eye contact with Felix, which made her story even more believable.

Bernabe was sure they would breathe a little easier once she left.

"Women have been controlling nations from the sidelines ever since men had orgasms. My father would never change taxes just on my own input. But he has a hard on for Lye, and I could very well use that angle. I'm not going to, but I needed them to understand I could."

An officer peered behind the bulletproof glass at the couple waiting for Lye. His lips were peered up in a sneer as he walked by. Neither of them paid any attention to him.

Lye finally came out of the bathroom; his school uniform now in the shopping bag Felix had handed him. He was dressed in a lavender dress shirt and black slacks. He had rolled the sleeves of the shirt so it ended in the middle of his forearms. He tried to smile as he looked awkwardly down at the black dress shoes he was wearing.

"How do you know my sizes, and why do I have to wear this?" he asked. Bernabe was trying hard not to laugh. He had never seen Lye in anything that could resemble dress clothes.

"I texted your mother. And lavender is my favorite color. It looks good on you," she looked over at Bernabe; stopping his laughter, "Wouldn't you agree?"

Unbeknownst to the trio, the officer behind the bulletproof glass kept sneering at them. The officer behind the glass had seen enough. He walked into the lobby; his well-polished shoes barely making any noise as he walked.

"Are these people with you ma'am?" he asked.

Felix responded with confusion on her face. "Of course. Why else would I be sitting with them?"

The officer didn't seem impressed by her statement. "Are you sure they're not bothering you. I can make them leave if you need me to."

Felix stopped what she was doing. "I appreciate you looking after me, but I promise the only threat these two are to me is a major headache." There was no malice in her voice; she answered without any sarcasm.

But that didn't satisfy the officer. He clenched his fist. Felix had threatened the entire police department, but this particular officer wasn't in the building at the time. He had no idea who he was talking to. "You're not dating that- that *boy,* are you?" He said, pointing a stubby finger at Lye. The officer kept his glance at Lye's disheveled afro, and the lanky demeanor in which he stood. There was no logic in his mind that could help him comprehend how the two could be dating.

Lye opened his mouth to say something, but Felix put her hand up to stop him. She put her phone in her pocket (not before announcing that her dress had pockets) and stood up. Without taking her eyes off the officer, she walked over to Lye and wrapped her arms around his neck.

"This boy, yes, I'm dating him. He's actually been chosen to be my partner, so you could say we're engaged. I must admit he is very lucky to have me. I would tell you about the sex, but we haven't had our wedding day yet."

The officer's behind the bulletproof glass tried their hardest not to pay attention to what was going on in front of him. The officer staring at Felix, unaware of the situation, continued. "You have to be lying. You would never be paired with-"

His outcry was interrupted as Felix firmly kissed Lye on the lips. Lye kissed her back once the surprise washed over him, and Bernabe laughed so hard he fell on the lobby floor.

Felix wretched her head back and wiped her mouth. "I'm sorry, he's a drooler. Do you have any other questions officer?"

The officer clamped his mouth shut, turned on his heels, and walked away. The fumes of his anger were evident. He attempted to slam the hydraulic door but failed. He looked back to see if anyone had seen his failed attempt and doubled back on his anger once he realized that Felix kept her eyes on him. The anger behind her discolored eyes dwarfed whatever beliefs ignited his own anger. He thought it best not to say anything else to her.

Once he left, she turned toward the delinquents. "Now, Bernabe-please get off the ground, you're embarrassing yourself- we're going to drop you off. Please take Lye's bike to school tomorrow so he can pick it up. And Lye, just stay in my sight. I don't need you getting into more trouble."

She walked toward the door and stood.

Bernabe clumsily rose up to his post on the floor and walked toward Lye. "Why is she just standing there?"

"She's waiting for me to open the door for her." Lye replied.

"I forgot how much I missed her being in our lives." Bernabe said, following Lye as he opened the door and walked her to the car.

***

Felix and Lye stood in line at Five Guys, and the heat inside the restaurant was causing Lye to sweat a lot.

"While I can't complain, why are we at Five Guys? I thought we were going on a date?"

"I go to Five Guys every week. They have the best burgers, and I am wearing a dress, so you had to dress accordingly."

Lye stayed silent for the rest of the walk. The cashier looked up from his register and noticed the regular.

"Hey Felix!" he said. He could've been no more than fifteen. He still had hope in his eyes. Lye envied the brown eyes looking back at him. He couldn't put an exact date on the day the light left his own eyes, but he was sure it was around the same age.

"Hey Scooter. I'll be getting my usual."

"Gotcha, large burger all the way with a large fry, and a chocolate milkshake. And what will the gentleman have?"

The couple had to stiffen their laughs at the idea of Lye being a gentleman.

"I'll take the same thing. Um, no mushrooms though."

The boy nodded as he put the order in. Felix found a booth in the furthest corner of the restaurant and sat down.

"I have to tell you a story, that's why we're here. I know I don't have to tell you this but remember where we are, and what's in double jeopardy."

Lye nodded. He looked around the lobby and saw six cameras watching. Two were focused on the corner in which they sat. Double Jeopardy meant she couldn't get arrested for crimes she was already punished for. But Lye, if he was caught on any camera admitting to a crime, could very well be. They sat down, and Lye found it hard to swallow as he waited for Felix to start.

"We're going to talk about that month I missed from school." She said, not waiting to see any sign of affirmation on Lye's face. "I was found with contraband two years ago by my father. Given he was my father and there were no cameras in the house, I thought I would walk away scot-free, but I was wrong. Dad went ballistic; the moment he caught me reading he called the police, afraid his good name would be associated with criminal activity. The police came to get me within an hour."

She stopped for a second to gather her thoughts. Her eyebrows scrunched every time she mentioned her father. Other than that, there was little emotion tied to the story.

"Of course, I was scared, I thought I was a little trust fund baby going to jail for the first time. In hindsight, I would have preferred jail. To this day I don't know the name of where they took me, no one ever told me. The first thing they did was strip me naked-"

"They made you strip?" Lye asked.

"I didn't say that. I said they stripped me naked. Anywho, they stripped me naked and tied me to a metal table. It was cold. Very cold. For some time, it was so dark I couldn't tell if anyone else was in the room. I think I was in the room for thirty minutes before *He* came in..." she trailed off, expecting Lye to interject. She noted his silence and continued. "I guess Lord President makes a trip when crimes such as that happens. There must be few of them within the country, it would take a lot of time to go to *every* case. I knew him from his voice. I still couldn't see anything. After a little soul searching, I figured the room wasn't dark; I was just blindfolded. The cold I felt on my head wasn't from a draft in the room; they had shaved my head.

"Lord President explained to me why I was there. The contraband I acquired used to be called books before they were illegal, and getting caught with one was considered treason. I thought I'd been there for thirty minutes, but he told me I'd been there for an entire day already. The lack of light and clocks had my inner clock all wrong. That's what scared me the most up until that point: I had lost my track of time. The next thing on my mind was the smell of metal. Not the table I was tied to, but- hot metal. And then the heat. I felt-our food is ready."

Lye had forgotten where they were, and the fact they had gotten food. He rose from his seat and headed toward the counter where Scooter waited with their food. Guilt no longer riddled his mind; it wasn't just a slight rain he felt when he usually thought of the time Felix disappeared. It was far worse. It came in waves, crashing over one another before the wave could reside back into rational thought.

You really are worthless.

"Not right now." He whispered to the voice inside his head.

The one person you loved, and you caused her all this pain. And this isn't the worst part!

"I said shut up!" he whispered.

"Sir, I haven't said anything."

Lye snapped back into reality to see himself face to face with Scooter.

"I'm sorry. I was- I was in my head a little."

"No, you don't have to explain. It happens to me too at times. I'll be having a bad day and *BOOM*, the devil on my shoulder has gotten drunk and decides to tell me how terrible I am. It's okay." Scooter said. Even when he described what Lye had just went through, he kept the little light inside his eyes.

The amount of food on the tray was massive. There was no question on whether they could finish the entire meal. Lye questioned Felix's thoughts on their attire. The burger she ordered threatened to shoot ketchup on his new shirt before he had a chance to sit down and eat it.

He came back to Felix and sat down. At the sight of her food, her eyes widened with glee, oblivious that she was in the middle of a horrible story. She grabbed her burger and tore into it, only stopping when she realized that Lye hadn't touched any of his food.

"Aren't you hungry? I didn't see you get any food in the cafeteria."

"I'm extremely hungry, I'm just emotionally invested in seeing whether you'll get stains on your dress."

"Honey, I've been around politicians all my life. The last time I got stains on a dress, you we're still crying to your mother because you wet the bed." The finality in her voice gave no room for questioning, but Lye still took the time to remember the last time he had wet the bed. For the sake of his pride he kept the age to himself. After giving up, he tucked in to his own food. Felix didn't resume talking until she had slurped the last part of her milkshake up.

"Where was I? Yes. The next thing sensation I felt was burning, not my entire body, just a certain point, right below my last rib. I heard yelling, and it took me a few moments before I realized it was me yelling. I was crying, yelling, and in pain. I could smell barbecue, and I threw up when I put two and two together. It's a terrible thought, knowing it was my own flesh burning. I'm grateful I was blindfolded. I wouldn't like the image of me tied to a table covered in my own tears and vomit to be in my head.

"There were speakers in the room. And at the time of the branding they kept chanting something about books being bad. I can't remember the exact words; I was distracted by my own pain. They had to make sure the branding would always show, so they placed the burning metal on me three more times just for safety."

She stared at Lye. Fear had pushed its way into her gaze as she thought of the table. It was the first time Lye had seen such an emotion from her.

"Everything was metal. For a few days, they would come back to see if it had healed. If it had healed more than they wanted it too, they would brand me again. All the while asking me where I got the book, who gave it to me, why I wouldn't give them up. Every time they would come with the branding iron, they would continue to say the same thing. 'Books are bad. America is great. Books are bad. America is great.' It got stuck in my head. It was a tapeworm that wouldn't leave. Soon enough I stopped crying, those words were the only thing I could think of. The only thing I could say. I don't know how long I stayed on that table. They fed me after the first few days. But it was hell."

Lye swallowed the last gulp of his drink. "I'm sorr-"

"The worst thing wasn't the torture; it wasn't getting branded and having my head shaved. It wasn't even the fact I still have the words 'books are bad. America is great' stuck in my head to this day. It was when I returned home, and you didn't have the nads to speak to me. You and I haven't spoken in two years. Not since I came back. Did you know I had to wear a wig for most of that time? I couldn't wear my natural hair until last summer. I went to school every day, hoping my then boyfriend would give me comfort. Would try to reach out. And what did Lye do? He avoided me. He decided not to look at what had happened."

The venom in her words was hard to ignore. Lye sat with his head down.

"You have people in high places placing bets on you. Trying to see how they can use your potential for their own means. There are more interracial pairings in this school year than I've ever seen, and I'm sure it has to do with my father covering his tracks on putting us together. So, if you're still going to stay on this crusade of the government is evil, I need you to understand something: there are consequences for your actions. And sometimes the consequences fall to those who love and look up to you. Do you understand?"

He nodded. Afraid to let his voice give himself away.

"I promise nothing like that will ever happen to you again. I'm sorry." He said.

Felix laughed a mirthless laugh. It was unlike her to be so ghoulish, but he knew that he deserved this punishment.

"He says sorry now. Listen, whether I want to or not, I'm stuck with you. But we have a lot to work through before I can trust you again. And don't tell me sorry now. You don't mean it now; your guilt is talking for you. Tell me you're sorry once you've had time to think this over. I am here to help. I am on your side. But no matter the love I have for you Lye, I swear, if I have to go through something like that again without your support, I will castrate you and sew your sack into a necklace."

Lye looked up at her. Her determined look, along with the finality in her voice, allowed for no question on whether she was telling the truth.

FIVE

March rolled in without a nuisance, there was little talk about Lye's lack of occupation, and school seemed to go without a problem. Lye sat in his backyard, watching Courtney as she practiced for cheer tryouts.

"How was that Lye?" she asked. The sweat of her brow fell in flecks. Mother Nature didn't care about the change of months when it came to Alabama. It was supposed to be spring, and the high of the day was a steady seventy degrees. It had been that way for the past two weeks. Lye searched the evening sky for any black birds. He was sure it had nothing to do with him, but there had been a slight increase since his date with Felix.

The children were startled by the sound of the backdoor opening. They stopped what they were doing to see their mother standing there.

"How is she doing?" she asked.

"We've been going at it for hours, and I think she's

ready to be captain of the varsity team. She wanted me to practice with her, so there's a good chance I might try out as well." Lye said, shaking the pompoms in his hands.

"That's good to hear. I need the two of you to come in now, The Choosing is about to start." She said. Courtney followed suit with glee. But at the reminder, Lye's legs turned into mush. He would much rather practice with his sister than watch the Choosing.

The Choosing was a program that came on television once a year in March. The entire existence of this program made the graduation ceremony obsolete, but tradition was tradition. It was an unspoken agreement The Choosing wasn't to be watched unless it concerned you or your family. It showed the roster of the local schools, along with the job the student would have once they got out of high school. Their partners and skills were not shown; that was no longer important. The Choosing always came on the first Sunday of March. Since it always showed on a Sunday, there was an awkwardness that always followed. Students looked at one another with envy and anger the following day; having to pass by people who had received their dream jobs.

Lye walked into the living room to see the television already showing the news reporter on the screen. He was a well-dressed older man. He looked the epitome of what a news reporter should look like, down to the parted hair too black to be natural.

"We have now received the results of the two thousand ninety-eight graduating class of Justice High School. For those who have never seen this program before, I would like you to know that all results are final.

Some of you will believe we have made a mistake with these, but I can assure all students and parents, these have been thought over with the greatest of leaders and brains . . ."

The reporter continued his speech, reiterating the things Mrs. Peeves said when the students first got their results. He continued to speak as Lye's heartbeat continued to rise.

"Before we show you the results, we would like to announce the Valedictorian of this year. It is our mayor's very own Felix Cambridge. A very bright girl I would say; very easy on the eyes . . ."

Lye blocked out everything after that until the roster came up. The names popped up in reverse alphabetical order.

Jonnie Yates. Plumber.

For once Lye wished his name started with another letter, he would have to wait the entire time to figure out what he was supposed to be. As the names continued to come Lye wondered why so many students had to attend his high school.

David Willburn. Teacher.

"Well, that makes sense. He's been wanting to be a teacher since sixth grade." Lye said to no one in particular. His family were too glued to the television to notice.

Zachary Hendrix, mayor.

Lye stared at the five letters on the page, confused. He had not mentioned to his family about the conversation he had with Dr. Cambridge, so they didn't share his confusion. He had assumed, even though he didn't want to do it, he would be the mayor of the city. And even if he hated the idea, the fact he knew where he had to go gave him some clarity. Staring at the screen had him floating in uncertainty. For the umpteenth he felt the tension he did when he stared at the blank space on his test results.

He sat down on the couch and waited for Davis to come on the screen.

William Davis, electrician.

The entire family sat on the edge of their seats, knowing that Lye would be the next name to appear on the screen. The name of William Davis stayed on the screen for what felt like an eternity. Later than sooner it started to fade, allowing the next name to appear.

Cecilia Clyde. Nurse.

Lye froze as he watched the name appear. He no longer noticed his family over the horror he was seeing. Still, through his horror he paid attention to the careers of his two companions (Alexis Bernabe, Veterinarian, and Felix Cambridge, Lawyer); other than that, nothing registered. Not the questions of his little sister, not the outcry of his mother. He couldn't hear anything.

Lye continued to stare at the screen, even as the reporter wrapped up his session. He stared at the screen even as the credits to the program ended. Distraught blossomed in his chest. He wouldn't graduate. He had never heard of anyone who didn't graduate. He forced himself to get off the couch, but before he could move, the presidential seal appeared on the screen.

Lord President was having a press conference, he stood behind the pedestal with a smile. His spray tan made him look a few years younger. Lye was sure the full brown hair he adorned was either fake or dyed. He had to be in his late seventies. The covered picture of Lord President in his room was taken at the inauguration. The president he stared at was decades older.

"Hello my fellow Americans. If my calendar is marked right, there are many students who have just learned what they will be doing for the rest of their lives. This is a time for reassurance for most families, as we have taken the fear of the future away from our children. They need no longer worry if they will make ends meet, if they will find the right spouse, or if they will find a job. We have taken care of that for you. And I am happy to congratulate all of you on your new endeavors.

"While you do know the next job you will have, the education you will need is still up to you. My seniors, I do hope you make the right decisions. The ties you make will decide whether you are a world renown doctor, or a doctor your local office. The decision is up to you."

He took a moment to take a breath. Of all the things Lye could use to describe Lord President, the one that came to him the most was tired. The smile he wore never reached his eyes. His eyes looked more of a night worker who had just got off his shift, not the representative for the Land of the Free. Lye began to pity the old tired man, but that pity was washed away as he thought of Felix.

"I'm sure many of you can see I have gotten a little old during my presidency. There are many citizens who cannot remember a time in which I wasn't their president. The thought makes me happy, but I am here to announce I will be stepping down as president soon enough. Actually, within the next few years to be exact. My cabinet, notorious for worrying about my health more than I, had begun to whisper I should begin looking for a replacement. And I have. Before I tell the people who I have selected, there are some things I would like to say. My replacement should not base themselves on the result of the Graduation test. Also, because we would like to keep the image of an All-American family leading the country, if the next Lord President isn't happy with the woman he is paired with, he can change it at any time before graduation.

"I must apologize to my fellow citizens, there must have been a typo in the speech I had written. While I did say every student in the nation has figured out what they will be doing in the workforce, that is not true. There is one student that doesn't have a job. I know what he's feeling right now, I went through the same thing. He must feel as though there has been a mistake. I can assure everyone; your government doesn't make mistakes. The man in which I am talking about resides in Justice, Alabama. A name suitable for the character of man this city has produced. This man, in such an unprecedented way, received a perfect score on his graduation test. Amazing, I look forward to meeting him in the near future."

He didn't have to say his name. The horror Lye felt before had only increased as he put the pieces together.

His family stared at him in various degrees of fear and reverence. His heart raced so hard he had to strain to hear the next words, even though he need not hear them. He already knew what was going to be said:

"I, Lord President, have elected Lye Aesop Davis to be the next Lord President."

With the final words, Lye's graduation picture flashed on the screen of his television. That was an understatement, his image was not only on his television. Everyone who could afford a television was staring at his graduation picture. It seemed as though he had taken the picture long ago. He wore a simple black suit. His mother had convinced him to do his hair that day. They all stared at the fake smile and tired eyes of the senior on their screen.

It took forty-seven seconds before every phone in the house started to ring. Even the landlines, which had accumulated dust from the lack of use, woke up to alert the family they needed attention. Courtney jumped up with joy, Mr. and Mrs. Davis hugged one another with celebration. Lye couldn't join in on the festivities. The ringing of the phones was an alarm in his ears. Even though the lights were on their dim setting, the light was blinding. He sat on the couch with his arms covering his head, trying to appear smaller than he was.

His mother, who had seen these symptoms before, gently grabbed him by the arm and led him into his room. Lye laid down on his bed, happy for the darkness and silence. There was nothing good that could come from him being Lord President. It felt like a sick joke. His mind raced trying to make sense of his new appointment.

There was a solid knock on the door. A knock made by the heaviest hand in the house.

"You can come in, Dad." He said, his voice quivering. Lye kept his body toward the window, but he could tell it was his father. The broad shoulders of the silhouette took up most of the doorway and blocked most of the light coming from the hallway.

"Are you okay?" his father asked, his deep voice rolling over the worry Lye felt.

"I don't know." Lye said.

"This can't be all bad. Think of the opportunities you could have. If you were president, you could bring about change across the nation. I'm proud of you."

Lye reluctantly took in his father's praise. The hesitance came from things he couldn't tell his father. The camera in his room still blinked, even if he was supposed to lead the country within the decade. And that blinking eye would catch things he couldn't admit to his father, things that were not his truths to tell.

"I'm just afraid I'll change. And not for the better."

"What do you mean?"

Lye rose from the fetal position and looked his father in his face. The towering figure in front of him held no malice, he still found the comfort of a child when being near his father.

"I'm afraid...that the reason I'm receiving this job may not be the reason that you think. I'm afraid that the government is trying to keep an eye on me, keep me restrained. Either that, or they want to use my face to make people who look like us believe they have our best interest in mind. One is a prison, and one is a lie. And I don't want to be a part of that type of life."

His father stood in silence for a second, trying to find a way to ask the question without putting his son in danger.

"Have you done anything that would make you believe the government is keeping tabs on you?" he asked.

Lye looked at his father and kept eye contact. "No sir." He lied.

"And if you were, would you tell anyone in this household about it?"

"No sir."

Mr. Davis nodded, and went to hug his son.

"Have you taken your medication today?" he asked.

"Sixty-nine."

"What?" his father asked.

"I was speaking gibberish since your question is gibberish. Of course, I've taken my medication today. I'm not acting out of mania right now, if anything, I'm acting accordingly."

Mr. Davis laughed. "Remind yourself I am still your father, and I demand respect."

"I'm sorry Dad. It's just hard when every time I do

something that's a little unorthodox, it has to be because I'm off my meds. Which isn't the case. I'm just tryna deal with the fact everyone in America now knows what I look like. Only a few minutes ago I believed I might not graduate high school. It's just a lot to take in."

"I got you. You're still taking your butt to school tomorrow."

Lye shook his head in understanding and flopped back on the bed.

Even after his conversation with his father, the thoughts that something bad was going to happen wouldn't leave Lye alone.

Maybe they'll have you killed. Or even worse, you become just like Lord President!

The simplicity of the thought allowed it to repeat itself constantly in his mind, creating a whirlwind of anxiety and unstable dreams.

"Maybe I just might kill myself before they do." He said to the camera after waking up with a cold sweat, unprepared to go back to sleep.

He woke up with a start. Something was wrong, there was a nagging sensation in the back of his mind, telling him that there was something he wasn't paying attention to. He rolled out of bed and looked around his room, wondering if anything was array in his immediate vicinity. Once he was sure there was nothing wrong in his room, he walked down the stairs, the nagging feeling still wrapping itself around his head.

"MOM!" he yelled to no answer. The nagging sensation wouldn't go away, it was though something was thumping on the brink of his brain, attempting to go in. He walked around the kitchen and saw no signs anyone was awake, or home for that matter.

"Might as well go check the mail." He said to know one in particular, once he realized he was talking to no one, he answered. "I need a pet, someone who's gonna listen to me when I'm talking."

Lye opened the front door to check the mail, and the wall of noise slammed into his ears. The nagging he had sensed earlier was the chanting of those who stood outside his house. If not for the annoyance the scene caused, he may have felt a little embarrassment that he went outside to a set of people with only boxers on.

"Lye! Lye! Lye! Lye! Lye!" they all chanted. He raised his hand to shield his eyes from the sunlight. It was barely time for him to get ready for school. He wondered how long they had been waiting for him to wake up. Most of the people who stood in his lawn was around his age. Two of them he knew from school. Most of the people he didn't recognize. He wondered how he could get them off his lawn without sounding like an ass.

"Guys, guys. GUYS!" he waited until everyone had calmed down before he began to speak. "I am happy for the support, I really am. But I still have to go to school y'all. And I'm only in boxers. I do have to ask; can you please give me some time to start my day before you go crazy? Please?"

The crowd answered by chanting his name again.

With a sigh of defeat, Lye walked back into his house in order to get ready for school. It was going to be a little harder now, but he figured he could manage. Before he went back to his room, he checked the other rooms to reassure himself he was alone. He spent most of his search racking his brain to remember an appointment someone had that he had forgotten about. Then again, the idea his family had guessed this would happen and left wasn't too far-fetched.

He took a quick shower and put on his uniform. In his frantic stupor he almost forgot to grab from the two pill bottles on his dresser. He went down the stairs and grabbed his bike from around the back. The crowd of people had not left. They continued to cheer him on. Some actually began to cry as he passed him by.

It'd be really hard not to develop a Jesus complex Lye thought to himself, *I'm not even in office and people are acting as though I just saved their baby from a burning building.* He threw the thought out of his head, a common exercise for him. One that he figured he would be doing a lot more in the near future.

He hoped on his bike and peddled, but not before turning back to the crowd. "Look, no one is going to be at my house since I'm leaving. I get the whole cheering thing, I really do. But can you at least show me the respect of leaving my house alone while I'm not there? That's all I'm asking of you right now." He worried he sounded like an ass but shrugged the thought out and continued on his way.

He peddled fast. Two blocks later he made the mistake of turning around. Some of the more able bodies of the group had decided to follow him toward his destination. Only two of them in the pack were supposed to be going in the same place as him. He was disgusted. What disgusted him wasn't the fact he had acquired a new posse. It was their faces.

They all had the face of blind admiration. His comment about a Jesus complex hunted him as he took in their faces. They all wished to touch the helm of his coat, all wishing to be healed of illnesses they didn't have. He was sure a mere two days ago, most of the people he looked at didn't know he existed. But their eyes were wide with love, they all wore the same childish smile. The smile of a child who had walked into a room and noticed their father had just gotten home from work. They all ran with the same enthusiasm, as though no one should be allowed to touch Lye but them.

It scared him.

Instead of his usual route to school, Lye decided to go the scenic route. At least this way he could lose a couple of runners. Once the last person had doubled over with the need to catch their breath, Lye headed to the prison he attended the last four years.

If he thought being at school would change anything about the way people were acting, he was extremely wrong. The moment he walked through the doors; the way people were acting toward him was evident. The cops gave him words of encouragement. Freshmen dared one another to touch him (it got to the point he made someone cry tears of joy by accidentally bumping into them).

Homeroom was as terrible as could be expected.

Mrs. Peeves stared at him the moment he walked into class. "There's my favorite student! I was just talking about you to the class. Telling them how I simply loved having you around, wasn't I class?"

Most of the class nodded their heads in agreement. Lye had to bite his tongue in order not to mention this very teacher had sent him out of class on numerous occasions because he was disrupting her class. The closer he got to the sitting students, the louder the racket became. Everyone wanted to talk to him. By the time he got to his seat the noise was deafening.

"Everyone, please be quiet."

Almost simultaneously, everyone was quiet. Bernabe and Felix were reading their own respective tablets, but the rest of the class eyed him with anticipation. As with anyone who was in his special predicament, he decided to see how far this could go.

"Everyone, stand up." He said. There was a slight tremor in his voice, but no one seemed to notice. The entire class (except for Bernabe and Felix) obliged, waiting for him to make another command. Even Mrs. Peeves was waiting for him to ask them to do something.

"Everyone, turn around in a circle while patting your head." He commanded.

The commotion of nearly thirty people turning in a circle and patting themselves caused Bernabe and Felix to look up from their reading. They quickly looked around and figured out what was going on. Both of them threw an accusative glance toward him.

"Okay, I'm done." Lye said, throwing his hands up in submission.

Everyone sat down and waited for Mrs. Peeves to start talking.

"I do want everyone to realize prom is coming. This would be the last time any of you have a choice about who your partner is, so choose wisely. And remember, you must wear the school colors of gray and red for the dance. There are no exceptions- well, except for Lye of course."

Lye, who had been wondering how anyone could concentrate when everyone would do anything he told them to do, snapped his head back to the present. It took his mind a few seconds to digest what she had said. A small thought had crept into his mind.

"Actually, I want everyone to wear whatever they want to wear for prom. Tell every senior and junior the next Lord President said it. Tell them it's a protest. The more color the better. And I mean that. I want everyone wearing blues, pinks, greens, and every color that you want. And go with whoever you want to go with. Girls wear a suit if you wish, guys, wear a dress. Do whatever makes you happy."

Mrs. Peeves' face was conflicted. The thought made him chuckle. On one hand, Lye was going against everything she had taught since they had been in her class. On the other hand, he was going to be Lord President, and she believed Lord President was right in all His ways. All the blood drained from her face when she said she would let the principal know what Lye had said.

Lunch time was the only time in which he found peace as Bernabe and Felix sat on the opposite sides of him.

"So what schools are you planning on applying to?" he asked his companions.

"I've already been accepted to Yale and Harvard. And I'm guessing they're going to want you to apply for the same schools." Felix answered.

"Why haven't y'all be acting funny today? Everyone's acting as though I'm the Messiah." Lye asked. He was grateful for the lack of change, but curiosity wouldn't allow him to go any longer without asking the question. Even as he spoke it, people continued to point and whisper as they walked past the table. Felix and Bernabe each stole a look at one another and reared their head in laughter. After they had recovered from the joke, they answered his question.

"We know who you are." Bernabe said.

"And you're just Lye to us." Felix said.

It had been years since the three of them sat at the lunch table together, and besides the constant look and snickers, Lye was happy to have that back in his life.

Not everyone seemed happy to see the trio, however. A pack of seniors found their way the table that the trio was sitting at. The leader of the pack was-

"Who are you?" Lye asked.

Bernabe looked up from his food.

"My name is Ashley." She wore her hair in a ponytail, and she smiled. The members of said nothing as the alpha was only one expected to talk.

"I got you. Uh...is there anything I can help you with?" Lye asked.

Ashley (or at least that's what Lye thought her name was, he was terrible at remembering names, no matter how recent he had heard them) smiled flirtishly. "Well, on the news it said you could have any partner that you wanted. I was just thinking that maybe you would want someone who looks better than plain ol Felix."

Plain ol Felix balled her first, but she said nothing.

"And why do you think I would want you?" he asked. His desire not to be rude was quickly forgotten. It wasn't the flirtation that ruffled his feathers, it was the attention itself. He knew no one would be giving him the attention he was getting had they not heard he was becoming Lord President.

Ashley laughed. There was a lot of laughter going on nowadays. "Well, look at me and look at her. It's easy to see who the better choice would be." She said. Her pack agreed in chorus.

"I have a question." Plain ol Felix spoke up. "What was the job you were given?"

Ashley answered. "Caretaker."

It was Felix's turn to laugh. "I'm actually kind of jealous. You will never have to worry about people's expectations of you. I would love to think that I too would peak in high school. If you want Lye, you can have him. The question is, once you've gotten older and wrinkles begin to show, will he still want you then? Do you have anything else to offer besides good looks that might last another ten years, maybe?"

"Felix, I don't think that's necessary." Lye began.

Felix shrugged her shoulder, focusing on the food in front of her. "But apparently it is. I don't care about her wanting you but I won't have someone talking down on me right in front of my face."

Bernabe, who, up until this point decided to stay out of the conversation, agreed. "I will have to warn you: she isn't someone to be messed around with. And we can't control her. Choose your next words wisely."

Ashley was not backing down. She sat down across from Lye, leaning over so he could peak down her shirt.

"C'mon Lye, do you really think she could amount to what I have going on here?"

By now Lye was seething "To be honest, I don't. I don't think she has it in her to stoop down to your level. I would appreciate it if you left though. I am trying to eat this prison food they serve us."

Ashley reared back as though Lye had slapped her. Realizing she was making no leeway, she turned to her pack and left.

Lye turned to Felix. "I have been meaning to ask you. As Ashlyn made painfully aware, I am allowed to choose another partner if I wanted to..."

"And you're second guessing us?" she asked. A curious smile crept on her face. Bernabe stopped chewing to listen in on the conversation.

"No. It's not that. I was just wondering if- maybe- you wanted someone else. That if there was someone that you wanted as your partner, I could take theirs and you could-"

Felix raised her hand, the curious smile never leaving her face. "I do appreciate the gesture. But that doesn't solve the problem. You're giving me a choice to choose who I want, but you got to think about it. Let's say I wanted to be with Alexis. That would mean you get to marry Elsa. And if that happens, neither of them has a choice on who they're to be with. I'd rather deal with the devil I know, and at least I can be happy with you. You wouldn't be giving anyone a choice. Unless you can pass a law that says *anyone* can choose who we want to marry, there's no point coming to me asking if I want to be with you."

"Do you want to be with me?" Lye asked.

At that moment Elsa came and sat at the table, near Bernabe. He embraced her and she kissed him on the cheek. The unexpected action caught the attention of the royal couple.

"Well, I guess I can't have Alexis either, so I am stuck with you." She chuckled. She grabbed his hand and squeezed it for reassurance.

"How has everyone been? Congratulations on your job Lye. I've never thought we'd see a black Lord President."

Lye had to stop himself from mentioning that America has had leaders of color before. He and Felix continued to stare at the odd couple in awe. The last he had heard about Elsa; she had angered his best friend. With Bernabe being completely enamored, he didn't notice the weird looks he was receiving.

"SO...." Lye began, making sure his voice carried "I'm not trying to get in to anyone's space. But-"

"Oh, my bad." Bernabe said, currently wrapped in staring at Elsa. "We have been going on dates lately. We actually have a lot in common. We're going to be going on a date later this week."

Elsa beamed at Lye and Felix as she talked. "Bernabe is such an amazing partner. He opens the door for me whenever we go anywhere. He pushes in chairs for me, and he's a great listener. I couldn't ask for a better partner."

"Bernabe? He allows you to call him Bernabe?" Lye asked, the pain evident in his voice. Only he was to call Alexis by his surname.

"Yes! I love that name. Elsa Bernabe. And I have to say he is such a- I don't know the word I'm looking for." She said.

Felix and Lye exchanged glances. "I think the word you're looking for is gentleman. I do have to ask; at what point did he start doing these things?" Felix asked. A cloud of suspicion hung over the duo, both stared at Bernabe with confusion. Bernabe, on the other hand, couldn't help but notice the extreme detail that went into painting the lunch tables.

"It was last month. He had gotten into some trouble with the police- bless his heart. They arrested him without even telling him what his charges were! But Bernabe talked his way out of a crime. He's such a smart man." She said, hugging him once more.

Lye winced every time the name Bernabe came out of her mouth. Most people called him by his first name: Alexis. Only one person, someone who shared the same birthday as him. Someone who had grown up with him most of his life, called him by his surname...

"Oh? He was arrested all by himself? And he did all these things by himself? And after being in a holding cell for an hour, he learned how to be a gentleman?" Felix asked, her smile growing bigger than a mere curious one. Her tone alerted the two boys that at any moment she might spill the beans. Bernabe threw a pleading look at Felix. Only Elsa was unaware of what was going on.

"Yes, isn't he amazing?"

Lye coughed into his sandwich, trying to cover up the laughter that tried to escape. Still hurting, he placed his hand on Felix wrist. Felix, understanding the gesture; rolled her eyes and changed her tone.

She instead put on a polite smile. "I agree. Sometimes I think Bernabe has taught this poor boy of mine his manners. I am happy you found a partner that treats you right. I was wondering Elsa, since Lye and Alex-Bernabe are such great friends, we should get to know one another. They are going to be the best man on each other's wedding. If it was an option, I think they would've just married one another."

Not wanting to miss a grand opportunity for a joke, Bernabe got down on one knee and stared at Lye. "I've been meaning to ask you. We've known each other for some time now. Will you marry me Lye?"

Lye put both of his hands to his face in a surprised expression, capturing the look of a woman being proposed to almost verbatim. "Of course, I will marry you! This is the greatest moment of my life!" he jumped in joy, pretending to be the happiest woman in the world. "I can't wait to tell my parents about this! You don't have to spend a lot of money on the ring, our love will get us through anything."

They resumed their positions at the lunch table, now holding each other's hand. Elsa gawked. Felix kept her composure; she was well acquainted with the boys' antics.

"As I was saying- they would have married one another. Would you like to go out with me somewhere? We can go shopping, get our hair done, go to the shooting range, paint our nails?"

Elsa was taken aback. "Shooting range?"

Felix smiled, sitting up in her seat. "Shooting range it is!"

Elsa put her hands up, trying to stop the flow of the conversation. "No, wait- I didn't mean-"

But Felix didn't hear that, or she just ignored it. She pulled out her phone. Lye looked over and saw she was making an appointment to the nearest shooting range."

"Okay, I'll pick you up after school today. You'll have the best of time."

"But my dad said that guns are just for boys-" Elsa stammered.

"Well your dad's a liar. Anywho, would you mind going to the bathroom with me?"

"Of course."

The two girls left the table, leaving the boys. They sat with their mouths open, so surprised they forgot they were still holding hands.

Bernabe was the first to regain his composure. "Did she just-"

"Become friends by hostile takeover? Yeah, I think that's what happen. It's kind of her style. I've been meaning to ask since I still don't know her last name. What's her occupation?"

"It's James. She's going to be a neuroscientist. She's actually great at that kinda stuff. Her dad always tells her that only men can be scientists though. She told me he didn't say anything to her while they were watching the Choosing."

The boys continued to watch the girls leave the cafeteria.

"Well I'm happy for her. I'm a little afraid right now, but I am happy."

"Me too."

A cloud of silence hung over the boys. Lye sucked his teeth and looked at Bernabe.

"I've noticed she doesn't have the decency to simply call you Alexis…"

Bernabe smiled sheepishly, "Yeah, I forgot to mention only you call me by my last name."

"Forgot to mention. Huh, ain't that a pity." Lye said, unimpressed.

The lunch bell rang. Only when the two stood up did they remember they were holding hands. They said their goodbyes and went their separate ways.

Lye was trapped in his mind for the rest of the day to retain any memory of it. He walked out the school doors, looking for his bike. His route was interrupted once he noticed the hastily parked limo a few feet from his bike.

The window rolled down, and the Mayor poked his head out.

"Lye! Lye! It's me!"

"You're embarrassing yourself!" Lye yelled back. He looked at his bike. There was a possibility that he could get on it and ride off. There was a bigger possibility that the mayor would order the driver to pursue Lye and run him over if he was able to get too far away. Still, a broken leg would feel much better than whatever conversation this man decided he wanted to have. He took one more glance at his bike; if he ran, he could get on it and cut through a few parking lots and sidewalks. He could get it away while the surprise of him being the future Lord President was still fresh. But- he had been ignoring the mayor for a few weeks.

He looked down at his legs and hopped. After deciding he would miss hopping more than he originally thought, he went to the limo. Lye looked around. None of the students saw fit to rescue him from the situation. Felix, Lye, and God were nowhere to be found to rescue him. He shrugged; to the rest of the students, it only made sense for the mayor to pick him up from school.

The mayor flung the door open, not waiting for the chauffeur. "Lye, I was so surprised to see that you had been chosen to become Lord President. I was hoping that I could have dinner with you tonight. Just the two of us?"

Lye sat down in the limo. It was only the mayor there, which meant Felix wouldn't be joining him. "Don't you have a job to do? I'm almost positive you have to do"

"That can wait. What we are doing is very important. And it's on me."

The idea that this meal was on the mayor, and not the taxpayer's dollar, crept into his mind. As the driver drove off, Lye reconsidered his position on how much he needed his leg.

SIX

Dr. Cambridge sat opposite of Lye in a high scale restaurant. He was dressed in a black expensive suit. Lye felt out of place. He still wore his school uniform, and honestly could think of many things he would rather do than sit here with the mayor. He looked at his leg again and figured he should get some use with it before he was in this situation again.

The two men stared at each other for a while. Dr. Cambridge waited for Lye to start talking. Lye waited for Dr. Cambridge to stop licking his lips.

The waiter had come by the table three times prior, but since this was the last table he was waiting on, he waited for either men to acknowledge him. The waiter through a pleading glance at Lye, who in turn nodded and turned to the mayor.

"He's been waiting for us for quite some time. Can you please order?"

The mayor ordered something Lye couldn't pronounce. Lye, realizing he was hungrier than he had first realized, ordered a steak.

"I take it there was a reason you wanted to talk to me?" Lye said.

Dr. Cambridge tried his hardest to appear innocent. The rendition paralleled a crocodile at a babysitting interview.

"Why can't I just want to spend time with you? Get to know you." The mayor asked. Lye waited for his smile to fade in vain.

"Dr. Cambridge, I promise this situation would be a lot scarier if we were here because you wanted to get to know me. Given the age gap, I feel like I should call someone if you don't stop salivating at the sight of me. You're creeping me out dude."

The mayor wiped his mouth. "I guess that's fair. I admit, I have been a little too excited with meeting you. I wanted to know-"

"You knew I was going to be Lord President." Lye interrupted.

Dr. Cambridge shrugged his shoulders; he'd been caught, there was no longer a reason to hide what he knew.

"Yes. He came to my house to talk about you. Well, he talked mostly to my daughter, she was the one who knew you the best. But he talked about you to me as well! The next day I planned to make sure that Felix would later be known as Felix Davis."

The waiter arrived surprisingly fast with their food. He took no time in leaving once he knew they were satisfied. Lye turned his attention to the mayor. "We already knew you did that, are you going to tell me why?"

Lye took a few bites of his food. He had been taught not to ignore free food, no matter how terrible the conversation he had to endure was. Even with the conversation he had to admit the steak was delicious.

"Well, I am in need for a new mayor by the time you become Lord President. That role will be taken by someone younger, less experienced than me. And when you become Lord President, you will be on the lookout for cabinet members. People who are wiser, more mature, more cunning. You will be looking for people who can keep your head on straight. It would be a shame if I didn't offer my own abilities to lead this great nation into more glory."

The reasoning behind everything was coming into fruition. While the mayor had a smile on his face, the taste in Lye's mouth had turned sour.

"And why would I ask you to be a member of my cabinet? You're kinda jumping the gun, aren't ya? There's no guarantee I'll be allowed to choose. Or that I'll make it there. We haven't had a good ol' presidential assassination in a while."

Dr. Cambridge made no hints in trying to hide his smile now. It was no longer a smile of innocence. He had held something dear to his heart, and he was waiting for the right time to use it.

"Do you remember the time where Felix disappeared?"

"I do."

"Do you know what happened to her?"

Lye's first instinct was to lie. To feign ignorance in an attempt for the mayor to say more than he intended to. But there was no real threat. Lye realized he was under no obligation to tell him when and where he learned those facts.

"Yes."

"Yes. I don't have to go around passing blame you already know belongs to you. I will tell you this: unfortunately for you, lovestruck girls tend to show appreciation for their dumb boyfriends. And Felix wanted to show her boyfriend appreciation the best way she knew. She wrote him a note."

Lye picked up the piece of steak and chewed it slowly.

"Before we get to the evident blackmail, are you paying for this, or is this taxpayer's money."

"What- of course I'm paying for it."

"Great. I'm famished." Lye called the waiter back to his table. It didn't take long for recognition to blossom on the waiter's face as he walked up. Because of this, he was more than happy to help in any way.

"Can I get another sixteen-ounce rib eye steak, medium? Yeah, same order. Thank you."

Lye took the last piece of steak and ate it. After he had finished, he began to speak, pointing his fork at the mayor as he spoke. "So, sifting through your need to be dramatic. I'm guessing the letter you're taking about is evidence showing who gave her that contraband. And you want to hold on to that as blackmail in order to secure your spot as a part of my cabinet? I'm getting tired of telling you this, but you disgust me."

The mayor folded his hands. "Sometimes we have to make difficult choices in order to secure our futures. It's common practice really."

"No, the blackmail is something I expect from you. That's not what's made me mad. What pisses me off is you had evidence that would've let her go. Evidence that would let your own flesh and blood walk free. You decided that on the off chance it would be of use to you- years to come- you would have your daughter get arrested rather than help her. That's what I'm pissed about." Lye said.

The mayor took a bite of his food and shrugged. "There wasn't much my daughter could give me. I feel her falling in love with a little black boy was the best thing she has ever done. Her imprisonment was a sacrifice I was willing to make."

Lye stood up from his chair, the force causing his chair to fall back on to the floor. Anger twisted his face. He didn't think of any consequences when he brought his hand back and punched the mayor in the nose. The mayor yelled in pain; blood ran in between his fingers. The people around the duo looked to see what was going on. Once they realized who sat at the table, they thought it better not to interfere.

"I hate people like you. People who will do anything to get ahead."

Dr. Cambridge's eyes filled with tears. He wasn't

crying, it was simply a reaction to being punched in the nose. "What do you know about people? Our nation is so divided right now, there is dissent everywhere we go. I'm trying to help you, and you can't see the bigger picture. That's what's wrong with you young people. All you can see is two feet in front of you."

The waiter came by with Lye's steak and looked at the mayor's face. "Excuse me sir, do you need any napkins?"

Lye kept his eyes on the bleeding nose. "No, he needs to remember what it is that connects him and his daughter. Let him bleed until he remembers what it means to be a father."

Lye grabbed his backpack and walked out of the restaurant. He was a long way away from Justice, but that didn't matter. The moment he walked out of the restaurant, people looked at him and pointed. His face was easily recognizable; his halo of hair even more so. It had been that way since every family with a television saw it on live television. He walked aimlessly, not knowing what direction led him to Justice.

"Excuse me sir, but do you need a ride?"

He looked behind him and saw an older white woman smiling up to him. She wore the uniform of the restaurant. She looked at him for a moment.

"If you don't mind, I would appreciate it. I live in Justice."

"Oh, well baby that's on the way. I have to visit my sister in Calera. C'mon, let's get you away from here."

Lye walked with the lady to her car. He was hesitant; the car she had stopped by was well out of a waitress's paycheck. He looked at her, waiting for an explanation. She didn't give one, so he silently sat in the passenger seat.

"What's ya name baby?" the older woman asked.

"You don't know who I am?" Lye asked, "I'm sorry, that sounded rude- and a little narcissistic- I didn't mean it like that. My name is Lye, Lye Davis, what's your name?"

The older lady pulled out of the restaurant parking lot. "My name is Ruby. But if anyone asks you about me, you can call me the gypsy lady."

"Yes ma'am."

"So why did you punch the mayor of your own city in the face? Don't get me wrong, I feel like the son of a bitch deserved it, but curiosity is getting the best of me."

Lye looked down at his knuckles. The lines on his fingers still held on to the dredges of the mayor's blood. "He did something that made me mad, and I lost my temper."

Ruby was so short she had to keep the chair pressed to the closest setting to the steering wheel. She peered over the steering wheel with a little difficulty. Even so, she whipped off the curb in a way that left no question on whose car she was driving.

"I understand why you're speaking in such a vague way, but I can promise you you're safe with me. I deactivated all the cameras and microphones in the car."

"You can do that?" Lye asked. The gypsy lady next to him had become more interesting.

"I can do whatever I want. I helped make most of the surveillance systems we have around here. Do you honestly think whoever made these didn't make a backdoor?"

Lye took in the woman for a moment. He had talked to enough people to know he shouldn't judge just based on what they look like, but he didn't- he couldn't- believe that.

"If I didn't know any better, I would think your doubting me." she added with a chuckle.

Lye couldn't think of any reason to lie to the lady. She seemed nice, and she was giving him a ride home. He admitted his doubt. She kept the smile on her face the entire time.

"When I was still in school, we didn't have all of the cameras and things you see. We also had the ability to choose what we wanted to do in school. I loved technology. I went to MIT. Before I knew it, I was in the CIA. And I loved it, I felt like I was doing things for my country. And when they asked me to develop a software allowing millions of people to be watched at all times... well the challenge took me over before I realized what I had done. Once I realized that everyone's lives were being watched because of me... I exiled myself. I wouldn't work anymore."

"If I may ask, why Alabama?"

She made a sharp left turn, causing Lye to slump

against the door.

"It's quiet here. The restaurant you were at is a place where many people of power come. I've seen the Louisiana governor with his boyfriend, the Chinese ambassador was there once... no one expects Alabama to be important, which makes it the perfect place to hide from importance."

Lye began telling her about the past few weeks. Her story allowed him to feel comfortable in telling his own. Even the parts he thought best not to tell his parents. It was too dangerous for both parties. He told her everything. Everything from Felix, to the contraband, to being selected, to how he felt about it. He even mentioned his medications. Something about the gypsy lady made it okay to talk about these things, he didn't feel any judgement in the car.

"What do you think I should do?" he asked.

Ruby was quiet for a little before she started speaking again. "To be honest, I am far too old to care about the future. The burden of the future is in the youth. I wish that others would understand that."

"But the mayor told me America has never been this divided..."

She laughed a mirthless laugh, a dry laugh. A mocking laugh that had been held in for much too long. "America has a history of segregation since the time she was born. Ironic, isn't it, that we are only divided the moment white people start disagreeing with one another? Child, you are in a position of power, and you are a target. And they messed up when they made both things true. All eyes are on you. What you do with that audience is up to you. If you want to make a difference, speak the truth. Shock the nation. Do something that causes them to look at the problems they don't want to see. If you want the power, just do with the current president does, or doesn't do."

"You just dropped a bunch of knowledge on me."

She put the car in park. "I'm just an old lady, that's what I'm here for. You're home."

Lye looked outside to see he was in front of his house. His mother was in the front yard, peering into the window.

"I don't remember telling you where I lived?"

"You don't? Well hopefully you remember the rest of our conversation. Now get out, I have other things to do. I have a little bit of trouble to get into before the day is over."

Lye opened his door and got out. Before he closed the door, he looked back inside on the old lady smiling at him.

"Are you afraid of getting caught?"

"Honey, if they could catch me, they would have decades ago. Now, keep what we talked about to yourself, and have a blessed life."

He closed the door and she sped off.

He turned around to see the fury of his mother. She had taken down her Kantu knots, so her hair fell down to her shoulders. She wore a faded t-shirt older than her children, and black sweatpants. Her eyes burned with anger.

"And what in the hell are you doing? I just got off the phone with the mayor, and he tells me he has a broken nose?"

"I broke his nose?" Lye silently damned himself as he realized he just admitted to whatever crimes his mother was accusing him of. He looked around to see if there were any black birds in the sky and tried his best to tell his mother everything. Everything legal, at least.

"You're still grounded. You've been famous for one whole day, and you're punching government officials. What am I going to do with you?"

To his surprise, she came up and hugged him. "I truly am sorry for what you're going through right now, I am. But you need to think before you start doing things, especially punching your future father-in-law for Lord's sake. You're not allowed to lose your temper, I'm sorry. Losing your temper allows them to be right about you, you understand?"

He nodded.

"Now, sit down on the front step, I'll be back in a second."

Lye listened. The fury he had saw when he first got out of the car was no longer there. Soon enough he heard the front door open up behind him, and his mother held two cokes. She handed him one and cracked her own.

"Now, I know you're holding out on me. And I don't want you to think just because you're going to be someone, that you can't come to your mama and talk about it. So, start talking."

And like he did when he spoke to the older lady, he told his mother everything. At the moment he didn't care who heard what he was saying to her. He told her everything. He spoke about the memorial, about Felix getting imprisoned, about getting arrested, about the mayor. There was nothing that had happened in the past few weeks he didn't tell her about. He even told her about the contraband he had in the house, about his police friend telling him not to bring it to school anymore. He told her about his fear he was being watched more than everyone else was. That no one would believe his story.

And when he was finished, he looked at his mother. He waited for her anger. If not anger, then something that told him that he had done wrong, that he should be punished for what he had done. He wanted someone, someone besides himself, to be mad at him. Someone to yell at him and tell him that he had messed up.

But those words never came. She simply hugged him. With the power that only a mother's touch could give, he felt better.

"Why did you think no one would believe you? Of everything you have told me, and God help me, that is the one thing that I can't understand. Why did you think you would not have anyone here listening to what you have to say?" his mother asked.

He looked into the Alabama sky. The evening sun had painted the clouds orange, and the lack of black birds allowed nature to show off all her glory. He stared at the sky as he waited to find the right words.

"I didn't think you'd trust me. I figured you would check it off for my anxiety acting up again. That I'm just seeing demons in shadows. I don't know. I figured if I were to come to you or Dad about it, you would laugh about what was going on. That you wouldn't see it the way I did."

Mrs. Davis followed suit into looking at the Alabama sky. There had been many days when the two of them sat on those steps around the same time of day. Mostly when Lye had a bad day, or when she was stressed over work. It had been a few months since they had sat on the steps together. A part of him wished he could go back to those times. A part of him was happy they were currently enjoying said times. She always sat him on the front step with a coke in each hand, ready to talk about whatever demons lurked inside her son's mind.

"I do have a question. You told me you were worried that we would think, or assume rather, all of the things you were thinking were only coming from your anxiety?"

"Yes ma'am." He answered.

"So, what part of you did those thoughts come from? When have I ever spoken down on you? Yes, we joke, we kid. But when have I ever told you that, whatever you're thinking, doesn't matter?"

"I guess I kinda got trapped in my head for a little

bit. But- aren't you mad at me?"

She took a long sip from her coke before she spoke, her words an oxymoron to the blank face she now wore. "Oh, I'm fucking pissed at you. You've managed to get yourself arrested, both of your only friends arrested, and you're telling me that you have been bringing contraband into my house for the past few years. But my anger in you will never stop me from being a parent. If you promise you won't bring those things into my house, I will look the other way. You're still grounded."

"What am I grounded from?" he asked. Even then he couldn't get the laughter out of his voice.

She took another sip of her coke. "Y'know, grounding you would be so much easier if you actually did things to have fun. I guess, uh, you're grounded from- I'll think of something. But don't forget, me and your father will always be there for you while we're here. Now, I've figured out your punishment. You have to clean the house for the next month. All by yourself. I'm going to go to bed, I have a meeting at six in the morning."

"Why?"

She looked up at the sky again. After a heavy sigh, she rubbed her temples. "To be honest, I accidentally put six A.M instead of P.M in the memo, and everyone had agreed to it before I realized my mistake. But that's what I get for writing a memo while I'm- never mind, you don't want to hear that."

She stood up and dusted the back of her sweatpants off. "Are you gonna come in the house or do you want to brood a little more?"

"I think I'm gonna brood."

She kissed him on the head and walked inside. Lye sat and looked at the sky once more, watching as the sun hid behind the house and finally allowed the temperature to drop. He wasn't sure what he was going to do, and he didn't think he could keep it up if his life kept in the path that it was going. There were too many surprises, too many things happening without him being ready. He took a deep breath. A red sedan passed slowly passed his house. The passenger window slowly rolled down, and a head popped out to congratulate him on the new job. He smiled and waved at them, feeling none of the emotion he was expressing.

He walked up the two steps, each step feeling like a mountain to be climbed. There was a lot to worry about, but he didn't have the time to worry about most of it. Right now, he had to worry about finishing school, and avoiding the mayor since he had broken the man's nose. Before he opened the door, he looked back at his leg.

He finally realized that his bike was still at school.

He shot a text to Bernabe and decided to follow suit with his mother and go to sleep.

***

Lye woke up in a start. He didn't know what had woken him up. He heard no noises in the room, and there was no sunlight coming from the window. He had the feeling, the unsettling feeling, that if he were to turn his head, he would see a grotesque monster staring at him, waiting to devour him. His curiosity got the better of him, and as he went to turn his head, the first feeling of dread came over him.

He realized he couldn't move. He was stuck looking at the ceiling.

The only noise he could hear was the ferocious pounding of his heart in his ears. The sound made listening for anything else in his room near impossible, but he was sure he was alone. He was a light sleeper, and he had closed his door behind him. The mere action of someone opening the door would have woken him up.

You could have been drugged

Oh, shut up. He thought to himself. There was no time during the day he could have been drugged. Yet, fear is a dangerous thing, and fear told him it was a possibility.

I've could have been drugged when I went to school today; I don't know who handled my food. I've could have been drugged when I went to the restaurant with the mayor. They could have slipped something into my drink. Or in my food. I've could have been drugged when I was riding with Ruby, how did she know where I lived? I never told her. She could have drugged me. I've could have been drugged when I was talking to my mom, they could have guessed what coke I would have drinking. I could have gotten one dose of the drug earlier today, and the other when I was at the restaurant.

No matter what he tried to do, he couldn't debunk any of the conspiracy theories his mind was throwing his way. Even with the idea of being drugged, the immediate threat, the fact he couldn't move, didn't amount to the certainty there was something was staring at him.

He willed his body to move. Move just an inch, but nothing listened. His limbs had decided he was no longer their master, they need not listen to the things had to say to them. An indiscernible amount of time passed, fear tearing at his mind the entire time.

At the familiar sound of his front door closing, his head snapped to the side. What little relief he felt in realizing he was alone in his room was diminished by the sound. Though he knew his front door had been closed, there was no light outside his window. It was far too late, far too early, for anyone to be coming in and out of his house. Once he realized he had moved his head, his control of his other parts soon returned. The sound of his pounding heart never left him as he put on shorts and walked outside of his room.

He had lived in the same house his entire life, and though he wasn't as good as his mother in the darkness, he didn't need a light to find his way to the stairs. He moved cautiously. His movements might have been comical if not for the impending danger lurking downstairs.

Lye made the distance in two eternities, his ears straining to hear anything that might give away the intruder. It couldn't have been his family members. They were all asleep. They all had things to do in the morning. His heart threatened to leap out of his chest to lead the way, or to leave his lifeless body in the staircase. He smirked at the thought. At least then he would find peace.

The only light in his living room was the constant blinking from the cameras, even still, he didn't believe he was alone. He dropped down to his hands and knees. If there was an intruder, it would be easy for them to notice him walking around like he owned the place. Technically, he did own the place, but the thought was cast away to make room for more pressing matters. He crawled his way to the kitchen. Some time ago his body began to sweat. His hands were now slick with dread.

He made it to the kitchen and reached from the floor to pick up a knife. Once he had a weapon, something that could protect his family, and by extension, himself, he went to find a light switch.

The sudden light was blinding, but he wouldn't allow himself to blink as he swept around the common area looking for the intruder. He found nothing, but 'nothing' didn't give him the relief he sought. It only made it worse. If there had been an intruder, if someone had miraculously materialized in front of him, he would feel relief. He then would see a tangible person who created this dread. But he saw no one.

However, he did see some*thing*.

On the kitchen counter sat an envelope, an ivory envelope he knew was not there when he had gone to sleep. His mother always checked the mail by the time her children got home from school, and she never placed any envelopes on the kitchen counter. He walked over to the kitchen counter. His grip on the knife never wavered, and he turned the envelope over. His heart skipped a beat as he read the letter had been addressed with him. There was no return address, only a presidential seal.

He placed the envelope down as panic gripped his throat, squeezing as he slid down to the floor. Somebody had been in his house. Somebody had been in his house and left a letter on his kitchen counter. While he slept; while his sister and parents were in their bedrooms. While everyone was vulnerable, someone had walked in. He lay on his side, his body racking with fear for a time too long for him to remember. The sun started to shine outside the front window by the time his body remembered he had things to do. He stood up, his body weak from the lack of sleep, and the panic he went through. It was no longer dark outside. His body still shook from fear, and his mind filled with nothing but half assembled thoughts running together, none making more sense the previous thought. He picked up the letter, and opened it with the knife he still held.

Or at least he went to. He stopped when he noticed he was bleeding from his hand. In his panic he had grabbed the wrong end of the knife, slicing his hand open during his lay on the floor. He cursed, running this hand under the lukewarm water. The water stung, but it shook him awake. He went into the restroom and patched himself up and returned back to the letter. He opened it carefully, making sure the gauze didn't touch any of the letter.

To Lye Davis,

I do wish to thank you for your new position. It's gonna be quite some time before you are in office, but I figured we should really get to know one another before then. I will be in town three days from today, we should get to meet one another. I am sure you have many questions, and I am sure you have more questions than anyone else who could've received this position. It's safe to assume some of those questions might be of the personal matter.

Lord President.

There was no doubt in Lye's mind that 'personal matters' pertained to Felix. He remembered she had said Lord President was there the day she was imprisoned. Of course, he would ask about the torture she had to endure. The torture she witnessed while she missed school.

He mustered whatever strength he had to climb up the stairs and go to bed. If it was only an hour of sleep, he would take it before he went to school. But sleep didn't come to him, nothing came to him. He stared at the ceiling of his bedroom while the sunlight bathed him its warm. Until he heard the sounds of life as his mother went to work. He lay there, his energy draining while he could do nothing to recharge it. When his alarm finally went off to set off the new day, he crawled out of bed. He dressed himself with weak movements. He was exhausted. He knew sleep would come to no aid to him. He wasn't aware of his actions as he walked down the stairs and continued the auto-pilot to his bike.

He stared at the space where his bike usually stood. Only after did he realize he had not able to retrieve his bike from school. He was too tired to wonder how his bike appeared on the side of his house. He didn't think about the fact that there was no reasonable cause as to why he was riding his bike at school, when he had no memory of getting it back after he had punched the mayor in the face the day before. He was much too tired to think of anything. All he thought about was how he should have brought himself a jacket, as it was colder than usual, even if it was March.

Lye didn't notice the crowd when he arrived at school. He didn't hear the screams of those happy to see his face. He only noticed how the cold air burned into his sliced hand. How the cold breeze bit into his shirt, and how he found it rather redundant how he couldn't get inside the classroom. None of the camera flashes broke inside the barrier of his tired mind. His eyes registered the bright light, but they didn't tell him why there was any reason for it to happen. He continued to go to class.

He blinked.

When he opened his eyes, he noticed the wind was a lot colder, and he was on his bike again. His panic almost threw him off. He looked around to see he was on the all-too familiar road to his memorial. He looked up in the sky, pondering why he had skipped school. But as he looked closer at the position of the sun, he realized it was already mid-afternoon. He couldn't remember anything about the school day. For once in his life he thanked God, or whatever higher being that could pass through American customs, for the occasional term of dissociation.

His head was clearer, but only slightly so; he still felt the pains of exhaustion. He hadn't slept since before he found the letter. His groggy mind told him that was two lifetimes ago. Whether it was from exhaustion, or his imagination, he did not know, but the familiar road wasn't half as welcoming as it usually was. Every tree seemed to cover a reporter, each nook and knoll hid the faces of those who wanted to congratulate him. Those who wanted to remind him of the goodness they had done in his life. He had no memory of what happened to him at school to convince him he needed the solitude of his memorial. Still, he was sure it had to do with him being chosen as Lord President. Lye couldn't tell what had him on this road in a specific manner. But his mind, his tired mind, his broken and fragile mind, only yelled out for a couple of things.

Peace and quiet.

Lye continued to pedal faster to his sanctuary, trying his damndest to get free of his city of cameras and crowds. His memorial had no cameras, it allowed none of the outside noise to penetrate its walls. Lye needed that. Through his exhaustion he felt his phone ringing, but that didn't matter, that was only more noise, and noise was not something he wanted to hear at the moment.

He zipped past Mrs. Pike store heading toward his memorial. The sight of the abandoned football field filled him with the dredges of joy.

In his desperation and weariness, his coronation was off. Instead of gracefully climbing off his bike, his body simply collapsed into a bush. With his mind deciding sleep was more important than pain, he didn't notice any of the scratches he received from falling onto the bush. He brushed off the needles and headed to the back door. He took out his lockpicking kit and unlocked the door only from muscle memory. If he had been conscious of what he was doing, he might have noticed there were even more scratches on the lock. The amateur intruder had been her once again. He locked the door behind him.

The relief was almost instant as he closed the door. The buzzing of his city was never allowed to come in, but his memorial always allowed him to breathe. He had been too tired to reach for his flashlight, but there was no need to look for it. He did not come here to read; he only came for rest. Rest did not need any light; it didn't want any light.

He made his way into the sanctuary of the memorial. If he had been awake, if he had been more conscious of what was going on, he would have noticed that there were different sets of footprints in the dust on the floor. Footprints that didn't obey the route he had painstakingly abided by. His paranoia alone told him that something wasn't right, but he couldn't tell what it was, and if he could, he was still too tired to care. As he reached inside his backpack and pulled out the lead box to put his contraband back into its to its shelf, only one thing struck out. Since he was sixteen, there was always an empty space on one of the shelves, the space was once preoccupied by the book he had given Felix. There was no space there. Every crevice was flush with books. He made a note to think it over once he was in a better state of mind, but for now there was only one thing he wanted to do.

Lye climbed on top of the pulpit, the circular desk in the center of the sanctuary. He looked around him, the small beams of light smiling down upon him as he closed his weary eyes.

He dreamt of peace. A world most like his memorial. A place without cameras, without yelling, without violence. He smiled at the dream he knew was futile. But the dream was in his mind, and even though he knew it would never happen; he knew no one could penetrate the happenings inside his own head. At times this brought him pain, but now it brought him nothing but peace.

Lye woke up peacefully, his mind mostly mended with hours of sleep. He stretched; a feline on an altar. He lay prone, looking up at the celling, much like an Aztec sacrifice. He shivered from the daft air.

Something wasn't right. Paranoia ripped him off the altar, he shouldn't be shivering. The memorial held in too much heat during the day for him to shiver. He pulled out his phone to check the time and cursed at himself. It was already nighttime, his need for sleep caused him to sleep the day away. He had countless missed calls from his mother and his sister, all wondering exactly where he was. Lye didn't know if he should call them, but he knew he had to be out of this memorial before he was caught. His panic fueled him more than anything else.

For a moment he thought about heading to Bernabe's, it was only across the street. He could easily sneak in. But Calera was harsher during nighttime, as no one had any reason to be out besides crime. Still, they were more than likely asleep, and he didn't feel right in waking them because he had been careless. He didn't know how he would explain to Bernabe's mother why he was out so late. The only thing he could do was go home. Even if he would be in trouble, at least he would be able to tell his mother the truth. He locked the library door, and pulled his bike from under the bush, wrapping his chain around his arms. Just in case.

He pedaled until sweat congregated on his back. There were no streetlights out; the only way to tell he was going the right way was the moonlight. As he pedaled harder; the sweat leaking into his badly bandaged hand; the moon laughed at his efforts.

Sooner, rather than later, he found himself on the stretch of road connecting Justice to Calera. He felt the joy of a child getting away with something, and his joy allowed him to pedal even faster.

A bright light flashed behind him. Lye looked back briefly to see what was going on. Someone was behind him in a car. Seeing he caught someone in the same crime he was committing, he allowed himself to laugh a frantic laugh. He felt sympathy for the driver, as surely, they felt the same feeling of anxiety he felt. He moved closer to the side of the road, giving the car more room to pass him. The bright light of the headlights bothered him, as he had spent much of the past few hours in near darkness, but there was a sense of solitude in the fellow criminal.

The headlights behind him no longer bothered him with its brightness. Sensing something was wrong, he turned around to see the car had stopped on the side of the road.

He stopped on the bike, wondering if he should keep going, or give him help.

It's none of my business. He thought. He quickly threw the thought out of his mind; it went against the way he was taught. He stopped his bike and laid his backpack on the ground. Lye slowly walked toward the idle car. The light was blinding to his eyes, so he couldn't see what the driver was doing.

"Are you alright?" he yelled. When there came no answer, he repeated his question, louder, hoping whoever was in the car had heard him.

The driver's response was a loud bang cracking the night air.

Pain seared into Lye's shoulder, the impact of

whatever hit him unraveled the chain wrapped around his arm. Instinctively he put his right hand to the source of pain and felt blood seeping into his fingers.

"The fuck!" he yelled, gritting his teeth in a vain attempt to focus through the pain.

A silhouette appeared in front of the lights. The broad shoulders of the silhouette betrayed it was a man, but Lye couldn't see any facial features. The pain from his shoulder thudded into his bones; he winced as he held the chain harder to brace the pain. The figure walked toward Lye, now holding a long slender object in his hand. Even before he reached the wounded teen Lye realized he was holding a baton. The baton could only muster the revelation an officer was headed his way.

"I was hoping I would see you outside, pass curfew." the officer said. Lye fought through the pain in his mind. Even with the pain, he had to bite down the rebuttal there was no official curfew. The voice sounded familiar. It wasn't someone he was well acquainted with. Lye looked at his bloody shoulder, of course it wasn't someone he was well *acquainted with*.

The officer brought his arm back and flung the baton across Lye's face. Several teeth flew out of his mouth as blood sprayed across the street. He fell to his knee, using his good arm to block the blow he knew was coming.

"You must think you're above the law. We give you an inch and you always take a mile!" The officer yelled.

Each word brought down another strike of the baton. Lye tried in vain to protect himself from the blows, but his mind was too occupied with trying to figure out where he had heard this voice before.

The night air was filled with the sounds of bones cracking, and the yells of a wounded animal.

Another blow to the face cracked his cheekbone, the vibration allowed sending his teeth chattering. His left eye no longer worked. The realization he could die here tore through his mind like a cornered, rabid animal. The possibility of death reminded him even if he was already a criminal, there is no reason to die on the street like one. He wouldn't just stand there and welcome death, even if his opponent wore a badge.

As the officer raised his hand for another blow, Lye flung the chain he still held at the man's face. He ignored the bone shattering pain in his shoulder as he flung his arm. The chain wrapped around the officer's neck, cuffing off his supply of oxygen. The officer dropped his baton and brought his hands up to his neck to attempt to free himself. The moment he dropped the baton, Lye back pulled with whatever might he could muster. The officer caught off guard and off balance and fell on his face. Lye's fear was quickly replaced with anger. Anger made it easier to ignore his body's cries to sleep. The fractures of his ribs and the broken ends of bone rubbing together as he breathed. Blood flowed freely from his shoulder and his face as he hobbled up. His right leg was unwilling to carry his weight for long periods of time. He rolled the officer over; the headlights illuminated his face. The impact of the road had knocked the officer out, but he finally realized where he knew the officer from.

He met him the first time he had ever been

arrested. It wasn't the arresting officer; it was the officer who had argued with Felix. He drove the heel of his foot into the officer's nose, making sure he wasn't the only one walking away from this with something broken. For good measure, he kicked the officer in the groin until he was sure something ruptured. Once he was convinced the officer wouldn't move for a bit of time he hobbled over to his bike. He prayed the cop would stay unconscious enough for him to escape. He asked any god who would listen the officer would lay still as he made it to his bike and pedaled away. He reached his bike with no problem, and silently thanked God in every name he could think of. He put the bike in an upright position and prayed even harder the cop wouldn't move.

He did.

Another bang cracked the night air, allowing Lye to know his prayer never passed customs to Heaven. Pain erupted from his chest. He felt as though he was drowning as blood began to fill his lungs. He fell to the ground, tangled into his bike. The headlights came closer, but the car sped by, disregarding Lye's condition. As he passed, Lye read the bold 'Calera Police Department' on the side of the car. He watched as the car drove passed him and sped off into the night as he gasped for air. His body was too tired. It was tired of fighting. If he just lay there, he would die. He would die.

But his mind would die too, his mind would be gone. And Lye smiled at the thought. He was tired of fighting. In his last moment of conscious, Lye saw a pair of headlights on the far end of the road, coming to where he was. He hoped the car wouldn't stop; that he was too near the side of the road to be noticed. He was tired of fighting, and soon he would not have to fight anymore.

He closed his eyes with a smile on his face.

SEVEN

Lye felt no pain. Regrettably, he felt other sensations. Sounds, smells, they all came back to remind him his wish had not been granted. He felt dizzy, and there was someone crying to the side of him; a god-awful cry. A cry that tore into whatever abyss he was enjoying, bringing him back into the world of the living.

"Please... please shut up." He croaked through his bruised face.

The crying stopped abruptly. "Lye?" said the weak voice.

Lye opened his eyes, or eye rather, as his left eye wouldn't open, and slowly turned his head, astonished by how much effort it took. Bernabe sat in a chair. They were in a hospital room, tubes and wires laced around Lye's body. Dried blood covered Bernabe's torso. The reassurance that it was Lye's blood, and not Bernabe's, brought some level of peace to the broken teenager.

"I-" Bernabe tried to begin, his tears catching his voice.

"You don't have to explain yourself; you were the car passing by?"

Bernabe nodded, afraid that his voice would cause him to start crying again.

The memories of the previous night flooded Lye's vision, but he quickly pushed them away. There was no need for both of them to be crying.

"Where's my family?" Lye asked, once again wondering why it took so much effort to talk. His lungs burned. Even as he did, he assumed they would be-

"They're speaking with a prosecutor." Bernabe said, confirming his suspicion.

"I do have to ask... " Lye began, each word making it easier for him to speak. "Why were you out so late."

Despite their current situation, Bernabe blushed. "Uh- I was out with Elsa, and we were- uh"

"Please leave it at 'I was out with Elsa'." Lye asked, albeit he made a note to ask later. "Are we in Birmingham?"

"Yes. There are a few security guards sitting outside. To be honest the entire floor has been evacuated in order to make sure there isn't another attempt on your life. I had to fight a gang of reporters to get here. I had to turn my phone off since it was blowing up. Everyone wants to talk about the fact you survived an assassination attempt."

"It wasn't an assassination attempt." Lye reprimanded. The look of confusion on Bernabe's face gave Lye the confidence to explain. "Remember that cop who caused Felix was having problems with at the station? It was him. He said something along the lines he'd been hoping he caught me outside of curfew. I don't think it was an assassination attempt. and if it was, it had nothing to do with the fact I am about to be Lord President."

At the mention of his future title the letter he read flashed through his memory, but as he did minutes prior, he repressed them farther into whichever crevice they came from.

Bernabe's face flashed with anger. He went up and pulled his hand back.

"And what is punching the wall going to do? You're only bringing yourself unnecessary pain."

"But you're in pain." Bernabe pleaded.

Lye shrugged and winced as he did. "Pain is good. You should welcome the sensation; it allows us to know that something is wrong. You should embrace pain. Learn from it. But you shouldn't bring yourself unnecessary pain."

"Do you have to be so philosophical?" Bernabe asked.

Lye shrugged. A sensation that caused discomfort in his shoulder. "Being shot does that to a person. But I promise I am so drugged right now I feel no pain." He lied.

Bernabe put his arm down. "What would you have

me do?"

For a brief moment, Lye wondered at the question. He had no authority over Bernabe. But he realized it was a delicate situation, so he accepted the authority, if only briefly. There was no anger in Lye's voice when he spoke. "Go to school, answer no questions about my well-being. Please bring Felix up to date with everything and let her know what I believe is going on. Take my phone, get on all social media, and blast every platform with the fact that it wasn't an assassination attempt. It was police brutality."

Bernabe nodded. He didn't ask why. There was something in Lye's voice, a steel that had not been there days prior, that told him that there was no reason for him to ask why. He dug into Lye's pockets, grabbed his phone, and existed the room. Once he was sure he was alone, Lye assessed the situation. Though he was in relatively no pain, he knew that was due to the medication blocking his pain receptors. His left arm was in a sling, and his ribs were wrapped, making sure that he wouldn't breathe too hard, causing the ribs to mend incorrectly. Thankfully both of his legs were okay. And by okay he meant not broken. Big purple bruises littered his body. He looked for any reflective surface to see his face, but he couldn't find any. He went to touch his left eye, but a gauze covered most of the left side of his face. He looked out the window. He was on the highest level, free from the sights of any onlookers. With the sense that he was alone, he wept. And realizing he was not alone in this situation, he wept even more. He wept until his head felt heavy, and he drifted back off to sleep.

He woke up late that night. Silence greeted him, but after a few seconds he noticed the slightest sound of snoring. He opened his eye again to see the women in his life sleeping beside him. His mother, Courtney, and Felix huddled together on a bench. Someone had brought it in while he slept to make it more comfortable. They looked so peaceful.

Lye, with a patience and steadiness he had never known before, scooted the cover off and walked to the bathroom. It was expectantly harder to do with both of his legs feeling like rubber, and an IV attached to him, but he was able to make do. Blood mingled with his urine, but it caused him no alarm as he thought about what had transpired in the past two days. As he made his way back into the room, he realized all members of the party were wide awake.

"Oh my gosh, I haven't had time to fix my face up." Lye said, smirking. The joke fell to deaf ears as they raised from their respective positions.

"I love you all, but for the love of God, do not hug me right now. I'm a little too tender."

Lye silently gave a prayer of thanks as they all sat back down.

He scooted, climbed, and otherwise embarrassed himself back into bed. Once he was comfortable, he looked at the trio.

They all looked weary, the past several hours had added years to each of their faces, and though he knew the aging would go away after much sleep, he felt bad. He didn't like them to worry, and he knew that he could do nothing to stop them from worrying.

"So, how's school?" Lye asked.

"Are you okay?" asked his mother, cutting his attempt to avoid the topic with ease.

"Physically? Well I'm on drugs, so I don't know. How does my face look, did I make it away with my devilish good looks?"

In spite of themselves, they cracked a gentle smile.

"They found the man who did it. It wasn't that hard; he was the only officer on payroll who came into work with a broken nose and a ruptured scrotum." his mother said. "How are you?"

Lye knew that she wasn't asking about how his body was holding up; the concerned look in her eye was evidence enough. His emotional being was in turmoil, but he didn't know how to answer the question.

"I- I'm angry. I am very angry. but not about what happened to me, but the fact that there will always be a possibility it happens to people who look like me. I am angry at my country, and I want to do something different. I want to change things. I want to make sure that no one has to go through what I just went through."

Courtney was the first to respond. "You're going to be Lord President one day. Then you can-"

Lye put his hand up before she could finish. "That's the problem. At least, that's one of the problems I see. Why do I have to wait until I'm 'of age' before I can make a difference in the world? Why can't I make a difference now? Who decides I have to wait until I am old to affect the youth? Why can't I do it now?"

"Please don't get too riled up Lye, you might rip your stitches." Mrs. Davis said. Her eyes kept sweeping over him; constantly taking in the damage and pain her son was in.

Still, Lye's anger roared with the fact no one in his audience could provide him an answer. Who, but old men, declared it an unwritten law the youth could have no voice? Why must they be allowed to make decisions without the youth's intake? It would be the youth that must live with their decisions after they're dead. Lye sighed, thinking it was an uphill battle trying to convince the trio. Looking out the window, he decided to ignore the rant bubbling inside of him.

"Please, for the betterment of my mental health, get some sleep. I'm sure I've slept more than everyone here. For good reason, but please. Get some sleep. We can talk in the morning."

Once the sound of gentle snoring entered his room once more, Lye thought about his dilemma.

"It makes no sense to me. The consequence of being a minor is I'm seen as only a minor occurrence. They don't listen to me, but they expect me to make great decisions in a matter of years. This makes no sense!" he said to himself, knowing no one would answer him.

Wrapped in his own dilemma, he fell asleep.

He woke to the sound of the door opening. It wasn't a respectable door opening, whoever had entered the room didn't care whether he slept well or not. He opened his eyes, and his anger of the previous night flared again, threatening to swallow him whole.

In front of him, in a three-piece suit, matching black gloves, and an air of authority that came from his title and not his name, stood the current Lord President.

He had the audacity to smile before he went over and locked the door. After he was sure no one would be coming in he walked gracefully toward the seat next to him.

"Well, Hello Lye. I must say, I am your biggest fan."

"What do you want?" he hissed.

"Would it be too straight-forward to say I want you? Is that wrong?"

Silence. Lord President took Lye's demeanor in for a moment before folding his hands.

"I'm sure you have several questions for me, despite your current condition." Lord President said.

Several questions popped in Lye's head. But one stood out from the rest.

"Is it true you were there when Felix was being tortured?"

Lord President clapped. A slow clap that almost sprinkled genuine intention. "You continue to make me proud Mr. Davis. You are exactly what I expected of you. So selfless, so kind. But to answer your question. No. Someone who was standing in for me was there. If my memory and calendar serve me right, I was in Wisconsin at the time. I had a voice actor there- it's fairly easy to convince someone I'm in the room when they're blindfolded."

"Fair enough. My next question, why me?" Lye's anger had turned cold. Their tones sounded more a small talk over a game of chess and less a discussion about torture and attempted murder.

Lord President smiled. He didn't look like the mayor in his smile. There was a cunning behind his gestures that Dr. Cambridge could only dream of having. A cunning that demanded reverence, even if Lye wasn't willing to give it. "I guess it would be an insult to your intelligence to ask you what you mean by that question. The only way I can answer that question, or begin to answer that question, is with another question. And my question is: How corruptible are you, Lye Davis?"

"Spoken like a true politician." Lye said, casually moving another piece on the board. "I'm not corruptible."

Lord President, who, up until that point, had kept perfect posture and did everything with calculated steps; brought his head back and bellowed with laughter. He was an actor who had finished rehearsal, and during his respite, allowed himself to be the person he truly was. It terrified the bedridden teenager. "That is what I told the man who picked me to be Lord President. I am sure that's what he told the man who came before him. It is easy to see you are clean before you've had the chance to touch filth. I was once like you."

Lye snorted.

The president glared at the snort and stood up in

retort. He took of his jacket and dropped it to the floor. The sound of impact was not that of cloth, but of padding. Lye looked at the president again and confirmed his suspicion. Without his jacket, he looked like the frail man he should be. At a look, he realized that the man's tan was completely artificial. His hair was dyed jet black, it was not his natural color. The president took off his gloves and threw them on the floor as well.

"The American people deserve the truth. I believed that when I first came into office. I believed I could make things better; that I could make a change. The American people need the truth, but the truth isn't what they want. Do you know how much taxpayer money is spent making me look like I am thirty years younger than I really am?"

"Then why don't you make a change?" Lye asked.

"I am too corrupted. I allowed what I believed to stop guiding me. What felt nice blinded me from what needed to be done. I got drunk off power. I have lived a life of regrets, young and power drunk. I come to you as an old man. A tired old man, hoping he can make amends, not for his past, but to the future. and I want you to help me."

Lord President smiled again. While he maintained eye contact it was obvious his eyes were looking at a problem far away.

"And how may I help you?" Lye wasn't sure if he believed what he was hearing, but he was willing to listen.

"By being incorruptible. You have this idea your Lord President is this evil mastermind, but you have to remember. I was given this world; I didn't make it. It wasn't my decisions that created the country you live in. Why am I the villain in your parable?" the frail man asked. Their tones continued with small talk, but there was nothing casual about Lord President's demeanor.

"You witnessed what was going on, but you did nothing." Lye yawned, fighting the urge to stretch. "I have a question though: do you think this was an assassination attempt?"

Lord President stopped to think for a moment. "No, I don't think it was. I looked into his file. He had multiple disciplinary actions resulting from his own beliefs. I knew his father; he was a great man. Best Grandmaster I knew."

"Had?" Lye asked.

"Yes. He was executed, along with his family for the attempted assassination of Lye Davis."

Lye shot up; the movement so painful it spoke even with the aid of pain medication. "You just said that it wasn't an assassination attempt!"

"I said I didn't think it was an assassination attempt. I believe it to be police brutality at its purest form. But the American people don't want to hear about police brutality. They would much rather hear about an assassination attempt. In this they can pour their support without having to make a difference. If they allow themselves to believe it was an assassination attempt, they can go to sleep thinking it was just one lone gun. But a white cop beating a black boy? Then there is something wrong in their backyard. They don't want to hear that. And before you ask, in my own corruptibility, I executed that order."

There was little attempt to hide the chuckle from his own joke.

"What would you have me do?" Lye asked. What he wanted to do was punch the man in the face, but he fought against it.

"That's the point." he said, picking up his jacket and putting it back on. "I'm not going to give you advice until you graduate. Last night you talked about the youth not having a voice. Once you get to the bottom of this hospital, there will be reporters coming to talk to you. Decide what you are going to say. How you will paint this picture."

There was nothing Lye could think to rebut. ""Fine. Anything else you wish to tell me?"

He stood up and put his jacket back on. After stretching enough that the padding stayed where it needed to be; he walked over and placed his hand on Lye's chest. None too firmly, in order to avoid any additional pain. Lye looked down. On his right hand was a small branding of the letter L. It had to be from his youth, but the frail old man in front of him made no gesture to show he was going to share that story. "If you need anything, let me know. Once Bernabe comes back with your cell phone, you'll notice you have a new number in it. It's my personal cell. Memorize it, I doubt you'll have your phone when you need it."

He walked to the door; before unlocking it, he looked back at Lye. "Two things, for the sake of our new agreement, as soon as I leave this room, don't trust me. I am the villain in your parable after all. Also, the cameras in this room will be deactivated for the next twenty-four hours. I'm also due to have a press conference with your parents in the next two hours."

With that, he put his gloves back on, and walked out the door. Leaving Lye with his worries and his thoughts.

His only visitor was a nurse bringing in his food. He sat there, mulling on the weirdness his life had entered in the past few days. He called a nurse in and asked her to bring him a remote. The tv had been off for the most of his visit, but he needed to see something. Lye continued to flip channels until he found the Common Connector station. He saw his parents and his little sister, standing beside the president. He had changed suits since he had visited him in the hospital, but the padding was still in his jacket. To the American people, it wouldn't be padding. It would be muscles that continued to care for his body in old age as much as he cared about his people. Lye didn't care to watch what he was saying; he knew it wouldn't be the truth. He turned off the television and closed his eyes.

The door opened. The feint smell of Five Guys fries entered the room.

"Are you awake?" Five Guys asked.

"No," he said with a smile on his face He had yet to open his eyes.

"Could you wake up for a little bit?" asked the most familiar voice.

"Sure, he said. He opened his eyes and smiled at Felix. She hadn't changed from her school uniform yet; she must've driven here as soon as school let out. He was somewhat happy Bernabe wasn't there yet. Only for the time being; he still worried how Bernabe was holding up.

"I brought presents." She dumped out her backpack on the table at the. Dozens of homemade (or class-made) cards flooded the area. "A lot of people wanted to make you get well cards. A surprising amount of these say, 'sorry they tried to assassinate you'. While the originality is lost in translation, I have to say you might be the only person in history that has ever gotten that card."

Despite himself, he chuckled. But as quickly his laughter came; a somber face replaced it. "Felix, I have something rather inappropriate to ask you."

"If you think you're getting a favor just because you're in a hospital, you really forgot who I am." She said, sorting the envelopes on the first flat surface she could find.

Afterwards, she sat by the side of the bed. She still carried bags under her eyes, but she looked a little healthier. Her shoulders were a little lighter.

"Can you lift up your shirt?"

She crossed her arms. "In what part of no favors did I-"

"May I see your brand?" he sat up; happy the movements didn't hurt as much as it had days prior. "Lord President came in a while ago, and he said some things that didn't add up. I want to make sure he was telling me the truth. Or at the very least, that he was telling me lies."

She stood up and pulled her shirt out from her skirt. she lifted the shirt until the skin of her branding showed. It was in the shape of the letter L, not as faded as the one he had seen earlier. But that had made sense; it hadn't been nearly as long as it had been with the frail old man he had met earlier.

The door flung open, and Bernabe walked in as she still had her shirt slightly raised. At the sound of the door opening she quickly brought her shirt down.

"Uh, am I interrupting?"

"No," the couple said in unison. Felix sat down as Bernabe walked over and sat near her. Relief poured over Lye as he looked at the two of them. He smiled as they said their own welcomes and pondered about each other's health. Once they had finished, Lye began to talk. He told them about the conversation he had with Lord President. He explained to them what he thought he had to do. They sat in silence. In the nature that was expected of him, Bernabe spoke first. "I'll go with you."

"No. I wouldn't be able to forgive myself. And I'm not asking the two of you to understand why I have to do it. I just think that's the best way to go about things. Felix, do you have anything you want to say? This will affect you the most."

She sat there in a daze for a moment. Of the three, only she felt sorrow in his words. "I know I can't stop you from doing it. And I don't like it, but if it lets you do what you wish to do, then I won't get in your way. The only thing I can really ask you is to think about the damage."

Lye nodded.

"Please, for the love of God, tell me something new. There is this cloud around us right now." He looked at them with pleading eyes; all three were unsure of what to do in his hospital room.

Bernabe began by speaking about his relationship with Elsa. "She's actually really cool, I would think she was the best woman in our class- if not for Felix of course. We are going to go on a date. Do you know when you'll be released?"

"I'm guessing in a few days. There's a lot of pain when my meds wear off, and my ribs still ache. Even without the pain being able to reach my head. But I think I should be well enough to leave in a few days. Did I miss prom?"

"No, prom has been pushed back to April due to your condition. Everyone believed that it wouldn't be right if we didn't give you enough time to recuperate before we had it. Actually, most of our school days seem to revolve around you right now. We've talked about every assassination attempt in the history of this country. People are comparing you to JFK and Lincoln."

Beside himself, Lye chuckled. "I think Malcolm X would be more accurate." It was an inside joke to himself; he had learned about Malcolm in his memorial, not at school. He made no move to explain; he knew they didn't know who he was.

Lye laid back down, and they talked about nonsense until smiles crept on their faces and the tears of the past few days were momentarily forgotten. Each of them continued to make Lye laugh. It became an unspoken game to see who could get him to laugh up until it became bothersome to his ribs, and as soon as he would wince, they would stop. They'd start again once his ribs stopped hurting him. Bernabe tallied the most points. He had years of inside jokes Felix never knew about, but she was a close second. They laughed until they were all greeted with the tired faces of the Davis family.

All three of them happy to see their son and brother laughing with his friends. All of them unwilling to think about the scene only Bernabe had witnessed. One that Bernabe had spoken of only once to the police officer and buried until he and Lye could speak once again.

"Lord President was kind enough to tell us he will be paying for your treatment. He doesn't seem as bad as-"

"I doubt it's him paying for my treatment, but I promise to thank the taxpayers once I get into office." The disrespect was customary. But he wasn't sure if he felt it. There was an air of confusion in his voice, an air he hoped his parents were not aware of. They sat down and spoke, the each of them. He was happy to see his family. Lye was sure they had visited him many times while he slept. He hated the idea they had lost sleep worrying about him, but there was very little that he could do about it now. Now, there was really nothing he could do about anything.

Bernabe was the first to ask the question lingering in the room. "Do you know what they did about the officer? I haven't heard anything about it."

"He's been executed." There was enough hatred and disgust in his voice that, for a moment, everyone in the room began to think it was Lye who had ordered the execution. The feelings he felt was not at his assailant, but the person who ordered his life to be taken away.

"The news will probably say he's been given life in prison or something of that nature, but the president assured he had been executed, along with his family."

As though summoned by the mention of this injustice, the tv screen flashed the image of the officer they spoke about. Lye turned the mute off the tv, so they could hear what they were saying about him.

"Officer Parker has been arrested today for the assassination attempt of President Elect Lye Davis. He will serve a life sentence in a federal penitentiary. The location of his arrest, or where he will be spending the rest of his days, were not disclosed. Parker's wife and three-year-old son were nowhere to be found as policemen searched his house today. It is assumed they have gone into hiding after the realization of such unpatriotic displays from their own family member."

Lye raised his hands in a defeated gesture. "As I said. There are so many cameras in this nation that no one can hide anywhere. You can't convince me we can lose a woman who has to take care of a three-year-old child. They have been executed."

There was no reaction from those who watched the screen. Everyone there was desensitized to the idea of innocent people dying. The only difference was the color of the innocent people. Mr. Davis was the first to break the silence.

"We also have good news, the doctor told us that you will be released tomorrow morning. Just after he checks you to make sure that you can, well move."

Lye's head snapped up. The random thought occurred he hadn't taken a solid crap since he had been in the hospital. But he hadn't eaten much either, so he chucked it off as something best not discussed with the doctor.

"Are you okay stink butt? You haven't said anything much since you've been here."

She looked at him, and for the first moment it seemed, he could see that her eyes were red from crying. Worse yet, he knew there was little he could do to help.

He scooted over, very gently in order not to rip any stitches or delay his getting out of the hospital. Doctors tended to take personal offense to someone ripping their stitches.

"Look, my bed has been so cold for the past few days, and everyone else here is much too big to get in here with me. How about you take your shoes of, and climb in with me?"

She nodded her head, finding it extremely hard to speak. She climbed in, and in an obedience nowhere in her nature she cuddled beside her big brother.

Courtney cried, burying her head inside his chest. Though he said nothing to her about it, the very moments of her pain sent waves through his body. The pain medication he had been on was beginning to wear off. Bernabe and Felix looked at their small comrade, carrying a burden she knew nothing about.

"I thought you were going to die!" she said.

He pulled her closer to himself. "Thankfully, I am not allowed to die just yet."

With that, they spoke of nice things until sleep took them all.

EIGHT

The doctor took no time in taking the IV out of Lye's arm and letting the family know he was free to go that following morning. Everyone was groggy from the uncomfortable sleep they had. Courtney had slept beside Lye; Felix and Mrs. Davis shared the bench beside the bed. Bernabe and Mr. Davis had slept on the floor. They were the groggiest when the doctor walked in. He came in with a wheelchair.

"I can walk." Lye said.

The doctor let out a tired sigh. "I understand sir, but it is protocol."

Lye was about to protest, but a stern look from his mother stopped him in his tracks. He got into the wheelchair, which was more comfortable than he has thought possible. Only after a few seconds did he remember he was still in his hospital gown. He undressed and redressed with the aid of his parents (everyone there had seen him in his underwear at one point, he felt no shame in it). The doctor took a more gentle turn in helping him get his arm in a sling. His mother smiled, but her eyes carried a sorrow that told him it was nowhere near a genuine smile.

The only occurrence that upset Lye was his inability to do a wheelie in the elevator.

Once they opened the front doors, his first instinct was to turn around into the protection of the hospital. Dozens of flashes followed his line of sight, until purple bulbs started to appear in his vision.

"Where in the world did they get a podium? And how long have they been waiting for us to leave the hospital?" Lye asked to anyone who could provide the information.

"It's been here since the day after I dropped you off. " Bernabe said.

Assuming the podium was meant for no one but himself, Lye tenderly climbed out of the wheelchair and walked to the podium. There was a chorus of applause as he got out of the wheelchair, but he decided it was futile to tell them he was only in it because it was protocol. Even while he walked, his movements were labored. His body was not used to staying still for three hours, let alone a few days. Practicing extreme patience, he walked up to the podium where a nest of microphone's met him.

An unnamed reporter called out the first and only question. "What do you have to say about the assassination attempt on your life sir?"

Lye swept his uncovered eye to find a face. This was live television, there was no way for them to censor what he was going to say just yet.

"It wasn't an assassination; it was an example of police brutality."

There was a murmur of voices between the crowd. The Alabama sky, which had never betrayed him yet, still shine safely, allowing him to think she was on his side.

"Would you care to explain?" Yelled someone from the crowd.

"Actually, since this will be the first time I speak in front of the American people, I would like to get a few things off my chest:" he stood as he watched the pack hungrily waiting to devour his next words.

"America leads the free world in complacency, legal slavery, and homicide. America is greatest in her ability to deny the injustice she has served her own citizens. We take pride not in what we are but what we are not. America had perfected the sleight of hand. We claim to care for the people when in reality we only care for the profit. Our people are led by ignorance and fear. While we don't fear our leaders, the xenophobia of our nation allows them to tap into the fear and distrust for those unlike us. The biggest example of this is our own bipartisan system. Even though we all claim to be Americans, our factions of politics, religion, and race has allowed us to believe the same people that share this great nation with us are against us. America leads the free world in separating her citizens, and then whispering the sweet nothings of discord among her adopted children.

"America is great in her ability to believe she was great in the times she was not. She is not as old as many of the first-world countries in the world, yet our country has developed dementia in her young age. She speaks of the times of greatness with a pen that washes away the sins she has committed. The genocide, the rape, the evils of this land seemed to be washed away in our textbooks. The silliest example is the idea that our children are being taught the natives of this land happily gave this country away, instead of being lied to, infected, and killed in order for our forerunners to live here.

"Most of our heroes are nothing more than rapists, liars, and murders, and corrupt politicians. What is the reason why this continues, the reason why we allow this to happen? We tell ourselves injustice is okay as long as the victim is not like us. If the victim is a poverty-stricken mother, a black man, a woman trying to make ends meet, or the immigrant. As long as the victims do not resemble the fathers of this nation, we are allowed to sweep the crimes we commit to them under the rug. This was not meant to be a nation for all, this was meant to be a nation for white men, while the rest of us were to carry the burdens.

"Police brutality stems fear in ghettos and low-income communities, while those well above the poverty line believe there is no such thing. The idea that 'Since I never had to deal with it, it must be false' has been a concept of America for much too long. Children from low income families do not see police as protectors, but as evil boogeymen, and those police officers that actually wish to help have to carry the burden of their less-moral brothers. The protests condoning the 'good ones' will always drown out those condemning the bad. The heavy presence of police in those areas only make sense. Note, I did not say it was right, or moral, I simply said it makes sense. Our country, in all her beauty, is only caring for profit.

"But police brutality is not the problem, it is a symptom. We are crying out about having a runny nose while ignoring America has been affected with the respiratory syncytial virus. America's problem is about control. Racism, sexism, and other forms of xenophobia are about control. While this country was made in the image of the benefit of the well-off white man, that man has realized his control of the other citizens of this nation is steadily depleting. Like a wounded animal, our representatives pass laws that attempt to reignite the control that helped them sleep at night. A woman cannot get her tubes tied without her husband's permission, a felon is not allowed to vote, children are taught since the age of five that while they are unique, only sameness will be rewarded."

Before he had realized it, he had gone on a tangent. Full of things he had read from his memorial. To his disbelief, the crowd still looked hungry for more words. With this he felt it easier to continue, as long as he remembered to stop.

"So, what do we do, as fellow Americans? Remind yourselves you are not to be controlled. Your differences are what make you who you are. You can be different from someone and still respect them. But most importantly, we must remind those in the government of their place. They are not our leaders; they are not put in power to be our leaders. They are representatives. They are there to work for us, and they have forgotten their job. Which was easy to do because we have simply accepted what they have thrown at us. When the future speaks of the evils that

America has gifted her adopted children, they will hold complacency as one of the harshest."

With that he walked off the stage, allowing the fullness of his words to penetrate their minds. His family followed suit, the crowd parted in front of him, allowing him to walk. From what Lord President had told him, he knew the American people wanted to be reassured, they wanted to feel as though everything was okay. But this wasn't the time for that. It was now the time to tell them the truth. He didn't want to give the people hope. They've had hope long enough. He wanted them to feel the fear he felt; the fear of the minority. Several of the police officers who stood to keep the crowd back stared at him with sneers. Even though it was their job to protect the crowd, and even more so their job to protect him, they didn't like the idea of him smearing filth on their name. But he didn't care, he wasn't smearing dirt on anyone, he was shining a light on the grime others didn't want to see. He would deal with that when it came time, but until that time came, he had other things to worry about.

He was really behind on his schoolwork.

Lye had firmly requested everyone get some sleep. For reasons no one spoke about, and no one dared argue, Bernabe and Felix had moved in with the Davis family since he had been in the hospital. It was never brought up how long they were to stay. Lye assumed it was until he was able to do things on his own.

The trio shared Lye's room, there was no hassle, and no one argued. There was once a time when the three of them would spend hours in there joking with one another. Bernabe had brought a mattress from a place unknown, and Felix shared the bed with Lye. Surprisingly, Mrs. Davis never commented on it. Lye believed most of it had to do with the idea that, due to his injuries, the idea of him desecrated her house was slim to none.

Lye welcomed the change, it made the school days more bearable, and given he wasn't allowed to ride his bike with only one eye working, he needed the rides to school.

Two weeks after he had been discharged, he was allowed to take the gauze off his face. He waited until everyone was asleep one morning, during the time he would usually be riding his bike, to assess the damage.

He stood in front of his bathroom mirror, and slowly pulled off the barrier from his face. His face hardened as he looked at his reflection, his left eye adjusting to the light. Thankfully, his left eye did not sustain so much damage that it wasn't working, but that didn't mean it looked better altogether. So many vessels had busted his entire iris was covered in red. A crescent of stitches covered the area between his ear and his cheekbone. His jaw had a bruise, it had faded slightly since the attack, but it still burned purple. He was happy he couldn't have seen what it looked like the moment he had it covered, because he couldn't imagine anything being worse than that.

He slowly unraveled the tape covering his torso. Bruises littered his body, and his ribs screamed at the lack of restriction. He hadn't controlled his breathing, and the deep breath he had inhaled expanded them past the point they had been accustomed to. They would be fully healed within a few weeks, but for now they weren't happy with being bothered, especially at a time in which they were still angry. Lye turned his back toward the mirror and slowly turned his head. Any jerking movements would spring waves of pain throughout his body. He looked at his two bullet wounds. Shattered bone had had to be picked out from his flesh during surgery. But thankfully the bones had stopped the bullets from hitting any organs or tendons.

He dared not take his arm out of the sling, nor did he try to peel the gauze that covered his bullet wound, but he still felt a sense of dread looking at his body. The body he had spent so long working on and working out. It had been two weeks, but the more he looked, the clearer the weight loss showed. He slowly dressed himself; making sure not to rip his stitches lest a doctor burst through his door. He got dressed and went downstairs, willing to take a nap as he waited for his companions to wake up and get ready for school.

"Damn, you look like crap." Bernabe's voice broke through his unconscious state.

"I figured in the rate you were moving with Elsa; you might get married before I do. It's bad luck for the best man to look better than the groom on his wedding day."

They chuckled; it felt better to hear his friend laughing on a regular basis once more.

The trio went to school in Felix's car. Blood stains still riddled the seats of Bernabe's backseat. No matter how much he tried to get the stains out, they would not leave. He kept a blanket there to cover them from sight, but that didn't stop them from creeping into either boy's mind whenever they rode together. The lack of blood in Felix's car made it easier for them to concentrate on their banter, which continued well after Felix parked her car in the school parking lot.

"Are you ready for everyone to see your ugly mug?" Bernabe asked. He opened the door and grabbed his backpack; slinging it over his shoulder as he looked for Elsa.

Lye went around to open Felix's door. "They had to look at your face for four years, I doubt they'll notice anything while you're next to me."

Felix merely yawned. She had spent the night reading on her tablet. She put her arms around the shoulders of both boys, making sure to keep her weight on Bernabe. "Can you to behave, just once?"

"No," they said in unison.

Though he had made jokes about his appearance, the idea of ignoring the staring looks was nowhere to be found. He had never been the type that worried about what others thought of him, and his expectations were the only one that mattered to him. The cloud of wool upon his head was evidence to that claim. But he had never seen so many eyes staring at him. When he had his bruises covered up, people smiled at him in sympathy. They even went out of their way to be kind to him. Those same people tried their hardest not to be caught staring at his face with horror, wondering how something so grotesque could be allowed in their line of vision. People continued to go out of their way to give him space, but it was no longer from pity, it was the burden of knowing what that man looked like without his mask off.

Homeroom was quiet. Lunch was the only time noise could be heard, as the trio became four.

"If I had known this was all it took for people to avoid me, I would have beaten my own ass." Lye said through his sandwich.

"So, are you still going to go to prom?" Elsa asked.

Lye perked his head up. "I have to"

"Why is that? Will there be a ceremony since you're going to be Lord President?"

Lye shrugged his right shoulder. "Nah, Batons and bullets might break my bones, but Felix scorned will hurt me. She's already bought her dress and a bowtie to match. So, unless I want to make it through the rest of the year, I'll be there. Have people taken heed to the whole 'wear colors' thing?"

Elsa smiled; she had been the only one to do so. "Actually, I have never seen it before. But a lot of people are excited about wearing something other than red and gray. Everyone's unsure as to what will happen though. A lot of teachers have told us not to do that. I think there's supposed to be policemen there."

At the mention of police officers, Lye looked around the cafeteria. There was a surplus of officers there. He wondered why it had taken him so long to notice it at first. Then again, he had been distracted by the events gone past to think of what happened in front of him. One of the officers broke rank and went to sit by the foursome. The tension of watching him walk up was punctured once the boys realized who was walking.

Bernabe was the first to acknowledge the officer. "Hey Will, are you okay? You don't look too good."

He didn't look anything like the Will they have come to know. His sweat had stained his shirt, and his hair was unkempt. The smile he wore was too heavy to keep up for too long; the only thing heavier were the bags under his eyes. The question wasn't a conversation starter; it was a genuine act of concern.

"No, I am not okay Alexis. I came here to tell you a few things."

He looked back at the pack of police standing along the wall. Some of them feigned the act to watch after the other kids, but most continued to stare at Lye.

"Most of the officers heard about what happen between you and Parker. Before you ask, I don't think he handled the situation correctly, but the fact that you went on live television to speak about it being police brutality didn't sit well with many of my senior officers. They told me to tell you to watch yourself. And we've heard about the fiasco you are planning at prom. For the Love of Lord President, please don't do it Lye." his words came out quickly and shamefully. He spoke to Lye, but he didn't attempt to make eye contact.

Lye did not share the same fear as his friend. "And what are they going to do if I don't listen to what they say?"

Will's eyes pleaded with Lye before he opened his mouth. "Please, I don't know what they have planned. But if I was them, I would arrest you for conspiracy, and insubordination. They can't do anything until prom night. But everyone knows you can't become President if you have been convicted of a crime."

Lye's head perked up. "I... actually forgot about that. So, you're telling me if I get convicted of a crime, I won't have to worry about being president?" The idea of being free of this responsibility allured to him, and he couldn't help but smile when he thought of what could happen. Bernabe shot his hand to his mouth to cover a yawn. When he moved his hand, the corners of his mouth were still turned upward.

"Lye-"

Lye put his hand up to stop Will from speaking. "Tell them I heard their threats, and I have changed my plans accordingly."

The diction of the message was the only thing betraying Lye had listened to anything that Will had said.

A pack of students had come up from the time in which will had begun talking, they waited for the policemen to leave before they turned their attention to Lye. Thankfully, they started talking before Lye could complain about the constant meetings he held in the lunchroom.

"Did he bother you?" asked a shaggy-haired senior. He wasn't in their homeroom, but Lye had seen him numerous times in the past years.

"Hey Justin." Felix said. Bernabe and Lye nodded; both were trying to remember the name of the boy in front of them.

"No, why are you wondering?" Lye asked.

Justin hesitated, as though he wasn't sure if he believed in the words he was about to say. His pride got the better of him, and he took in a heavy breath. "All of us heard what you said on the television, and most of us have been too afraid to say something to you. The day after you said that, police have been around the school even more than usual. I think I've seen about three more black birds on the way to school today. Whatever it is, we don't want you to get hurt even more so than you have."

A nasty plan crept into Lye's head, but he quickly threw it out.

Another student walked up, she was smaller than the rest of her pack, but that didn't stop her from finding the courage to speak. Even as he watched it, Lye wondered what made them so worried about talking to him. He was still Lye. He was still merely a student. He had no power.

But they believed he had power, and they wanted some of it.

"You said some things on the news I know we didn't learn in school. How can we know the things you know?" she asked.

The idea of bringing them to the memorial was laughable. There were too many people around to give away his secrets. A field trip full of criminals was the last thing the school needed.

"I have an idea . . ." Felix said, everyone looked at her. The gears of her head were moving at such a speed the look in her eyes showed she was not present with them. Not wanting to admit it, Lye was sure he had seen the same expression on the frail man in the hospital. "I have a way we can get everyone to know the things we know and get it to where we can wear what we want to prom."

She stood up and stepped on the lunch table. The immediate party's surprise infected everyone else in the lunchroom, until everyone was looking at her. she cupped her hands and began to yell. "SENIORS! ALL SENIORS, I NEED YOUR ATTENTION." Everyone stopped speaking, and the seniors that hadn't already had their attention on her readily gave it up.

"I'm sure all of you know about what has happen to my poor boyfriend. I know, I know, he's a mess. I felt like, since we're all seniors, we could all give him a pick me up. And the best way to do that, is with a party!"

At the sound of the word, all the seniors cheered. Bernabe and Lye, who didn't know what she had planned, decided to go along with it. Only Elsa believed that Felix would want to have an actual party.

Once the cheers had died down, she decided to speak again. "And so, what we are going to do, we're gonna have a party. If you're not doing anything this weekend, the party will be at my dad's manor. At seven. And this party is gonna be amazing. We'll call it a get-well party, because I am tired of my boy looking so sad."

They all cheered, and for the time it took her to speak, the police officers turned their attention away from Lye.

"Now, I do have to warn you. We can't be doing any illegal things there. There's gonna be a bunch of cops and black birds. But you don't have to fear, you only need to know that they're there to make sure another person doesn't try to attack my baby. He's gonna be such a good Lord President."

As the crowd cheered, Bernabe leaned over to whisper to Lye. "Sometimes it scares me how she controls a crowd. Turning into a different person almost at will."

Lye returned the emotion. "You're telling me, I still don't know what she plans to do."

"Now say it with me! LYE! LYE! LYE!"

The chant of his name continued as Bernabe stood up to help Felix down from the table.

"I do have to ask," Elsa began, trying to put together pieces the boys weren't willing to ask for. "I understand a get-well party, but how in the world are we going to distract the officers enough to have an entire prom without them arresting us?"

Felix looked at her, her eyes flashing in excitement. "Oh, that's easy. We're going to burn down a school."

NINE

Lye sat in the passenger side of Felix's car as they left the school parking lot. Bernabe's truck sat beside them as they reached the mouth of the parking lot. The drivers had gone separate ways, Bernabe was heading downtown, but Felix had turned right, taking them toward Montevallo.

"Aren't you headed home?" Lye asked.

Felix smirked. "I thought we should take the long way." She smiled as she rolled down the windows, letting the afternoon air come in. Lye did the best he could to lean out the window. Maybe we needed some fresh air."

"I couldn't agree more; I've been cooped up like a sick bird for days."

With all its negative assets, the back roads toward Montevallo were still one of the most peaceful parts around. The back roads have always been a peaceful place for everyone, no matter the age. The roads had the grand buildings from before the secession -Or at least made in their copies- for mere minutes. They were still a sight to see, making everyone think of a calmer time. It wasn't the scenic route; but the calmness was worth going out of their way.

Before long they stopped at the gate of the Mayor's manor. The robot at the gate wheeled himself up to the driver's side. Felix handed the robot her card. It did not take long for the gate to open. Felix put her car in park when she arrived at the front door. Her hand hovered over the ignition as she thought on whether to turn her car off or not. The door was open before Lye could get out of the car.

Dr. Cambridge had aged since the last time Lye saw him. His once tidy hair had grown a few gray hairs in the short time since he had seen him. He wore casual clothes, unlike the suit and tie Lye was accustomed to see him wearing. The house itself still looked marvelous. But the man with blue jeans and a pink button up seemed out of place. He walked up toward his daughter, completely ignoring Lye for a few moments. He made no move to touch her. His straight face was unreadable.

"Felix, what a pleasant surprise, and Lye, you're here too."

"Hello Father, Lye and I wanted to talk to you." Felix kept a smile on her face, but her fists were balled as she spoke. "We wanted to have a get-well party for Lye, and I wanted to check up on my family..." She held her hand up at Lye." And he wants to talk to you about something. I don't know what."

"Of course, I will listen. But I severely doubt there is

anything you can say that would possibly grant you the privilege of a party, at my house." He led the way into the house. Felix and Lye took no time following after him, they knew the man would not wait for them. The Cambridge's shared small talk as Lye watched. Felix still carried her smile on her face, but her fists were still balled. For their plan to work, Dr. Cambridge would have to believe Lye was telling the truth. Lye shrugged his shoulders. He ignored the discomfort, bring his arms up for a salute.

Dr. Cambridge brought them into his office. He offered them soda as they sent down. Neither senior declined. The mayor looked at Lye, waiting for the boy to start. Lye cleared his throat; he hadn't planned anything to say.

"I would like to talk to you about a couple of things. But I have to ask that you are completely honest with me. And I promise the same in return. May I have a pen and paper?"

The mayor looked at Lye once again, and once again the man's face was unreadable. He pulled a piece of paper from the drawer at his desk. He handed Lye the paper, along with a pen to write with.

Felix looked over at Lye, making rolling gesture with her hand, encouraging him to begin. He cleared his throat. "Firstly, I would like to apologize for punching you in your nose. That was very foolish of me. I would also like to mention that was out of anger, and for that I am sorry."

Not many people were accustomed to Lye apologizing. The mayor nodded. A smile slowly crept on his face, but the lines of suspicion never left the mayor's forehead. "It's okay." he mumbled. "I was in the wrong, you had every right-"

"I came here to offer you that job." Lye said. The pity in his voice made even Felix slightly recoil. Being apologetic was one thing; pitying someone was another.

"What?" the mayor said, he looked for any sign of deceit, anything showing him Lye was lying to him. His once stone face finally broke, as his eyebrows shot up in interest. Lye kept a pathetic smile on his face.

"Given the past two months of my life, I realize that I- I don't know as much as I think I know. Because of that, I realize you were right. I would need someone who knows the ropes in order to watch my back. And think about how it would look to the American people? My father-in-law a part of my cabinet? It's a conservative's wet dream. You can have any job that you want." Lye finished, trying to read his face. It was a relief for both parties that the mayor broke out in a generous smile. He straightened his shoulders beaming at his daughter. Lye noted it would have been an insult to the mayor's intelligence if he didn't believe Felix had done something in order for Lye to offer such a position.

"What made you change your mind?" Dr. Cambridge finally asked.

"To be honest, it was Felix." Lye started, confirming the mayor's suspicion. "Trust me, I am still very angry with what you did to her, but she demands that I forgive you. It would be too ill of a message if we had discord between the two families. This is simply a peace treaty."

Behind his smile, Lye prayed the mayor's ambition

would outweigh his suspicion. A paranoid Dr. Cambridge might remember Lye wasn't known for his ability to follow directions-he wasn't the type to forgive someone because he was told. Paranoia would give him away, but ambition would put him in a different light. Ambition would cause the mayor to think Lye's inability to make eye contact as submission. Slowly, he watched as ambition took over and a smile swept across the mayor's greedy face. "And what do you want in return?" Dr. Cambridge asked.

"Absolutely nothing for me. I want you to clean your act up. You look terrible man. I want you to show some support in what your daughter is doing. And I want you to be a dad. As from what I want you to do with- or for- me, that is still, and will always be, nothing."

He smiled. And Lye smiled.

"Why did you want a piece of paper?"

Completely forgetting the paper and pen he held in his hand. Lye began to write down what he had told the mayor. Having the words he said in writing would falter most of the disbelief he was sure the mayor still felt. Once he finished, he passed the paper back to the mayor. No matter what he thought of the man, he was still going to be his father-in-law. A father-in-law who had already proven he had no problem forgetting past crimes if it benefitted the man.

"There, this way you know I'm telling you the truth when I say this."

The mayor stood and shook Lye's hand. Thanking him for the future job.

"Lye, could you give me and my father some time alone?" Felix asked. Lye nodded and walked out of the office. Michelle wasn't there, and since there was nothing else in the house that needed his assistance or attention, he walked out. He sat on the front step, thinking about how different his life had been two months ago. He would have been in therapy at this time of day. But things change, and so must he. He readjusted his sling to a more comfortable position and sat on the doorstep, watching the Alabama sky.

She smiled at him, and her warmth almost made him forget the issues that had risen in the past two months. For a still moment, he wasn't going to be Lord President. He was only a high schooler enjoying the blues and whites of the sky. He could still go home and be at peace. He thought about a times years prior. Before the burdens he shared with his friends were conceived. Before he had to wear a sling. He tenderly touched his face and grinned. *Hell, I'd go back a few weeks, before I was target practice for the Calera Police department*, he thought to himself; the slightest of touch sending waves of pain throughout the left side of his face.

"Are you done daydreaming?"

Lye still had his hand up to his face. There was no reason to look back and see who was talking. "I prefer the term 'brooding', it carries the proper weight of what's going on in my head." He stood up, Felix kissed him tenderly on the bruise on his cheek, and they went along their way.

She continued to drive past Justice, entering the city limits of Calera. A cold hand grabbed Lye's heart as they rode on the road, he had lay dying on weeks prior. Earlier, Felix avoided this road when they took the scenic route to her house earlier. He silently thanked her for doing so, he couldn't help searching to see if he left any blood on the pavement. Her new car seemed out of place in the poverty-stricken area. Anyone with a hungry stomach would be looking for anything new to steal.

"I wish I had my chain on me," he said as he scanned the area for anyone staring at them for too long.

Felix took her eyes off the road for a second, chucking. "You don't pose much a threat, Mr. Sling. I have a concealed carry license. I promise what's in the glove compartment will protect us a lot more than a bike chain."

They continued on their route, approaching the road where his memorial and Bernabe's house stood. Lye tried to see if he could see his friend's car in the driveway as he passed, ignoring the fact that trees had been planted for the simple purpose to block the eyes of bystanders. Felix turned on the road heading toward the abandoned school. The car climbed the small hill where the antiquated Calera High School stood, albeit without any of her former glory. The duo got out the car once she parked, looking around. Looking around was only habit; the parking lot always stood empty during the day. The back of the school held a school bus graveyard. The busses hadn't had a student on them in living memory. The front parking lot was a different story.

From the entrance of the door to the first tuff of grass held on lunch tables, chairs, and beds too big for those who wanted shelter for the night. A parking lot that once held the cars of the teachers and visitors only held dry and abandoned furniture. Felix sat on the top of a lunch table in silence.

Felix kept her eyes on the school, the gears of her mind flying. Lye looked down at his memorial, his heartstrings being pulled as he wished he could retreat inside of his sanctuary.

"Okay, we can talk now. What's your plan?" Lye asked

A few seconds went by before Felix answered. "We're going to sit this school on fire." she said matter-of-factly. She said the words in the same tone as reading off a grocery list; it was as simple as that. The more she looked at the school the faster the gears in her mind turned, piercing together information that no one but her could see.

"The shell of the building is brick. There's no real hope in trying to light the shell of the building on fire. But the place is filled with forgotten desks, tables, and books. Mostly everything the place holds would catch on fire. And the building hasn't been used in decades, so the fire suppression system no longer works. It wouldn't be that difficult of a job to get everything in flames.

"How are we going to light a fire?" Lye asked. He had never walked inside the school, but it would be a nuisance for the trio to move furniture around in order to make sure the fire catches the right way. Especially in the small window of time they had.

Felix stayed quiet for some time again. She stared at the boarded-up doors of the school. Some pieces of plywood had been taken down already by people who wanted the shelter for the night years prior. She put her hand to her chin and turned around to look down the hill at the wooden area that surrounded his memorial. "Fire always burned up hill. If those trees catch fire, it is inevitable this school will set fire." She looked around and pointed at the dead trees that went down to the street.

With a sharp intake of breath Lye rubbed his face again. He had already connected the dots in his head on what they had to do. But he held a small piece of hope when he looked over at Felix. "And how are we going to set the trees on fire?"

She looked at him, and for a second, the fury in her eyes dampening as she smiled a sad smile at him. "We have to set your memorial on fire."

He looked down at the hill, and his eyes teared up. He had spent years going inside that building. The beautiful sanctuary he had come to love. Like hearing his lifelong pet would have to be put down in order to alleviate future pain, he choked at the idea.

"But what about-" he couldn't finish the sentence, his voice broke as he envisioned the building in flames. Felix put her arm around his shoulder in an attempt to reassure him. "I'll be right back." She said, heading off to her car. As he waited, he continued to look at his Memorial. He couldn't imagine a world without his place of safety. Without a place to escape. His eyes swelled with tears when Felix came back with her tablet. She passed it to him with the same sad smile she wore when she walked away. He looked down, recognizing the words he read on his tablet. He had read the same words in his bathroom a few weeks ago, when Will told him to keep his books away from school.

"I've been sneaking in to your memorial for some time now. But instead of taking the books out, I took pictures of the pages. That way I could read them without getting caught. It's worked so far."

The idea was simple, but Lye couldn't agree with her. There could only be a few books on her tablet. A small amount compared to the surplus of knowledge she so readily planned to burn down. Felix noticed the hesitation. She shrugged. She knew it would take more than that to convince Lye of her plans.

"Our classmates want the information we have. There's nothing that resembles these stories on the Common Connector, but if we were to get it online-"

"It would be damn hard for anyone to take it down in time for no one to see it." Lye finished the thought. Felix nodded, continuing on before Lye could offer an objection.

"And, too many people would be curious of it not to download it for themselves. Now, if we take twenty of our classmates, and have them all take pictures of the pages, we could have your entire memorial uploaded into a drop box in a day." Interest slowly replaced the pain on Lye's face. Felix decided to continue her argument. "Of course, everyone who wanted access would have it, but we would also upload the entire drop box on the Common Connector. The people can read these books, they can see what we see, and there can be change. I know not everyone will be able to understand what's going on in a day... but you're always the first to mention change that comes easy is not change that lasts."

As much as he hurt to admit it. He understood. And with the points she stated, he was almost mad at himself for not thinking of that idea months prior. But months prior, none of his classmates would have agreed to commit treason. His brush with the police caused them to open their eyes, and if they didn't make a move while the small outrage was still fresh, he would lose the soldiers so ready listen to direction.

"Who have you chosen to do that? How are we going to get twenty people here without the police coming? Are we going to show-"

Felix held her hands out in a reassuring gesture. "I announced in front of the whole school we're having a party for you at my house Saturday. The entire police department is mad at you, don't you think they're going to keep their eyes on you? Black birds and police cars are going to be at my house, watching you. In the time it's taken everyone to start planning for this party, I've already talked to five people who want to learn. The group of seniors who talked to us at lunch spearheaded the search looking for more students to help. At this moment, I have more than twenty who are willing to bypass the party to help with this crazed idea of mine."

Lye nodded. He moved his hand from his face; realizing he had been rubbing his cheek the entire conversation. There was nothing he could think as a rebuttal. "And when is Prom?"

"Two weeks. We have two weeks to get everything in order."

"What would you have me to do?" he asked, more

224

than happy to give someone else the reigns of his crusade for a moment."

"Just be you. You're a distraction enough. I'll take care of this plan. You don't have that much time to get everything prepared for prom, so you shouldn't burden yourself with all of this." She went over to hug him. "I know you're sad about your memorial. The less you have to think about this plan, the better you'll feel. Let's go home."

***

There were more cars in his driveway than he was expecting when they pulled up to the Davis house. His mother's car, his father's SUV, and Bernabe's truck were there. But there was also a gray van, and a blue sedan in the driveway as well. Lye recognized all the cars. He hoped nothing wrong was going on. His eyes swept over the neighborhood as he got out the car much too quickly. The last thing he needed was doctors coming out the woodwork yelling about ripped stitches.

From the other side of the door, he heard laughter and shrieking. He caught his breath as he opened the door, taking in the different voices and the smells of cooking food. Felix followed suit with his sense of urgency, quickly appearing behind him as he walked into the foyer. Her worried look washed away as she noticed the voices and smells.

"Abuela!" Lye yelled, moving as fast as his healing body would let him to hug the small woman in the kitchen. The smells of her blessed cooking filled his nose, and he forgotten how hungry he was. "I thought- I heard that you were-" the last he had heard of Bernabe's grandmother, she was in the hospital.

"Yes, I am doing much better. I can't pass on when I know the two of you are causing so much trouble. You would not allow me to get rest, and so there is still many more chastising I have to do. I am happy you are doing better, my love." Lye bent down to allow her to kiss him on the cheek. She turned from the stove and reached inside a pan, pulling out a tamale.

"I will allow you one. But no one else." she tenderly patted his shoulder and turned to look at Felix. "I've already met Alexis' girlfriend. I take it you're the one he's afraid of?"

Blood rushed to Felix's cheeks as she accepted a tender embrace. "I could be. I didn't think he had it in him to admit that."

"You do well child. I expect you to keep these boys in line. Hopefully you can teach the lovely lady Elsa some of your tricks. Now get out of the kitchen, I am not too senile to know when someone is trying to take my recipes"

They laughed, and Lye tore into his tamale. With her cooking in his hand he was king of the world. Everyone was there. The Davis Family, the Bernabe family, even Michelle had made an appearance. They sat in the living room, enjoying each other's company. Michelle and Courtney listened to Bernabe telling a story about his boyish ways with Lye. The parents were all smiling, talking about days long gone, and speaking of the days to come. Everyone smiled as the couple walked in the room. His house looked the same as every house in the neighborhood, down to the exact measurements. Even with that, Lye knew the amount of love held in these doors were not replicated.

"What's the occasion?" Lye asked.

"Mrs. Bernabe was feeling miraculously better, and she wanted to cook tonight." Mrs. Davis told him "So we told her about the situation going on with his living. Before we knew it, everyone had decided to have dinner here." Her face was a little flushed. The adults had been drinking slightly. Not enough to get drunk, but enough to be merry with each other's company.

The trio continued to enjoy each other's company, and the festivities continued as Felix and Lye retired. Though no one noticed it, Lye cried as he walked up the stairs. Few people knew of the plans they concocted in the last few hours. It only made sense to him this would be the last time they shared this much laughter in this house.

***

"Get up."

Courtney's voice woke him up from a good dream, Lye stared at the celling for a moment before he acknowledged the welcomed intruder.

"What is it?" He propped himself on his good elbow. Felix and Bernabe were nowhere to be found. "Where is everyone?"

"Mrs. Bernabe had to be taken to the hospital early this morning. She wasn't feeling well, and Dad believed it was something bad. So, we don't have school today."

"Where is Felix and Bernabe?" He hadn't heard them leave in his sleep.

"Alexis is with his grandma, and I don't know where Felix is, she said she had to leave about an hour ago. She told me to keep watch over you."

A look of horror swept over her face as she looked at the bed Lye was laying in.

"Your stitches have busted!"

He looked at her confused and looked back at the bed. There were drops of blood in the bed. He looked down at his gauzes and noticed there were bright red blotches of blood showing through. He sighed annoyingly; waiting for his doctor to burst down his bedroom door.

"Thank you for telling me, don't worry, I'll clean it up."

But she didn't listen, she took of his linens and hurried to the door.

"Go to the bathroom while I'm doing the laundry."

With no haste whatsoever, he walked to the bathroom. He was annoyed. He was still groggy; he didn't feel like cleaning his stiches. But if it would reassure his sister, he wouldn't complain. And he didn't as he cleaned himself and changed the gauze. It was more difficult that it should have been since he had to do it with one arm.

"Did you clean the stitch?" she asked.

"Of course," he said as he walked back into the room.

After he walked into his room, he went to find his phone. He had no notifications, so he called Bernabe, not waiting to figure out what had everyone to disappear while he slept. He was afraid to hear bad news. Abuela loved him like her own, and the love and respect were reciprocated. He didn't want to think of her in pain. Bernabe spoke to him briefly though a shaking voice.

"Abuela is okay." He told his little sister as she walked back in the room. "Her heart stopped a few times, but she's doing better now. They still don't know what's wrong with her though. Bernabe said hi, he's pretty shaken up."

"I'm sorry to hear that. Mrs. Bernabe is a very nice lady."

And she was. There were very few memories of her that weren't lathered in joy and laughter. Even in times they were in trouble, there was nothing but love from her. Courtney didn't have the same bond with her, but even her voice held sorrow for what the elderly lady was going through. Lye felt his eyes water, and he let his tears fall freely as he got dressed for the day.

He felt the hangover from the joy they all felt the night before. A joy quickly tarnished by the pain Abuela was feeling currently. But that was life. It was always there to remind them why joy was so important: because it could be easily taken away.

To distract himself from the pain, or to accept it even further, he spent the day with his Courtney.

During the evening, most of the gang came home. Most were too tired to talk, and so Lye sat on the doorstep with Bernabe. He walked into the house for a brief moment and grabbed two cokes. He passed one to Bernabe, and they talked.

"It- it feels weird. Just last night, we were having such a good time. What was the point of last night if we were only going to be sad in the morning?"

Lye thought back to how he had thought about the same subject earlier that day. He took a sip from his coke before he answered.

"Well, maybe...and I'm not sure how you feel about getting spiritual, but maybe we were given a happy day yesterday because someone knew we would be sad when the morning came. I know it hurts now. But the fact you feel sad now doesn't stop the fact you were happy last night. And the fact you were happy last night doesn't soften the fact you're sad now. I know it sucks, but you will feel better later on in life. But now, you just have to allow yourself to suck. She's still here with us, and I feel that should matter for something."

Bernabe looked over at his friend. "Yeah, but we were so close to losing her today. I don't know what would do when she's gone." his words quivered as he spoke. Lye decided not to mention that Bernabe said *when* she's gone and not *if*. Everyone would have to die one day, but Bernabe had accepted his grandmother didn't have much time as it is.

"Lucky for you, " Lye began. "I still have one shoulder that's not in a cast. You can cry on it, it's all comfortable and everything."

A dry chuckle escaped Bernabe's lips as he laid his

head on Lye's shoulder. It didn't take long before his tears saturated Lye's shirt. Neither of them spoke until Bernabe took his head off of Lye's shoulder and wiped his eyes. The moon shined above them, listening to them tell stories about Abuela. Most of them held the accounts of them getting in trouble in the days of their youth.

Saturday evening created a buzz not unlike many high school parities. As Felix had assumed, the house buzzed with black birds in the sky, and no less than a dozen cop cars stood in the yard. This didn't matter to the students, as they were more worried about loud music and having fun. Felix had made it a mission to let everyone know there were to be no alcohol, and anyone who was found with any paraphernalia would be kicked out immediately.

In the kitchen, Lye handed a drink to Felix, and went back in order to find one himself. Though the party was supposed to be about him, most people cared only about the music and the company. He didn't mind. He was grateful for the fact, especially since the party was a façade to begin with.

"So, who do we have here?" Lye asked after he returned.

Felix looked at him, taking a sip from her drink. "I'm not sure who's at the house; I'm pretty sure it's not just seniors here. But the drop box has been filling up quickly. Fifteen students are in the library, and five are with Bernabe to make sure the fire actually makes it inside the school once we light the memorial on fire." Lye nodded. There was no reason to hush their voices. There were no cameras, and anyone close enough to them were too preoccupied with the music to listen in on their conversation. Felix pointed across the room. Two students stood awkwardly, looking over at Lye. Lye felt for them; they both seemed uncomfortable at such a big setting.

Lye felt the same way.

Felix signaled for the duo to follow them. She led the way to her bedroom, a quiet place from the party. After yelling at a couple who had made their way up there to make out, she closed the door after them.

There was no reason to introduce each other. They've all gone to the same school for years. The first was Darnell Brown. Darnell was the richest student at Justice on his own accord. When he was thirteen, he created a piece of binary code he sold for thirteen million dollars. Lye didn't know what the code was for, so he never asked. The other boy's name was Wes Daniels. Wes had been arrested a few times for letting off explosions on his parents' property. As far as Lye knew, he was never convicted; his parents wouldn't press charges. Both boys met Lye with handshakes and laughter.

Regrettably, both boys looked at Lye with admiration, as though he had done something amazing. While Darnell was taller and bulkier than Lye, and a tad darker, Wes was very skinny and very fair. They both had the same look in their eyes, as though they've met a celebrity.

"Do the two of you have dates for prom?" Lye asked.

Both boys shook their head.

"Okay, so prom is on a Saturday evening. And I want you to do a huge thing for your country."

Lye explained his plan for the two of them. As he spoke, he watched their faces for anything that showed doubt, hesitation, or any hint they would tell on someone. He was grateful that he saw none of those things.

Wes was the first to speak. His face showed none of the emotions Lye looked for, but the guilt riddling his face was evident. "When I listened to you talk, I was surprised. I have to admit; I wasn't raised to believe-"

Lye put his hand up to stop him. "What's understood doesn't have to be said. And I understand. Soon you will too. Just because we're different, doesn't mean we can't want the same things. They've taken away our individuality, our ability to learn anything they didn't put in our face. So, we are trying to take it back. Us southerners have the added burden to prove not everyone born under the Mason Dixon line still think like it's the Civil War."

Wes sheepishly grinned, happy he didn't have to explain what he wanted to say. After a few minutes of ironing out the kinks of his plan, Darnell asked a question.

"How do you know we won't turn on you? Or turn you in?"

Lye pulled out a small black object from his pocket. "I've recorded the conversation. Crimes not yet done are excusable, but we've committed treason speaking ill of our government. And, as for turning me in. Well, Wes' signal is seeing me in handcuffs." All three boys nodded in understanding. It wasn't the lack of trust that created the somber tension. The admission Lye had thought of a contingency plan helped them realize how heavy their decisions were to be.

At that moment, Felix came in and handed a USB drive to Darnell, and promptly walked out. To a bystander, it would appear that Felix wasn't supposed to be a part of this all-male meeting. Lye quickly covered his smile at the thought. He had tried to convince her she should attend. Her argument was ironclad. She was the hostess of the party; it would raise suspicion if the hostess disappeared for a long period of time. Her absence in the meeting would insinuate she had little to do with what was going on. In her words: "Very few will think I'm associated with this when, in reality, I'm the one who orchestrated it."

The boys said their goodbyes and continued with the party.

***

The week leading up to prom was tense. Many seniors still felt the excitement of going to prom. In between every class was a reminder the students were required to wear the school colors at the dance. More than a few seniors were given detention when a teacher heard them speaking of what flashy colors they would wear. Police officers looked at Lye with itchy fingers, every day the posse speaking to him grew and grew as more high schoolers stayed on their tablets. It was not against school rules; tablets were the only way they could retrieve the information they needed. But even the most clueless of teachers noticed how students would speak of historical figures the teachers had never heard of. On a daily basis, teachers would ask questions on who Hamlet was. Twice a teacher had ran across the street to see if the Common Connector had any information about these heroes in vain. The teachers, happy their students were more than willing to go out of their way to learn more, never thought of bringing this peculiar happening to the cops.

A few hours prior to prom Lye sat between his mom's legs. He tried with all his might to get comfortable, but his sling wouldn't allow for such luxury. He sat on a pillow in their living room. Felix had gone out to pick up her prom dress. Mr. Davis was out with Courtney.

"Stop squirming." his mom said through clenched teeth. In between her teeth she held five miniature black rubber bands, all which would be used to tie the ends of Lye's braids once she finished braiding it.

"You're pulling my hair too much." he gritted.

"It's not my fault your hair is so thick. You definitely did not get my grade of hair."

She took her wide tooth comb and forced his curls into submission. Soon she took her skilled hands to turn the wool on his head into fine rows of hair.

"Why did you want to get corn rows? You want to look good for your prom picture? Then again, I would appreciate it if you did, I can't show my grandchildren ugly prom pictures." Lye thought of the still-healing bruises on his face and the sling around his arm.

She laughed at her own joke, and realized her son was not laughing.

"What's up?"

"I'm afraid of having kids." he said. Even though he was not able to see her face, she knew she wore the mask of confusion. "I- I just don't want to give my kids the problems I have. How could I look at my kids knowing the reason their mind is out to get them is because of me?

She stopped her braiding. Her fingertips were slick with hair grease as she listened to her son's feelings.

"When did you begin to feel this way?" she asked.

"I've felt it for some time. I just never said anything about it. I don't want to give a child depression. I don't want my child to have suicidal thoughts because his brain is all messed up. I don't think I could look my daughter knowing I caused her to be this way."

Mrs. Davis listened intensely. This wasn't what she expected to hear on anyone's prom night. But that didn't stop her from doing her duty as a mother. "It's almost narcissistic of you to believe you have that much power to *cause* that. Would you say I *caused* you to feel the way you do?" she asked calmly.

His head snapped up, something he immediately regretted since his mother still had his hair twisted around her fingers. "No. I mean, I wouldn't-"

"At which point do you think I see you less than my son, and only a mental illness? Have I done anything to make you believe that?"

He thought for a moment, though he knew there was no reason for him to do so. Never in his life had his mother made him feel any less loved, or any less adored because of what went on in his head.

"No ma'am."

"Do you think, after you have watched the baby grow inside their mother's wound, after you had taken them to the hospital back home, that you would think of anything besides making sure they are okay?"

Lye couldn't help but retort. "You sound like you're talking from experience."

She snorted. The air in the room turned colder as his mother thought on how to word her next message. "I guess it is my fault. I never told either of you. Forgive me. I had the same worries. I didn't talk to my mother about it, I never went to the doctor about it until after I had you. One would argue you inherited all those mental demons from me."

Lye stayed quiet for some time. "I didn't know-"

"And I apologized for this. I'm on medication just as you. Now, knowing I felt way, knowing that you inherited all those chemical demons from me, do you see me any other way? Am I just a lady with mental illnesses?"

"Well- no, you're my mother."

"Exactly. Every time I popped one of you out, I knew there was a chance you would be like me. And I still did it, not because you were meant to rule the world. Or that I thought you had great things to do in this world. Simply because you are my child."

He said nothing as she continued braiding his hair. He never knew. But it would only make sense. She always knew how to help him in his worst of days. It would make sense; she knew exactly what he was going through.

"Thank you, I don't feel as-"

"Alone? I understand. Forgive me for not letting you know these things when I could have. I'm sure I could have avoided a lot of confusion in your life."

"That's okay. I understand." He said. There was shame in her voice, and he couldn't help but say anything that would take that shame away.

With that she finished her braiding, and he walked up the stairs to edge up his hair. When he came down, Felix had returned. His mother helped him into his tuxedo. It would have been hard for him since he had restrictions on how he could move his arms. Once she was done, she stepped back and looked at her son.

"You look handsome." She looked at Felix. "I take it you're going to get dressed at Alexis' house?"

Felix nodded. Mrs. Davis kissed her son on the cheek. "You have fun now, and think about what I said. And no baby making." She smiled.

The couple wore tired smiles as Bernabe opened the door for them. Lye had to admit he was somewhat taken aback looking at his long-time companion. Social media already whispered about the Justice school prom. Various students had already posted their dresses and suits, wearing the brightest of blues, oranges, and greens. The most popular picture was of a girl who had handstitched her own rainbow dress. But nothing compared to the awe of looking at his best friend dressed up.

Bernabe smiled at them, moving out the way so they could come in. He wore a maroon tuxedo with black trimming. His shoes matched his suit, but his shirt and bowtie were the same black as the trimming of his jacket. He had shaved his face, and-

"Did you wax your eyebrows?" Lye asked. Felix stifled a laugh while Elsa walked up. True enough, the thick eyebrows they were accustomed to were gone; and trimmed photogenic imitations sat in their place. Bernabe nodded, restraining himself from touching his face.

"I think they look nice." Bernabe said.

"I agree." Elsa said as she walked up, kissing Bernabe on his cheek. Elsa grabbed her make-up bag and led Felix to the bathroom. She had waited for Felix to come before she got dressed. Bernabe sat in his living room as they waited on them to get ready. Bernabe's house was old enough to have individuality; there were no pictures of Lord President. The furniture had been handpicked by the family, and it didn't share blueprints with the entire neighborhood. But Lye could only concentrate on Bernabe's eyebrows.

After his fifteenth jab, Felix and Elsa walked out the bathroom. Elsa wore a maroon dress. She smiled uncertainly as she looked at Bernabe. Felix wore a turquoise mermaid dress that held to her figure well. Both women wore matching high heel shoes. Both men were breathless when they took in their respective date, and they hugged each other in congratulations on who would hold their arm. Seeing the two hugging, Felix couldn't help but make another comment on the possible marriage of the two.

From her purse, Felix pulled out a bottle of vodka.

"I couldn't find any whiskey in my dad's cupboard, but I did find this. It's ninety proof, so it should do the trick." Elsa looked around at the boys, wondering at want point did they agree they would be drinking. Neither said anything as they went outside to Bernabe's truck.

Lye helped Felix climb into the bed of the truck, which had been padded with old blankets in response to the night requirements. Bernabe helped Elsa into the passenger seat. And slowly drove toward the railroad. The air was expectedly warm, so a ride in the bed of the truck would be nowhere near uncomfortable.

"Do you have a handkerchief?" Felix asked Lye. He sheepishly denied having such a thing. With a sigh she brought her leg up, reveling the knife she always carried in her. She cut the helm of her dress seven inches, leaving a ragged tear on the otherwise perfectly cut dress. As she did Bernabe stopped in front of the memorial.

He opened the window connecting the bed to the truck and directed his words at Felix.

"I took down a board in the front. I'm sorry, but you only have one shot. It shouldn't take more than that."

But Felix wasn't listening to that, she had already taken the bottle of vodka from her purse and stuffed three inches of cloth into the bottle. She took a lighter from Lye and lit the piece of dress that hung from the lip of the bottle.

"You underestimate me yet again Alexis." she said, bringing her arm back and throwing the Molotov cocktail toward the memorial.

There was a muffled sound of glass breaking, followed by a *whoosh* as the dry air, along with dry books, dust, and a room full of wood, caused the fire to erupt within seconds. As soon as the teenagers were sure the fire would sustain itself with the constant dry food they had given it, Felix fell down to the bed of the truck and Bernabe sped off in the opposite direction, toward Montevallo.

Felix licked the vodka from her fingers, watching the orange glow in the night.

"Viva la Revolucion."

TEN

The brightness of the orange glow was dull compared the colors popping at their prom. As was tradition, prom was held at the American Village in Montevallo. The American Village was a slice of the past. Most of the buildings were made to imitate the eighteenth century. It had been a tourist attraction for years; statues and replicas littered the place. Lye couldn't help but smile at the amount of different colors people wore. There were different shades of blues and oranges, pinks and greens. Many people greeted Lye as they walked toward the dance floor.

The photographer had objected to them wearing such colors. He had threatened to call the police. Realizing an unprecedented amount of colors lined up for pictures, he quickly grew quiet. At every prom he had seen, there was always one person who didn't want to follow the rules. But this time the number of criminal students was something he was unprepared for.

"Are you sure this is going to work?" Bernabe said

as they entered the dance floor. The DJ had set up shop a few feet in front of a portrait of George Washington. Many students had already begun to dance. There were some students who had not listened to Lye's request. But they were in the minority, and they kept themselves away from their criminal counterparts. Lye smirked, taking a swig of his drink. "Not at all, there is a good possibility we will all go to jail tonight."

The foursome broke up as they danced with their respective partners. Laughter and happiness once again crept into Lye's heart. Soon he forgot about the conversation he had with his mother. He looked over at Bernabe. His friend held a strained face, as though he was somewhere else as he danced with Elsa. Lye didn't think to bring it up, but he was sure his friend's thoughts were on Abuela, and of course, Lye himself.

Soon enough the music stopped. The students looked over at the stage. Lye could only guess it was the prom committee. He sifted through his memory to find who was on the prom committee but had to accept he had been too distracted to worry about what some would call the best night of their lives.

"It's time for us to declare prom king and queen!" said the bubbly girl holding the microphone. She wore a slim purple dress. She reminded Lye of Mrs. Peeves. Everyone clapped as she continued. Lye continued to look around as she spoke, hoping against hope their plan would work. Every shift in someone's posture seemed like a cop coming after him. Every clap sounded like the shot of a gun. He tried to breathe evenly as he saw monsters in the shadows.

"For Prom Queen, it is our very own Felix Cambridge!"

The crowd continued to clap. Lye looked over to see that Felix had already made it halfway to the stage. He watched as they placed the ceremonial sash around her shoulders, and a crown upon her head. He snapped his fingers the best he could.

"And for Prom King, of course, we have our very own Lye Davis. I'm sure everyone knows that he's going to be Lord President soon, so give him a round of applause."

Lye slowly walked toward the stage. The applause they awarded him sounded forced compared to the one Felix received. He wondered if anyone there thought it treason not to clap. As they decorated him with his own sash and crown, he agreed with himself only his future title had given him the vote of prom king.

After giving thanks, they went back to their spot on the dance floor. Multiple people gave Lye handshakes as he walked past. The only one who seemed uninterested was Bernabe. Lye looked at him and returned his strained smile. It would soon be time for hell to break loose.

They continued to listen to the sound of music. Felix and Lye smiled at the congratulations their peers gave them, but tension continued to grow from the trio. They continued to give each other strained smiles until Lye figured what caused it. There was another sound in the background, but Lye couldn't identify it. Whatever it was put his mind on edge. He smiled as he looked at his classmates, his own smile tougher to keep on than it was only a few minutes prior. The room was filled with colors.

Quite a few members pushed the charged for sameness even further. Quite a few girls wore suits. The varsity quarterback wore a silver dress.

'This is going better than I had thought. It's been an entire hour-"

The sound that Lye couldn't identify roared in his ears now. Everyone stopped as they heard police sirens outside the building. The music stopped as they looked at Lye, all wondering what they would do next.

George Washington stood idle in his portrait as twelve police officers came in, all smelling like smoke and ash, all furious at the scene of insubordination. One of the officers, in his fit of anger, went over to the DJ stand and flipped it over. The leader of the pack, while he didn't like what his subordinate had done, said nothing. All of the kids looked at the officers as they stood.

"We want Lye Davis, if you move away from him, we will forgive you for what you're doing right now. " he said. He scanned the room looking for the boy. Lye had gone into the corner of the room only minutes prior. There was rage in the officer's voice as he spoke again. "We know all of you are acting on his orders, we will look the other way if you help us."

Lye took his hand off Felix and started to move toward the officers. Before he was able to finish the trek across the room, someone put his hand on is shoulder. Lye expected it to be Bernabe, but a glance to the left showed that Bernabe stood a few feet away; Elsa behind him. The owner of the hand was the quarterback he had witnessed earlier. He stood in front of him, protecting him from the cops, defying the officers.

In response, they all drew their weapons, pointing at the human shield who dared protect the prom king.

"If you don't get out the way, we will shoot you." One of the officers said in a trembling voice. It was the lack of conviction in his voice that betrayed his identity. Lye peered into the pack to see Will holding his gun with equally trembling hands.

In true teenage spirit, the crowd made no move to submit to authority. Many of them had stopped dancing, and walked in front of the quarterback, putting more bodies between Lye and the officers. The students who didn't listen to Lye's words started crying in the corner. The officers yelled, but the students wouldn't budge. Their hearts, once they had tasted the fruit of individual thought and clarity, would not allow them to go back into the state in which they were. The photographer, who prior to this had tried to refuse to take pictures, found an opportunity to make money, and started taking pictures of the opposing forces. To his left stood the conformed and uniformed officers. Each one with their weapons drawn. The faces of the officers twisted with fury and spite. There were some who seemed to salivate to the idea of shooting. Lye noticed their itchy fingers, twisting as they waited for the order to open fire. Only Will showed hesitation; he was closer in age to the teenagers he held his gun to. The photographer continued to take pictures, this time of the teenagers.

They showed no anger; there was no fury. And while the photographer didn't see it, that did not mean it wasn't there. They all, besides the ones who stood in their uniform, felt the anger of knowing they had been lied to, they had been misled. But their faces were stone. They stood as the barrels of the gun pointed at them. They dared the policemen to shoot. The silence was deafening, as both sides waited for the other to make a move. It was so silent in the room the sound of text notification sounded like thunder compared to the controlled breathing of both parties. Lye realized that it was his phone, and so he pulled it out.

"John 19:30" the text rang.

Not really the subtlest way of saying things, Lye thought to himself. He began nudging his guards of out the way, standing in no man's land between the officers and the student guard

Lye put his right hand up; his left arm resting comfortably in its sling. He grinned at the sound of twelve guns cocking; like he was sharing an inside joke with the bullets.

"I will go with you, just don't bring any harm to them. You're being recorded. And I'm sure they have no problem uploading this to the Common Connector."

"What do we have to worry about a bunch of kids for?" the leading police officer asked.

Lye shook his head. "Oh? Kids we are? We know things are not as they should be, and kids grow up. The problem with us kids is we outlive nasty adults like you. We realized this world is flawed. And we want change. And we will have change; Father time has granted us that ability. The battle against the youth is a losing battle. Either you help us get what we want, what we need, and what this country deserves. Or we will build a country truly free ourselves, with your rotting corpses as the foundation."

"Why are you telling me that?" it was Will again. Lye felt a surge of guilt as he looked at his friend on opposite sides of the war. As quickly as the feeling came, his conviction washed it away.

"I'm not talking to you. I'm talking to everyone who will see this video." He said, aware that many of the students had pulled out their phones.

The officer in charge had gotten tired of him speaking. He quickly slapped handcuffs on Lye's wrists and slapped the crown off his head. His classmates roared their thoughts at the officer, but the cop said nothing. Neither did Lye as the pack of officers led him outside toward the cars.

The cops' anger gave birth to fear as they walked outside. The orange glow in the sky; the sound or explosions rocked the pack as they ushered Lye to the car. This was not the fire they had taken care of. They threw glances of fear and suspicion at Lye as they ran to their own patrol cars. The officer pushing Lye shoved him into the car none too lightly.

The officer forgot to buckle Lye's seatbelt as he threw him in the back of the car. From the back of the cop car Lye could hear broken sentences, coming from the radio, letting the officer know what was going on.

"No casualties-"

"The Common Connector-"

"Someone had bombed-"

Each car sped off in the night toward the Common Connector. The cop driving Lye looked back at him, his face twisted in suspicion and rage... and fear. He had noted Lye had mentioned the Common Connector only minutes prior, and now the building was no more.

"Did you have anything to do with this?" The officer asked Lye, hoping the boy would confess with him. If humans could foam at the mouth from anger, it wouldn't take long for the officer to start.

Lye brought his handcuffed wrists up in a submissive gesture. "Sir, I've been at the dance the entire time. There was no way I could set off a bomb. I don't know the damndest about bombs."

Which wasn't entirely false. Lye didn't know a thing about the making of a bomb, but he *did* know who to talk to in order to have a bomb happen. That was the problem with announcing everyone's future job to the entire town. Everyone knew what everyone was good at.

The officer drove him in silence, they passed the Calera Police Department, and continued into the night. The buildings were soon replaced with hills, and the hills replaced with flatland. They drove until the country night was all they saw. The officer said nothing to Lye as he made the long drive.

Country night was a saying Lye had heard since he was young, but he didn't understand it until he sat in the back of a car. The darkness of the night was not one kept back by billboards and city lights. The headlights of the car did their best to keep the consuming power of the darkness back, only the stars above seemed to be able to keep it at bay, and still that did nothing.

The cop parked him to an unknown building. There were lights from the towers, and from the lights Lye could see guards walking the perimeter, watching to see if there was anyone who dared try to escape. The unnamed building was a prison; that was easy enough to see.

The cop still said nothing as he ripped car from the Lye, half guiding, half dragging him into the entrance. The walls of the building were painted with the same gray of the school he went to. The dullness made it feel as though they were siblings, if buildings could be related.

"Where are you taking me?" Lye asked, the cop still said nothing. The anger the officer felt was the only thing on his face as he looked at Lye, breathing with flared nostrils. Lye continued to walk, suddenly tired from the aftermath of the night he had.

The silent officer kept pulling him until they stopped in a room. The room had dust-covered posters of protocol long forgotten. A solitary man sat at the only desk in the room. He barely gave them notice as the officer slammed Lye into a seat. Lye couldn't help but figure the man was expecting him.

"Name?" said the man at the computer, not taking his eyes off his glaring screen.

"Lye Davis."

The man tore his eyes off the screen to look at him. After sizing him up, he began to speak in a hoarse voice. "When you speak to me, you will answer my questions with sir, do you understand me?" The hoarse voice showed the man didn't spend a lot of time speaking. His lips moved clumsily, as though they would soon forget how to perform their own function.

"My. Name. Is Lye Davis."

The two men stared at one another, a cold war to see which side would blink first.

The man at the computer took his eyes away from Lye and went back to his computer.

"Empty your pockets and put everything into the basket." Computer man said, gesturing to a plastic bucket to the left of him.

Lye took out his wallet and cell phone, none too kindly placing it in the basket. Forgetting to turn his phone off, he reached toward the basket.

"What are you doing?" asked the officer. Lye's hand hovered a few inches from his phone.

"I was going to turn my phone off." He said.

"No one asked you to. Don't touch it." He said. He brought Lye toward the back of a room and stopped once he had Lye facing a camera. Lye hadn't noticed the camera beforehand.

"Hold this."

The officer handed him a board that read "Justice Police Department." Lye stiffened a chuckle as he thought about what was going on. He was getting a mugshot in a tuxedo. The cop said nothing as he brought Lye back to his seat.

"I'm pretty sure I'm the best dressed person in this building, am I right?"

The officer said nothing else, instead he gave the floor back to computer man.

"Height?"

"Six foot even." Lye answered.

"Weight?"

"One hundred and ninety pounds, on a good day."

"Race?"

Not for the first time in the night, Lye laughed. "I'm thinking from the sheep wool on the top of my head it's obvious to see I'm black."

"I didn't ask you to make jokes, I told you to answer my question." the man said. He said in a sense of finality admitting he wasn't one who expected, or was accustomed to, people not giving him the respect he had grown to love.

"Do you have any physical ailments?"

"Nothing besides bullets and bruises one of your fellow men gave me."

Anger flashed on the face glued to the computer. "He was simply doing his job. If you had not been out past curfew, you wouldn't have a sling?"

Lye swallowed several quips about the lack of an

official curfew. "So, you admit it wasn't an assassination attempt?"

The man stood up and slammed his hands on the desk, leaning over so that his face was almost touching Lye's. "Listen here, you ungrateful spat. I don't know who you think you are, but you are nothing here. You do not say anything I didn't ask for. You listen to what I have to say. And you only speak when you are spoken to."

"You sound like my principal." Lye said.

The man brought his hand back in order to strike, but thought against it, and sat down. His previous anger all but forgotten as he went back to his job.

"Do you have any illnesses." Even though it was a question, it sounded more as a threat. Lye registered it and decided to answer the man's questions.

"Nope, I would claim I am as healthy as a horse."

"Do you have any mental problems?"

Lye sneered. "I wouldn't call them mental problems. But I do have mental illnesses-"

"I'm not here to hear you preach boy."

"Manic Depression, ADHD, GAD, and the ability to submit to improper authority."

"That would explain it," Mr. computer said in a huff. "I wondered how Lord President could have been so wrong with you. I guess he didn't know you're mentally ill. I guess I have been a little tough on you, considering you're not in control of what you do. "

"I am in full control of what I do." Lye said in defiance. He didn't like the idea his actions were being excused to an illness, as though he had not thought all of this through.

Another officer came in, they spoke in low tones so Lye couldn't hear what they were saying. The officer nodded and walked away.

Mr. Computer rose from his throne and walked toward Lye, none-so-gently raising him up and taking off his sling. Lye yelped a little in pain, but he did not say a word.

The officer brought him to a machine on the other side of the room.

"Give me your hand."

Lye complied. He stood in silence as the man scanned his fingerprints. Once the man was done, he guided the teenager back to the seat.

"What are my charges?" Lye asked, remembering the similar position he was in with Bernabe. The man continued to do what he had planned to do, unawares to what Lye was asking.

"I'll ask you again, in case you didn't hear me before. What are my chargers?" Lye asked, no longer keeping the venom out of his mouth.

The man on the computer said nothing, he continued to type as another officer came into the room. He held a jumpsuit, and a bundle of leather. They commanded him to strip as the officer handed him the jumpsuit. He had no option but to comply. His mind continued to wonder what the leather was for. Once he had zipped the jumpsuit up, the purpose revealed itself.

"A straight jacket? Really? Don't you think that's a little too far?"

"Mr. Davis, this is common protocol for anyone who is mentally ill. We do not want you to hurt any of the guards who work here." Mr. Computer stated.

"I'm not mentally ill. I have mental illnesses. And I can assure you there is more danger in me hurting myself than I do in hurting anyone else."

Still he complied with what the officer was asking. They tied the straps of the jacket. The pain in his shoulder subsided, the straight jacket acted as a sling for his arm.

As he tried to get accustomed to the new restraints, two officers led him out the room. They brought him into another room, just as bare as the one he had come from. A lone chair sat in the middle of the room. An older man stood behind the chair, dressed in white. He was so pristine it looked abnormal. The officers wasted no time slamming Lye into the chair, buckling a restraining strap across his chest.

The sound of clippers tore his attention from everything else in the room. As the clippers grew louder, Lye could feel the cool air on his head. He had grown his hair all his life; this was a feeling of which he had no memory. As he felt the twists of hair fall from his head, he resigned himself to keep a straight face. Though the tears threatened to come to the surface, he made no sound, he did not blink. His insides boiled with anger and hate for the man who cut his hair. But reason told him, as much as he wished to take a razor to the man's throat, his enemy was not the man. His enemy was whoever gave the order.

The thought did not quail his hatred as he saw more curls fall from his head.

Once they had fully humiliated him. They guided him to yet another room. This room had no man waiting for him. There was only sink, a bed, and a television. The only things Lye registered when the officer closed the door was the emptiness of his soul, and the coolness of his head.

The television propped on as soon as the officers locked the door.

An older man, dressed in a black suit and a red tie, began to talk.

"Hello citizen, you are here because you have forgotten what it feels like to be an American. That is okay. It is okay to be ignorant, but the biggest sin is to allow ourselves to stay that way."

The recording itself must have been years older, the technology of the film was dated. Since this was the only thing in the room that had any movement, his eyes held on to the movement on the screen.

"America is great. America is the greatest country in the world. As a citizen of this great country, you must understand we are here for you. We will never lead you astray. You will comply to us, as we have your best interest in mind. There are many things you may not understand, but dear citizen, as Lord President, I promise never to lie to you. I am one of you, I am for the people."

At the mention of Lord President, Lye's interest in the taping peaked. He studied the man in front of the green screen portraying the American flag flying in the distance. This man was younger than the man who visited him while he was in the hospital. He looked as though he believed in the words he said. But this was not the man that he knew. The President from the recording wore no gloves, his hands had nothing to hide on them. He had blue eyes instead of the brown of his predecessor.

You're going to die here, the intrusive thoughts of his mind inquired.

"Long time no see, I was wondering when you would pop up."

The appearance of one of the voices in his head briefly tore his thoughts from the tv. Although, without constant distraction, his eyes quickly went back to the only thing in his cell that moved.

"-America was once divided. Everyone had different thoughts, beliefs, morals, and understanding. The only way to reunite a country so diverse, is to take away the diversity. In doing that, we have shown that people can be one again. There is nothing that matters but being an American. Our children are American, our beliefs are American, our goals are American. And as long as we keep this dogma intact, our country will grow. We were once a country foolish enough to believe our diversity is what made us strong, but we were wrong. What made us strong is taking away the things that made us different. Soon, we will show you that different, is not good."

The recorded president smiled. The smile reminded Lye of a used salesman who finally saved enough money to buy a commercial. It was terrible. Still, it kept Lye's attention; it was the only thing in this room besides his bed. He was allowed a sink, but there was no toilet. That would be a problem in the future, but for now he didn't need to use it.

"*Nothing that I did mattered. I can't do anything here.*" said the little voice in his head, a little persistent.

"Shut up," Lye told the inside of his mind. He realized to the people watching him on the other side of the camera, he did appear mentally ill. He didn't know which was worse, the fact that he was talking to himself, or the idea he was talking to a recording.

Once again, he noted his thoughts took his attention away from the ongoing television.

He thought of Courtney. Images of her being arrested, being tagged along with whatever revolution he thought he had been doing, confronted the forefront of his mind. How many of his peers were in the same predicament because they believed they could make a change? He had no way of knowing whether the cops had kept their word in not harming his classmates. What of Bernabe? What of Felix? Were they safe? He didn't tell his mother anything, all she would know was the bombings, and his arrest. She couldn't be sure where he was. Was she out, looking for the prison he was in? Looking to see if she had seen his body on the side of the road as his friend had?

Images of scenarios that should never happen

popped in his head. The room he sat in disappeared until his brain took over everything, allowing him to see the imagined horrors that those who agreed with him would go through.

A moment of clarity rushed him from his thoughts as the guards opened the door. They held a collar in their hands, connected to three feet of chains.

Lye made no movements as they locked the chain around his throat, leading him out of the room.

At times they would tug on the chain as they walked down the hallway, causing him to stumble. They laughed as he almost tripped. His hands were tied but he was sure footed, so no matter how many times they would tug, he did not fall.

They led him into a room twice the size of his cell. There was a tray of food on the floor. The guards undid the chains and took of his jacket off.

He stood still as blood rushed into his stiff arms and fingers.

The guards looked at him. "Food and recreation. You have one hour."

They exited the room and locked the door behind him.

Lye looked around him, and almost laughed. There was a poster on the opposite side of the room, a poster that would have been more fitting in a school classroom. the words "Don't forget to smile" were on the poster, mocking the situation that Lye found himself in. He stretched, making sure to work out the muscles in his shoulder lest they get too stiff. He looked around the room, but there was no reason to do so. Only the poster about smiling decorated the room he was in.

He looked at the food on his tray. Despite of his current situation, or simply because of it, a small chuckle escaped his bruised lips. The food on the tray was taken from the textbook of prison food. The mush that sat on his tray may had resembled meat at a time long ago. Lye picked up the dirty plastic spoon and began to eat, wondering how someone could keep a dirty plastic spoon. If he had expected the food to taste any better than he looked, he would have been disappointed. The food had been freezer burned before it was cooked, and it was well past its expiration date. Still, he was never one to eat for anything more than bare sustenance. Lye silently ate the food. His stomach protested with the muck he fed it. Several times it threatened to bring up the food he had only just swallowed. After a game of tug of war involving his gastral acids, he stretched and decided he would attempt to do some yoga.

After a series of grunts, aches, and yelling at his muscles as though they were separate entities of his body; he stood up, drenched with sweat. His train of thought was derailed by the sound of a bell. He had heard the exact sound countless times at school, waiting for the period to end. Guards came in, holding his straight jacket and the accessory chains. He stood still as he was restrained. As they led him out of the rec room, Lye found it hard not to make similarities between his high school and his prison.

He was more than used to being in long hallways.

They had even painted these walls the same dull shade of gray. After a few steps it was easy to imagine every door held another classroom. To him, the long and empty halls only attested he was late for class.

He stood at the entrance of his cell, wondering why there were so many guards around him. One held the chain, and two stood directly behind them with rifles in their hands.

Most people may feet fear in this situation, but Lye laughed. Even if this was protocol, he felt a sense of pride of being seen as this big of a threat. That even with this straight jacket, the guards only felt safe if they had armed themselves against their prisoner. But he lost his smile as he entered his cell. Once he was safely inside his cell the guards took of his jacket and closed the door on him.

The television showed the same Lord President, but no longer did it show the American flag on it.

"Prisoner, I know you feel as though you are here because you are being punished. My friend, I do want you to know why you are here. You have forgotten the patriotic way. While it is true, this nation was once a nation of revolution. Of new ideas, and of even protests. But I do want you to know, this is not such a time."

Lye shrugged and laid on his bed. His shoulders slouched and screamed in pain, which he routinely ignored. As this was the only distraction to the sameness of his room. He felt there was no harm in listening to the lies upon the screen."...this is no longer a time for revolution, this is a time for peace and sameness. That is the only thing that can and will protect the American people. The sameness that we feel with one another. At times, I will admit, we will make mistakes. But we are only human.

"I want you to know however, my friend, some of us are better at being human than others. But even if you believe we have done things you do not agree with, that doesn't mean we do not have your best interest in mind. Your president, your congress, and all of your appointed leaders, we care so much for you. All of our babies, children, and stock, we love you are dearly, as God intended. Your congressmen love you so much, that sometimes they do not burden you with the responsibilities of knowledge. We know that the American people are too busy, too kind, and too occupied to constantly hear what we are doing in order to better this country. And so, we will not always tell you what is going on. Would a child dare spend his time asking his parents how they take care of the household? No, the child simply eats the food that his parents have paid for. He sleeps in the bed his parents have paid for him. He rests under the roof that his parents have slaved for. And what does the child do with his time free of the burdens of responsibility? He plays, he enjoys life. He frolics with his friends. What he does not do is worry. What would you like to do, my friend? Would you like to be a prisoner of worry, or would you like to be a friend? A carefree friend?"

The tv went blank.

"Who in the world still uses the word 'frolic?'" was all Lye had to say.

"You're going to die here."

Lye leapt from his bed as fast as he could; ignoring the pain shooting from his shoulder and torso. The voice did not come from the television, and it didn't sound as though it was coming from an intercom. It wasn't one of the voices he routinely heard in his head. The voice seemed to come from behind him. But there was no one. No one could have entered without his knowing.

Lye ran into his bed, covering himself up in a blanket in a juvenile attempt to hide himself from the voice he heard. He didn't want to admit it to himself, but if anyone else would have heard the same voice they would swear it came from him.

He closed his eyes, hoping that his unconscious self would release him from the sound of his pounding heart.

His dreams were filled with images of his family being arrested. His friends being executed, and his classmates being tortured. The restlessness of his sleep, paired with the ever-shining light in the ceiling, made it impossible for him to know when he had fallen asleep. Nor did he know how much sleep he had gotten. He stood up and immediately threw up the meal he had eaten, or at least tried to. Only this made it certain that he had slept long enough to digest a meal.

"Bang your head." cried the too familiar voice.

He rose his head so fast in attempt to look for the voice he did indeed, hit is head. After rubbing his head, he tried to remember the last time he had taken his medication.

"I've been here for two days. So, it can only have been a week since I- no wait. You've been here for a day.

So, it's only been six days since you've taken your meds. How long does it take that stuff to wash out of your system?" he stopped for a second. "Why am I speaking in the second person?" Conscious of the fact that answering that question would only make him question his sanity even more, he decided not to answer.

"Whenever you're in a situation where you feel you no longer have control, take a breath and relax." he told himself, regurgitating the advice Mr. Mike gave him last year, before the second increase of his medication. He sat on his bed cross-legged and began to meditate.

Lye thought of a situation in which he was in control. The only image his mind could conceive at the time was his bike. As his heart rate lowered, he thought of riding his bike unburdened. He imagined himself he was riding down his familiar Alabama roads. There were no black birds in the sky, and there was no camera in sight as he passed the roads. Tranquility slowly obeyed his command, until both his breathing and his heart rate lowered, and he threatened to slip into sleep.

As he fell deeper into unconsciousness his mind turned against him. The Alabama roads he ventured on were the same, but soon he noticed there were people on the side of the road sleeping. As his curiosity piqued, he got off his bike and looked.

His mother and father laid together. Lye smiled at first; until the crimson on their shirt and faces wiped his smile away. He trembled at the amount of blood surrounding his parents. Their too-still bodies mocked his efforts. He yelled at them to move, shaking them and yelling their name. They never did. He looked around and saw a familiar body. He ran to see Courtney. She too, was riddled with bullet holes. She too, would not move. She too, covered in crimson that should never be on her clothes. The more he looked around, the easier it became to recognize the bodies that lay on the side of the road. Bernabe and Felix crumpled in unnatural positions. It was obvious and heartbreaking to know their limbs no longer listened to the laws of a living body. More of his classmates appeared on the road.

Soon enough he realized where he was. He stood on the road to the memorial, He stood in the spot where he had been shot. Screaming and crying, he looked down at his hands. The sight made him puke in fear. His hands were covered with the blood of those who had helped him in his obsolete revolution. He looked down, and at his feet glistened the gun that had riddled his comrades' bodies with bullets. The trigger and barrel slick with blood. As he looked more his stomach could hold no longer as it emptied its contents over the gun.

He opened his eyes screaming. The vomit he had dreamed was entirely real. Gray vomit, mixed with stomach acid, ran along the front of his jumpsuit. He took it off and tried to wash it off in the small sink he was allowed. His hands began to shake uncontrollably as he tried to get the vomit from his clothes.

"Please, please not right now." he pleaded with the only prison that mattered to him. His body couldn't muster anything above a whimper. His heart began to pound. Sweat began to leak out of his pores. Soon more of his body began shaking. Lye stood there in his underwear and socks, rubbing the spot of his puke stained jumpsuit. Minutes passed and he continued to rub until his hands started to crack and blood started to stain the spot where vomit once stood. Realizing he had gotten himself in a loop, he threw his jumpsuit on the ground and crawled into bed once more. His body continued to shake. His body continued to sweat. and his mind continued to race as he thought of the well-being of all those who had tried to help him. He curled into the fetal position, shaking all over.

The television turned on again, but he didn't hear any of the words. His racing thoughts drowned out anything that attempted to catch his attention.

Lye lay there, too tired to move, and too afraid of his thoughts, to attempt to go back to sleep. He brought his hands to his face in an attempt to block out the ever-shining light from the ceiling. Lye brought his hands up, but the smell of blood caused his stomach to turn. He lay there, dry-heaving in his bed. A pathetic sight for a teenager who was Lord President-elect and revolutionizer. The thought of him in this state conceived anger.

"My name is Lye Aesop Davis. I am seventeen years old. I attend Justice High School." he said, inhaling the smell of his own blood with every breath. "My name is Lye Davis. My favorite color is orange. I am an African American male."

His breathing fluttered for a moment. He continued to speak his mantra of self-identity.

"My name is Lye Davis. I am a target." no, he thought to himself, positive thoughts. "My name is Lye Davis; I am seventeen years old." he repeated his mantra until his breathing and heart rate slowly went down. His energy fell in waves until he was much too lethargic to move out from his current position. He heard the door click after hours of lying there. Almost immediately he heard a bell ring as the door opened.

"Rec Time." said the guard on the other end. Lye knew the guard held a strait jacket for him to get in. He knew they carried weapons and batons in order to reinforce his obedience to their authority. But he didn't care. He was drained.

"I SAID REC TIME!" the guard yelled at the lump of muscles on the bed. There was no response.

"I'll give you three seconds and if you haven't moved since then, I'm coming in." he barked to no response.

In a heave, the guard slammed the jacket to the ground and swiftly made his way to the bed. From the sounds he was making, Lye could hear that he was pulling something out of a case. Next came the pain as the officer brought his baton down in swift motions.

"Get! UP!" he yelled. But still the lump in the bed didn't move. Even as he brought the baton down, the body before him made no movement. Not even the involuntary action to brace for pain emitted from the blows. The guard continued to bring his baton down until sweat dripped from his brow. But the body wouldn't move. It didn't care how many times it was hit. Once the guard realized he was defeated; he sighed and walked away. He grabbed the jacket off the ground, walked out, and locked the door behind him.

The physical pain was nothing more than a papercut on the broken hand which was his mind. He was too weak to speak, and the images of those who had helped him continued to creep until his mind until that was the only thing he could register. He was too weak to notice the bruises forming on his body. He was too weak to get into a more comfortable position. He was too weak to remove his bloodstained hands from his face.

Lye, for the first time in his life, was much too weak to fight.

ELEVEN

Weeks had passed, but there was no way for Lye to tell. The cell had no clock, nor did any of the hallways that he walked from shower or the rec room. After his third day (or at least, he thought it was his third day) the bell from the rec room followed him everywhere he went. A bell rang whenever someone came to open his cell. The bell rang whenever it was time to leave the shower or the rec room. The bell rang when it was time for him to eat. The bell was nothing new. The memories of the classroom were still fresh on his mind, and submission to a bell had been reinforced since he was four. The camera alone could tell the difference in Lye in the past weeks. Lye's eyes had begun to sink in to his skull, hiding away from the sameness of the cell. His cheeks followed suit, giving him an appearance of a skeleton. Black bags hung loosely under his eyes. There would be days he would sleep for double digit hours, and days where he would stare at the wall to pass the night.

Today was a day in which he slept. He had spent

the last ten hours sleeping, at least he thought so. There was no sunlight, so there was no way for him to know if he had overslept or had slept for too little. Time was an illusion for Lye, as there was no way for him to know.

He opened his eyes to the never changing scene but realized in the time it had taken him to get a peaceful rest, someone had changed it.

The walls were covered in red words. Someone had dipped two fingers in a paint can and wrote a paragraph on the wall nearest to the door, and farthest from Lye. Lye sat in horror as he read the red words.

"I'm sorry to everyone who to everyone believed in me. I'm sorry because I realize I had told a lie. And that Lye has brought my family great shame. I no longer can live with the shame that I feel, and I do apologize for the pain I will bring my family with this revolution. I hope one day you can forgive me, and if you do not, I at least wish one day you will understand. I won't give you all the reasons I had to do it, just know. I'm going do it. And I really had to do it. I hope you realize what I learned on my deathbed: America is Great."

Paranoia and horror clenched his throat as he realized he had just read his suicide note.

"I think it's my best work, what do you think?"

Lye looked over toward the sound of the voice and subdued toward the furthest part of his bed. Sitting on the edge, was Lye. At least the man looked like Lye. Identical to what Lye had looked like before he had been arrested. The doppelganger even had the braids that were cut off the first day of his imprisonment. He smiled at Lye and licked what could only be blood off his fingers, smiling the entire time. Blood caught on the edge of his teeth and gums; giving his smile a gory tint.

"Who the fuck are you?" Lye asked.

The doppelganger rolled his eyes. "Well, obviously I'm you. It's not like anyone here would waste taxpayers' money just to mess with your head. Then again," he said, pondering his words as he mockingly looked around the cell. "It's really hard to sell that argument to someone in solitary confinement, wouldn't you say?"

"You can't be-"

"I can't be you? I can't be real? My dear you just read a suicide note. And I *know* you thought that was real. I *am* you."

I must be hallucinating, Lye thought to himself.

"Well of course you're hallucinating. Do you know how long you've been in here? Well, I guess you wouldn't. And since you don't know, I don't know." he still smiled at Lye. "You really should control your breathing; you're heading toward another panic attack homie." The doppelganger smiled again; this time the notorious smile of mischief he learned from his mother.

Lye quickly listened. His breathing had increased, even if he didn't want to admit it.

"Why are you here?"

"I don't know, maybe your brain thinks you're lonely. I've been trying to talk for you for weeks. But you never would listen, would you? Also, I want you to call me

Aesop, it's better if we don't share the same name. For whatever sanity you have left."

"You never answered my-"

The bell rang on the outside door, telling Lye it was time for him to get up. In the weeks past, his mind had held on to whatever structure it could. At the sound of the bed he instinctively walked toward the door and held out his hands. The latch opened, and Lye walked up toward the steel door until his hands pointed out of the other side. Through his obedience, Lye was allowed out of his cell without the need of a strait jacket. No longer did he cause the guards any trouble.

"Step away from the door prisoner."

"Yes sir," was his simple reply. There was no sarcasm in his hollow voice. There was nothing. He sounded like a recording. A piece of data coming out of an automated machine after a button was pressed. The emotion of his youth, the tenacity of the man who helped orchestrate the arson of a school. Nothing was there.

The door flung open and the guard grabbed Lye by the shoulder, pulling him out of the cell and pushing him toward the way of the rec room. The guard held no chains for Lye, nor did he wear any weapons. Those were no longer necessary. Lye maniacally lead the way to the rec room. There were exactly three-hundred seventeen steps from the entrance of his cell to the entrance of his rec room. Every day he would count every step as he walked down the long hallway. The guard said nothing. He kept his eyes on his phone as he followed Lye to the rec room. Lye stopped at the entrance of the rec room. His head shot up in alarm. He had only counted three-hundred twelve steps, and not his usual number of three-hundred seventeen. He looked back down the long hallways and tried to envision the spots in which he had overstepped. When he realized he couldn't find it, he stepped in place for five paces. The guard opened the door, and silently Lye walked past. Lye turned around exactly one hundred and seventy-nine degrees; holding his hands out for the guards to take his handcuffs off.

The nameless guard casually grabbed his wrists and unlocked the metal restraints.

Lye walked toward his food and sat down. There was a burger and a bowl of clam chowder. A glass of coke sat next to the tray. He sat with his knees together and his buttocks on his heels. He ate in silence.

"You are embarrassing to me." Aesop's voice, or his voice, lingered in the air. After the initial realization it was a hallucination, he ignored it. After he finished the meal, he rose to his feet and began to jog the perimeter of the rec room. The room was ten feet by twelve feet. Jogging around the room exactly one hundred and twenty times would equal jogging one mile. He had jogged thirty times before Aesop appeared.

"You disgust me. I don't even know who you are."

Lye ignored the rebuke, continuing to focus on the number of laps he had jogged. Lye's face no longer showed emotion. He continued to breathe out of his nose while he ran. Aesop looked at him in a sneer, disgust slathered in every word coming from his lips.

"Listen to me you institutionalized fuck." Aesop

said, but Lye still ignored him. After he had jogged the entire mile, he dropped and began to do push-ups.

"The prison regimen is such. One hundred and fifty push-ups. one hundred sit ups, and fifty burpees." As he got down to a prone position, Aesop appeared again.

"Is there anything in that robotic mind of yours that resembles me?" he yelled.

Lye continued to ignore the mirage. His blank expression was the only thing Aesop received.

"I really wish I could actually hit you."

The bell for the door to open rang again, diverting Lye's attention yet again away from the hallucination.

Lye quietly rose again from his position and held his arms out for the guard to place the handcuffs on him. He quietly walked in front of the unarmed guard. He counted the same three hundred and seventeen steps, this time landing on the same amount he had come to expect.

The guard opened the door, and Lye looked into his room. His blank expression quickly froze and turned into one of fear. A yell escaped his lips, and he hurryingly tried to shelter himself with the guard.

"What the hell are you doing?" the guard asked him, oblivious to the things his prisoner saw. Lye backed away from the entrance of his cell. For the first time in weeks he fought against the pushing of the guard.

In the center of his room, suspended from the ceiling by the bed sheets tied around his neck, was Lye's body. His lips had already turned a faint blue hue from asphyxiation, and his muscles twitched as his dying brain tried to send any impulse throughout his body. The image sent chills down Lye's body. As the guard grabbed him again, he threw up, covering the guard in the vomit of the freshly eaten food.

The guard stepped back in disgust and reached for his baton. There was nothing to grab, however. He had stopped carrying any weapons as Lye became more obedient. Realizing he had nothing to subdue the teenager, he reared his hand back and hit him across the jaw.

The final sounds and sight Lye saw as he fell to the floor was his own blue lips parting and a demented laugh escaping them. Then everything turned black.

"Wake up."

Lye moved a little, but kept his eyes closed.

"Please stop being a prick with me. I'm in your head. I know you can hear me."

"You're not real." Lye said. It was the first words out of his mouth that didn't sound robotic. He opened his eyes and tried to stand up. Looking down, he realized he was in a strait jacket once again. The guards hadn't placed him on the bed. He sat on the floor near the sink. They had made sure he could still see the television and nothing more.

Aesop squatted directly in front of Lye. "You keep complaining I'm not real, yet I keep showing up. It's time we talked."

"Why did you show me that?" Lye accused.

Aesop stood from his squatting position, deciding to walk around the room. He stared at Lye, unsure how to start the conversation. The resemblance was uncanny. As Aesop's brows scrunched up and his lip rose into a snarl; Lye didn't have to search far to imagine what it took to put that picture on his face.

"Do you know why I keep doing this? Because I'm only showing you what you want to see, your imbecilic ass." Aesop reached behind him and pulled out a gun. Lye almost pissed himself as he looked at the standard issue Glock nineteen. The smell of blood flirted with his nostrils as he took in the red coated barrel and trigger. He had seen this gun before in his dreams. Lye watched as Aesop brought the gun to eye level. He tried his hardest move away from the gun point. But he was restrained; he could only watch as the gun came closer.

"You keep asking me to do this to you. You keep asking me to remind you what you're doing wrong. Your brain, our brain, is freaking out and the best thing to do is create me to teach you this lesson."

"What lesson?" Lye asked, unsure if he wanted to know.

Aesop put the barrel of the gun on his tongue, using the barrel as a tongue depressor.

"Dis es wat yur doi do yorself." and he pulled the trigger. Blood splattered on the opposite wall. Gray matter splattered over Lye like confetti. As Aesop fell the blood leaked down Lye's own sleeves."

Panic pounced upon him. His breathing continued to rise until he was highly ventilating.

The restraints would not allow him to move no matter his persistence. A change in the cell brought Lye's eyes to the camera. The light on the camera. The freshly installed light was blinking like crazy.

"OOOhh, that's new." The words came from the stiff body across from him. His stiff body. Aesop brought himself to his feet. He stretched and yawned, as though he had taken a nap, and not blown his brains out. "I wonder what's that's about." He turned his head toward the camera. The back of his head had been completely blasted off. Seven braids were gone; in their place lay a crater of brain and blood pumping through his hair with every beat of his dying heart. Aesop was unabashed at the gaping hole in the back of his head; more concerned with the camera than anything else.

He looked back at Lye with a childish grin in his eye. "Oh, it's started. And I can't remember what that means. Do you?"

Lye said nothing. Aesop threw his hands in the air in mock defeat. The blood from his bullet wound started falling on his shoulders as he walked closer. "Why did you have to start hallucination when you're at the most boring version of yourself?"

"I-I can't breathe."

Aesop turned his nose up at Lye. "Why are you telling me that? I know you can't. Oh, you're not talking to me." Aesop looked back the camera again, revealing his bleeding head to the original and rightful owner. "You're talking to whoever is supposed to be watching you."

Lye vomited yet again and passed out.

When he came to, he tried to wipe his nose, but noticed he couldn't move his hand more than three inches. He opened his eyes and tried to look around, but he couldn't move.

"And the little one is up." Aesop spoke.

"Oh, you're awake." said a different voice.

Lye attempted to look over but remembered he couldn't. The voice was female; it sounded friendly enough.

"Please do not try to resist. Right now, you're restrained to a bed. I know it seems like an unnecessary precaution, but you were struggling while you were unconscious. Now, 389-84-5484, tell me, what's been going on?"

"Why did you read out my social?" he asked.

"That's your name. Your real name. There can be several 'Lye Davis's in Alabama, let alone the country or the world. The only way our benevolent leaders can tell the difference between the mix is by your real name. The name you were assigned at birth. Would you like it if I shortened it for the sake of our session?"

"I would appreciate it if you called me Lye, the name my mother named me." Lye snapped. Though he couldn't see Aesop, he could hear his fingers snapping with sass.

More scribbling from a point out of view. "The man you attacked told me you were being so obedient as of late. I must ask you, what is new? What is going on?"

Lye said nothing. He looked at the ceiling, as it was the only thing he could see for the time being. He began to count the number of white tiles that he saw.

"389- Lye, would it be better for the sake of the conversation if I undid your straps?"

"It would help." He answered.

She chuckled as she walked closer over to him. She began to undo his restraints, and soon enough he was able to sit up straight.

The room around his was no longer gray. He was in a white room. The woman in front of him was dressed in white too. She wore a pant suit coupled with a friendly smile and a familiar face. No matter how many times he raked his memory he couldn't decide if he knew her or not.

"I don't know what's wrong with me doctor." He wasn't sure she was a doctor, but he thought she was a doctor, and so he called her doctor.

"What's wrong with him is he needs his medication." said his voice beside him. He looked over and saw Aesop. This time he was wearing the tux Lye wore for prom, thankfully his head was intact as he sat there.

"I think I need my medication."

"Lye, why would you ever say such a thing like that? Why would you ever think you would ever need to alter the way God made you? Are you saying He made a mistake when he made you? You don't need medication. You never needed medication. You were never on any type of medication. You just believe you do. I'm sorry that you do."

Lye thought for a moment, he couldn't remember much. But he could have sworn that for some reason he needed medication. There was something different from him.

"Don't you trust me? There's no reason for you to believe you would need such a terrible thing."

"Firstly," Aesop said, interrupting Lye from talking. "This hoe's finna get dog walked. There's enough medication for limp dick to go around but God forbid you take your medication for mental health."

"Did I take medication?" Lye asked, beside himself.

The nice lady smiled. Her smile made her seem like a friend. Lye relaxed. He hadn't noticed he had been keeping his shoulders tight. He took his tongue off the roof of his mouth and unclenched his jaw. He was holding in a lot of stress, stress that he couldn't remember why he was holding in.

"No, I promise you. You never took medication. That's why you're in the hospital. Because you need help. We are here to help you."

"Here to help me?" Lye said. he couldn't think straight. There was something that wasn't right about that information. He couldn't remember going into a hospital, but he couldn't remember much outside of his cell. Every memory he could think of slipped through his hands the harder he tried to think about it.

"Yes." She said. "I am here to help me. Is there anything that you want to talk about?"

Lye took another look at the nice lady. He took a deep breath, ignoring the look of insult Aesop was giving him. "I- I have been having hallucinations doctor."

Aesop put his hand to his heart and let out a hurt gasp.

"Tell me more about these hallucinations." She said.

Lye took a deep breath. "I keep seeing myself dying, what would that mean?"

"It means you're getting better. Many people have hallucinations in your position. That is your brain getting all the toxic parts out of you. Sometimes we must purge ourselves for the sake of ourselves, wouldn't you agree?"

"Yes ma'am." Lye nodded. He thought he agreed. The kind lady didn't look like she would lie to him.

Aesop walked over to the nearest wall and banged his head on the wall. Lye tried his hardest not to look at the hallucination, knowing it would call for more questions. "You're not in a hospital, you're in prison. Of course, you need medication, given the fact I'm here." He stole a look at the nice lady in the pants suit. "I swear if this woman turns me into a plot device, I will haunt your dreams." He threatened.

"Do the hallucinations talk to you?" the lady asked.

"No ma'am, they never speak to me. But- I think they have helped me see what I have done wrong. I think I remember why I was in this hospital. I went against the American way, and I went crazy. If I had only stayed on the route of the American way, I wouldn't have this problem."

The nice lady, dressed in all her white clothing, gleefully clapped. For a moment she reminded him of another woman who clapped in such a faux patriotic way. The other woman stayed in a gray room, not a white one like this, but he couldn't remember who the lady was.

"Ma'am, do you know when I will be able to get out of this hospital? I would like to get home to my family." Lye said. he remembered his family at least. His mother who would share a coke with him on bad days, his dad who made him laugh, his sister who asked questions.

There had to be a reason why they took so much time with him.

"We do not know that for sure Lye, whenever you seem to get better, we will let you out. But for now, let's talk about you. How are you feeling?"

Lye stole a side-eye glance; his mirage of a companion was nowhere to be seen. He took in the room a bit more, everything was dressed in white, to the point where it was almost unnecessary. He smiled at the nice lady. "I feel lonely. At times I wish it would all leave, y'know? I don't want to die..." he trailed off and found his confidence in his voice once more. "I don't want to die. I just want to get rid of this empty feeling. I don't want to feel other people's pain anymore."

"What about your own pain?" she asked.

"I can live with my own, that's not the problem. It's others', it's worse when I try to go to sleep. It's like I can hear people screaming, people who can't make it. I want to help them all, but I can't. And that bothers me."

"You have taken in too much responsibility my dear." The nice lady said, "You are trying to carry a burden that doesn't belong to you, and that's the reason you feel the way you feel. You are only a teenager Lye, what can a teenager accomplish in this world? Very little. That is why you feel as though there is this high expectation on your plate. Because you won't allow yourself to be a child. And that is the problem. You must let the adults do the worrying. Let the adults handle the decision making. Let the adults do all so you don't have to worry about such things. Do you understand what I am saying? You are much too young to believe you know what's going on in the state, in the country, in the world. Hell, most teenagers your age don't even know what's going on in their own households. But I will tell you this, you have to let everything go, that is the only way you will truly be free of your own worry."

"I think I understand." Lye said; the words falling meekly from his lips. Somewhere behind him he heard himself snort.

And when he was brought back to his cell. He immediately tried to bash his head in the wall.

The cell door flung open, and a pack of guards came in to subdue him.

They did not handcuff him. One of the guards produced a needle and rammed the needle into the scrambling teenager's arm. After a few moments the he fell asleep.

TWELVE

The self-induced torture of Lye's mind had been so great it could be seen physically. His eyes continued to shrink inside his head, as though to escape the lack of sleep. His weight continued to fall, giving him a more prominent skeleton appearance. His wounds have healed, but his body was stiff from the constant restrictions of the straight jacket. No longer did Lye's eyes show the gleam that welcomed everyone he spoke to. No longer did he show a grin whenever someone mentioned something he did. The officers who guarded him always showed a look of triumph. They had broken the teen, and they had no guilt and showing their happiness in doing so. The destruction of his spirit had become so great, the old man with gloved hands decided to give him a visit.

The only difference in Lye's cell was the new chair to accompany the older man. Lye sat in the corner of his bed as Lord President walked in the room. Lye looked up. His empty eyes focused on the man, but they showed no recognition. Lord President had a look of hurt in his eyes.

Not genuine hurt, but the hurt of a man whose prize horse had collapsed on the track.

"You look terrible." he said, his voice hurt, his eyes soft.

Lye said nothing to show he heard what the president had said. It had been weeks since he had said anything at all, and it didn't seem as though he would start now. The only time he heard his own voice since the therapy session was through Aesop.

"Will you at least talk to me?" Lord President said.

Lye continued to stare at the man, his eyes lacked any recognition of who he was talking to, or listening to, to be more accurate.

Lord president seemed defeated. Unbeknownst to the older man, the camera in the corner of Lye's cell began its irregular blinking again.

"I had hoped that you could bring change. That you would do something in this country. And if you wish to know something, I was not entirely wrong." He began, trying to bring Lye back to reality.

Lye shuffled in his seated position, still he showed no signs he was listening to what the man in front of him was saying. The older man took off his jacket and nodded to the camera. The blinking had stopped when the president looked at it, but once he turned his attention, it resumed its irregular blinking.

"In the time in which you've been here, the American people have grown angry. I don't know how you pulled it off, and honestly, we don't have enough evidence to say it was you, since most of the evidence had either been burned or bombed. But in the months since your incarceration, there had been a hard dump of documents available in the Common Connector. Someone had taken pictures of the pages of books they found. They have been the most downloaded thing in the history of the Common Connector. The dates in which these things were published are causing outcries that the people have been lied to. I would like to believe that this was your doing."

In his impatience, Lord president leaned over, waiting to see if any of the words he had said had reached his once successor.

"My group of advisors are split in half over a decision. Half of them believe I need to resign before I am impeached. Half of them had forgotten either of those things could happen. Because of the overload of unfiltered information, many of the politicians believe their best bet is to leave the country before the common man decides to take off their head. A few were brave enough to try and take the money they've made over the years, but when news of that came over, their accounts had been hacked. There are people who are calling you a terrorist. There are people who are protesting telling us they want you freed. More people want to hear what you have to say. They want guidance. And they no longer believe they want the guidance of a frail old man. Still you have nothing to say about that?"

Nothing.

"And you lay here, broken and defeated. I must say I am disappointed. I believe I had failed you."

Lye made eye contact with the man. For a brief moment, something flickered behind the dark fog in his eyes. Lye opened his mouth, and for the first time since his therapy, he spoke.

"What have you heard about my conditions?" he asked. His voiced creaked like the door of his Memorial. It had been too long since anyone had needed its guidance.

Lord President looked at the boy. Like many adults in his position, he looked to see if the boy had anything up his sleeve. Once he realized he couldn't find the signs he was looking for, he began.

"At times you don't sleep for days, sometimes you sleep for two days at a time. The guards have noticed you talking to yourself, gibberish that wouldn't make sense to anyone here. The doctors can't find a reason for your twitching, you seem you can't stay still. Which itself is a feat considering you're in a strait jacket. You've become hostile, I heard you tried to bite one of the guards, on multiple occasions. Then there are times you've been having hallucinations. You've been asking help from a man named Aesop? You cry for no reason, and at times you believe you share this cell with a demon. But the worst I've heard if your inability to care about what's going on to you. Guards have tried to move you out of bed, you don't eat at times for days on in. You look terrible."

Even as he spoke, the older man couldn't help but notice the little light behind Lye's eyes growing brighter. For a moment he thought of ignoring it. He was safe. This boy had been locked in a cell for months under twenty-four-hour surveillance. But he couldn't help the anxiety he felt looking at the restrained teen. Fear blossomed in Lord

President's heart as the prisoner's cracked lips spread into a smile.

"I've noticed the little hesitation you're having right now," Lye began, becoming more coherent with every word. "I would like to say... everything you've spoken about could be counted off for the fact I haven't been on my medication for the better part of two months. Honestly, I do appreciate you getting me out of school for the past two months. But I haven't learned at thing here.

Lord President laughed. "You're bluffing, there is no way this cell had had no impact on you. Just look at yourself."

It was Lye's turn to laugh. The sound of the mirthless laughter bounced off the walls of the cell. "I never said there was no impact. I just said the impact was not due to you. I knew you would most likely put me in a cell. Even worse I was sure I would get similar treatment to Felix, where there would be a constant attempt of brainwashing going on by my favorite government. Everything you mentioned, while adding the fatigue and muscle soreness, if you cared about that, was not only something I expected to happen, but something I *encouraged* to happen. I had stopped taking my medication six days before prom started."

"You Lie!" the president accused. There is no way this boy could have done such a thing. No way he could have *planned* such a thing. In his anger Lord President stood up but composed himself long enough to carry the conversation.

"Why would I lie? I'm stuck in a cell; I don't get

anything out of lying to you. At most I might get you to worry, but I have bigger problems. I've been waiting for you to come and visit me. I wanted to have a conversation with you."

There was no longer a suave older man instead of him. Lord President was getting angry. Angry at the idea Lye dared to bluff at a time such as this. "What can you possibly have to say to me? Are you ready to give up your accomplices? You realize that people have begun to call you a terrorist? The news is saying you're in hiding. That we can't find you. Even with the things you've uploaded, that won't be enough for people to believe you. You're just another-"

"I said another conversation, not a mudslinging competition. What were you going to say, dear president? Was it nigger? If it was, you can say it, I'm sure you do many things when you know that no one is going to hear. You don't understand what it's like being black in America." Lye said.

"We've all heard it before. It's like having a target on your back. Blah blah, when will you ever get over it?"

Lye chuckled. The smile hadn't left his lips since he started talking. "What happened to the nice president? And we will get over it when there is change. When the narrative is changed so that a black man can face the same type of scrutiny as our white counterparts. If a white man was accused of the things you accuse me of right now, he would be called a lone wolf. That he was mentally ill, and he needs help. I am a terrorist. Don't get me wrong, I'm used to the double-edged sword. Y'know the saying, give me liberty of give me death? That statement has been hammered into my head I was arrested. Do you know what our people would do to me if I started yelling that on the rooftops? It would cause riots. They would make an example out of me."

Lord President sat down and composed himself. There was nothing wrong with a conversation. There was no way for Lye to do anything to him. He could tell the teenager was prompting him, but there was no harm that could happen here.

"Well don't you think white males have it bad as well." he countered.

"The presence of privilege doesn't negate the absence of a struggle. But you can't tell me having fair skin doesn't open doors in our country."

The president threw his hands up. But his curiosity kept him in his seat. "White children have their own set of fears, Lye. It's been too long since our boys didn't have to carry the fear of touching a woman the wrong way. Of-"

"Consent?" Lye interrupted. "I speak of racial injustice and your counter argument is white boys have to fear consent?!"

"They worry about being falsely accused." Lord President said, realizing he hadn't thought his argument through.

"Of rape? They fear the responsibility of a decent human being? And let's talk about being falsely accused. And how much of our nation is of black boys being falsely accused? How much of that history has been washed away? The difference is when black boys are falsely accused, we don't get fifteen minutes of fame, we get executed. "

"So, what do you believe? What do you want?" Lord President asked.

"I want blood and broken bones. I want your head on a pike. But I know that's only because I am angry. And anger tends to tear us away from our common beliefs. I believe in loving your neighbor. I believe in watching out for your fellow human. I don't believe they should be like us in order to get help. I believe we were created and evolved to be different. In our difference we can be unique. But I believe we should unite against our common enemy."

"Me." The president sighed. "I thought we were on the same team Lye. That we wanted the same thing."

"Don't overestimate yourself. The common enemy is not one man. It can't be shot or stabbed. The common enemy is the system. Wars are not fought to protect people; we sacrifice our people to protect the system. Laws are passed based on how they benefit the system. Police brutality is profitable; victimless crimes have double digit-sentence, and senators get away with the *fears* you mentioned because of the system. Once we tear down the system, we can make change."

"You mean how you commanded people to break the law?"

"If you're talking about the prom fiasco, that wasn't by any means me commanding people. I gave them a choice. Either they could choose to be their individual selves, or they could continue to submit to the sameness we are taught. I allowed them to do so by taking the consequences of their actions. I knew everyone would blame me, and I was okay with that. But I didn't command them. I reminded them they had a choice."

"You threatened almost every person older than you. If I recall, you said you would build the foundation on our dead bodies."

Lye brought his head back in laughter; mirroring Lord President the first time they met in the hospital. "I did no such thing, I simply told them the facts. Father Time is on the side of the youth, he will always be. You will all breathe your last before we do. I never said we were going to kill anyone. Either help us achieve the human rights we so deserve, or we will wait until age does our job for us."

Curiosity slowly took the place of anger as Lord President asked his next question. "Am I a part of the system?"

"You are a pawn. It was decided we should fall long before you came into play. We are governed and conditioned to believe that the way of America is us versus them. Black versus white. Police versus poverty. That is not how it should be. If anything, it should be those who see people as profit versus those who see them as people. It should be the people, versus the issue. Not the people versus the people."

Lye stared at the president, the light in his eyes no longer hiding behind the dark fog he had only minutes prior. "We deserve to be individuals. We deserve our human rights. We deserve to be diverse. And we can no longer sit back and wait for old white men to decide on how diverse the youth should be."

Lye looked at Lord President again. The fire had returned to his eyes. Dread washed over Lord president as he listened. "Don't let them continue to tell you that you can't do anything because you are young. Don't let adults tell you that you can change the world, and then get mad when you attempt to do it. Believe in yourself, believe in your voice. We will create a world where they failed us."

"Are you having another illusion?" The president asked.

Lye ignored him and continued to speak. "You must remember that together, we can change things. Our enemy is not one person, and so one person cannot destroy. We must destroy the system. We cannot wait for those who benefit from it to destroy it. We must help those who are oppressed, even if the oppression doesn't affect us. We must stand together and let them know that we are here to stay. We are the youth. We are aware, and we will not back down."

"Who are you talking to?" Lord President yelled.

Lye attempted to stretch his back before he resumed the conversation. "Like I told you, I knew I'd be here. The information upload was just a distraction. I will give you a tip though. If you're going to make sure all the information in the country goes through one filter, make sure it can't be hacked. For future reference. It took ten minutes for someone to hack into the Common Connector. It took a month for them to locate the exact camera that's connected to my cell and send me a message to let me know. But it only takes about five minutes for someone with that knowledge to relay and stream a conversation to anything connected to the Common Connector, which is connected to every electronic device in the country. Maybe they were wrong about the revolution being televised. The entire nation has heard the youth, and they just witness the graduating class of Justice putting the American government in check." Lye chuckled. "Y'all really should have let me turn my cell phone off when you booked me."

The television came on. To Lord President's horror, he was not looking at the recorded speeches of his predecessor. He looked at himself looking at the television, with Lye sitting on his bed. The angle showed the recording was coming from the camera. The camera he was sure had been turned off. With realization on his face, and the horror of the situation, he launched himself at Lye, wrapping his fingers around the boy's throat.

A gurgled laugh came out of Lye's throat, echoed through the cell from the television. Guards came into the room, prying the elderly man off Lye. They soon subdued the boy, putting another needle in Lye's buttocks. Soon he fell into sleep.

But he fell with a smile on his face. Every second of the conversation since the older man walked in had been witnessed on every electronic device in America.

THIRTEEN

Without warning, the door to his cell flew open, it was the only sound of an outside world for the last ten hours, and so Lye's eyes instinctively clung to the door. In came a guard holding a set of keys.

"You're free to go, come here."

"What happened to Lord President?" he asked, standing from his bed and awkwardly walking to the door. He had been in the jacket for the better part of the last three months, and it had been easy for him to learn how to walk without his arms as a counter balance. But the fresh bruises of yesterday caused his footing to be ever so off. The angry guard hesitated before opening his mouth, "He stepped down. He's out of a job. To be honest, all of us are now out of a job because of you."

Lye stood still as the locks of the jacket were unlocked. "What do you mean?"

"Your little plan worked. The last of his executive

orders were to pardon you, and to close down our prison." he said through gritted teeth. As he finished the sentence the jacket fell to the floor, and Lye began to stretch. The guard produced handcuffs seemingly out of nowhere. Lye obediently held his wrists out, not listening to the sound of his bruises pleading him to take it slow.

The guard grabbed him by the arm and began to lead him out of the cell. For a few minutes they sat in silence. In the silence Lye found himself stuck in his thoughts. He was so wrapped up in his thoughts he didn't notice a pack of guards stood at the exit when he walked up.

"How may I help you fine gentlemen?"

They all stared at him, neither of them willing to speak the first word. Lye let out a sigh. "I'm sure you want me to apologize. To say that I'm sorry. But if what I've been told is true, then my actions have cost you all a job, a rather high paying job if I had heard correctly. I can reassure all of you. I am not sorry. I do not feel any worse about this than I'm sure you felt when you decided to raise your weapons against a teenager that was not only unarmed, but completely restrained. So, if you would like to fight me as a man, you can take off these handcuffs, but if you are simply going to stand there and be mad, you can disperse."

He said nothing afterwards, allowing his words to hang in the air for someone to catch. Against his own impulses, he hoped that someone would take the bait. That someone would unlock his handcuffs so he could take his anger out on someone. The last few months have been hell to him. He almost begged that a guard would rush him with a key to release his chains. The teenager almost pouted as the crowd of newly unemployed men walked away to collect their things.

Sooner than later Lye was back in the clothes he wore when he arrived. Ironically it was the tuxedo he wore to prom, though he was missing a lot of the weight he wore when he had first put the clothes on. The tuxedo, which had been comfortable the last time he wore it, now hung loosely over his body. It was more a blanket than a tuxedo.

He dully noted his cell phone had been smashed, but that didn't matter much to him. The deed had already been done. He reached inside the bag of his belongings and pulled out a piece of satin.

"Oooh, I had almost forgotten about that." He delightfully placed the sash around his chest and followed the guards out of the prison. He tried his best not to bring up the fact he was the only one smiling as he headed out.

As he walked, he noticed a familiar SUV sitting in the parking lot. He couldn't remember if there was a parking lot the last time, he had seen the outside, but at that time he had other things on his mind. The doors of the SUV opened, and out poured his mother, Courtney, Bernabe, Felix and surprisingly, the Mayor. Mrs. Davis ran to meet him, and at her heels came Bernabe. They all wore jeans and a t-shirt. Felix walked slowly, as though she was afraid to damager something she was holding, and Courtney walked the same strife to keep her company. Bernabe reached him first, holding him close. In the time it took him to make contact, Bernabe began to break down, weeping into his friend's shoulder. It took Lye a few seconds to realize this was the longest time they had spent away from one another since they were five. Even without the current circumstance, this was a heavy toll on both of the boys.

"Hey, it's okay. Bernabe, it's okay. I'm here." he said, trying to calm his friend down.

He broke up the hug and held him at arm's length. Bernabe, even without the torment Lye had endured, mirrored the boy's appearance. His brother in arms had lost unhealthy amounts of weight since the last time he saw him. He seemed to take him an indescribable amount of strength to put on a smile. Lye knew, even though he had no idea what had happened in his life since the last time they were this close.

"I thought they killed you Lye. We didn't know what was going on, and we thought they killed you."

"Oh, not yet." Lye said, attempting to put a smile on his face.

Mrs. Davis walked up quietly, without a word.

"Mom!" Lye exclaimed, seemly remembering the fact he had a slash around him. "I won prom king! To be honest I'm sure they only did because I'm supposed to be Lord President, or at least I was supposed to be. But I made prom king!"

She too, started to cry when she saw him, laughing all the while at his exclamation.

While the others followed suit, a sense of guilt ran throughout his body. He had known what would happen to him when he was arrested, but not once did he think about what would happen to the others. Not once did he think, he didn't even wonder. He couldn't allow himself to think about their emotions. He just hoped they would be okay with it.

Soon he joined the chorus of those who cried on his shoulders. and they all cried until Felix arrived there. Once the first person acknowledged her presence, they broke apart, Bernabe led the way to the car as they all gave Felix and Lye their space.

"You're not as heartbroken as everyone else." he bean, chastising himself as he thought of the way he decided to start the conversation.

"You've told me everything, I was the only one who had due time to prepare for what was going to happen. Even then, I was the only one who kinda knew what you would witness. It didn't make it easy for me it just made it easier."

Lye nodded. "How are you feelin?"

"I guess you can say it's a little complicated. Physically I'm doing okay, emotionally I would have to admit I am out whack. We all are, Bernabe is over there looking like a skeleton. Courtney is the only one whose weight hasn't changed since prom night."

"I'm sorry to hear that. It's all my fault."

They stood in silence. Lye was unsure what to do with his arms since he had spent so much time with them across his chest.

"It is. but we can talk more once we get you home." Felix said.

They filed into the car, all making sure their fragile prize was secure. All of them looking over their shoulder at the prison behind them, all of them worried that they were dreaming, and Lye was, in reality, nowhere near them.

As the drive continued closer to Justice, the roads became even, and buildings soon replaced trees. Most of the people in the car felt a sense of relief at the sight of a black birds. Lye still looked at the drones with distaste. One black bird in particular made a show of following the car for several miles. The passengers in the car saw this as a sign that they were closer to home. The little jailbird saw this as the only sign he needed that there was still work to be done.

Everyone was either silent or sleeping as they dropped the mayor off and went home. Since his incarceration, not much had changed in the house. Bernabe and Felix were still sleeping in Lye's room; at least they were there. After catching the jailbird up to date with what had happened since he had been gone, everyone decided they would take a well-deserved night's sleep.

Lye climbed the familiar staircase with ease. He opened the door to his room. Fortunately, everything was the way he had left it. His bed was still undone, and the mattress Bernabe slept on was still dressed in military fashion. There were clothes on the floor, but all of them belonged to him. The only things that changed was the items on the dresser. The picture he kept of him and Bernabe now had another companion. The picture of the four of them at prom, dressed in their various colors, hours before he was arrested, sat contently on his dresser.

"How are you doing?" said a voice behind him. There was no reason to turn around, he knew the voice.

"I would like you to know y'all are beginning to sound like broken records. If another person asks me how I'm doing my head might implode." Lye said, his eyes darting to find the solemn camera in his room. He was angry to note the light still shined bright. Even if the president had resigned, that did not mean things had changed.

He buried his anger quick enough to turn around with a smile. The remaining party of the trio looked at him, wondering what his next words would be.

"But are you okay?"

He went over and hugged the two of them. "Let's get out of here. Go somewhere. Eat something that isn't served to me on a school lunch tray, hmm?"

They studied him.

"You're not going through a mania attack, are you?" Bernabe asked. The question was pointed as a needle; Felix and Bernabe watched as Lye visibly deflated while he thought of an answer.

Lye would have been insulted if it had been anyone but Bernabe. He may have been insulted if the past two months never had happened. But for once, that question did not bring offense, just happiness. Happiness that his friend still cared.

"Nah, I'm really hungry. And I don't want to be in my house right now. So, who's driving?" he asked.

"I myself am going to sleep. I'm sure you boys have things you want to talk about without me. Wake me when you get back. Actually, don't wake me up, though I would like something to eat. I'll see you when you get back." She kissed Lye and gave Bernabe a hug and proceeded to lay in the bed.

"Does she do that often?" Lye asked.

"I can still hear you." Felix reminded them, stifling a yawn.

Bernabe ignored Lye but started to pull out some clothes from the dresser drawers. "C'mon man, you're still wearing your prom tuxedo. Take a shower, and I promise I will get you some food. Also, you have an appointment tomorrow morning so that you can refill your medication. And I really don't want any lip from you, not right now. Just do what I say, okay?"

Lye looked at his friend. There wasn't any anger in his words. He wasn't saying that out of malice. He was near his breaking point. Lye obeyed and didn't leave the bathroom until the stench of prison had left him.

Bernabe lazily opened the door of his truck, and watched as his friend got in. There was little time that passed before Lye opened his mouth.

"How are you really doing?" he asked. "You look like me, and I know I look like crap."

Bernabe took his eyes off the road and looked into

Lye. "I thought you died. I seriously thought they took you away from us and somewhere your body was under the jailhouse. There was no way for us to know anything. And with Felix and- I just- I'm not sure if you're even here right now. I think this is a dream. I have had this dream before. You get home, we go out, and then I'm driving you back to jail again."

Lye kept his eyes ahead, trying to ignore the words of Aesop in his head. "I understand. But I can promise you I'm here right now. In this truck. Now we both look like we're late for dias de los muertos, so how about we get something to eat?" He reached over and put his hand on his friend's shoulder. "They haven't killed me yet. You worry too much."

The guilt of selfishness seeped into his psyche.

"I'm not going to sit here and act as though I was worried about how everyone would take that. And I -for various reasons- didn't think too much about anyone while I was incarcerated. And I'm not going to act like I knew what I put you through. But I do ask that you forgive me. I didn't do anything out of a sadistic manner. I-"

Bernabe put his hand up.

"I don't want you to rationalize this Lye. I don't want you to talk about the need of the American people or hear how everyone needed to be aware with what's going on. I'm here with you til death. I just want you to be aware of the emotional damage we caused. All of us. Yeah, I agree with you. I'll walk into the gates of hell with you, but that doesn't stop the fact you need to understand what we did. Courtney spent the first month sleeping in your bed with Felix. I had to listen to her cry every night, and we couldn't get her out of it. Everyone is drained. Everyone was crying, and they're all so worried about you they're putting on a mask right now. So, *you* don't see the damage."

"And you're telling me, so I know?" Lye asked. It wasn't a rude question; Lye could have guessed that was the case. But to hear it made it realer than he wanted it to be."

"I'm your best friend. It is my obligation to remind you of the damage. You don't receive any blind loyalty. Even if you were meant to be Lord President."

They sat in silence for a while. Neither boy knew what to say to lighten the mood. Lye reached over and turned on the radio.

"...is the fifth incident of copycat actions of Lye Davis. Families are getting worried that-"

Bernabe turned off the radio, Lye threw a worried look at his driver.

"I'll tell you about that tomorrow. Tonight, we will not talk about anything political."

Lye said nothing. They rolled into the driveway of Whataburger and ordered their meals. When they got to the front window, the lady, no more than fifteen years old, worried none about them as she grabbed Bernabe's credit card.

Lye bent over Bernabe and called for her attention. "Excuse me, could you put a few packets of ketchup in the bag?"

"Yeah, of course," she said. She looked over at the boy leaning over the driver and her eyes widened. Recognition animated her face as she let out a little squeal. She turned around and ran from the window, leaving the boys with a confused look on their face.

"Did I say something wrong? Are we not allowed ketchup anymore?" Lye asked.

Bernabe shrugged his shoulders. "I've come here at least five times since you've been gone. I've never seen her act this way."

The girl in question came back with three people, all teenagers.

"You're lying. That can't be him." said the first.

"I looked it up, it said he was a fugitive of the state." commanded the second

"Nah, he died in prison." pleaded the third.

Lye had not moved, as confusion had frozen him. They all stared and gawked at him.

"Um...so, how about the ketchup?" Lye asked.

"What's your name?" asked the original teen. She continued to cheese; already aware of the answer.

"Lye . . .?

Once again, the group squealed.

"Dude, we saw what you did online. You're my

hero!"

"We all planned that we would wear our own clothes for our prom. I'm gonna wear a suit!"

"I read the Art of War!"

Lye once again found it hard to find something to say. "Thank you, it means a lot to see that people had noticed what was going on." He had grown accustomed to unwanted attention, but that didn't make it any less unwanted.

"Lord President stepped down!"

A fury of comments and praise came from the window. Blood drained from Lye's face. Bernabe noticed the change and looked at the workers.

"Guys, I really appreciate what you're doing. But he just got out of prison, he needs his rest. I promise I'll drive him up here at a later date."

They all agreed and gave them the rest of his food. As they were driving home Lye questioned the amount of food they had in their bags. "I think they gave us the wrong number. We only ordered three meals. We have like seven burgers in here. There's a bag full of fries-there's no holder; they just dumped all the fries they could into this bag"

"Good, maybe you'll actually eat something." Bernabe yawned.

They sat in their own thoughts for the rest of the drive. As they pulled in to the driveway, they shared a chuckle.

The walk up the staircase stopped for a moment. Lye looked down the hall at Courtney's bedroom door. He gave Bernabe the rest of the food and walked down the hall.

Before he had a chance to knock, he hesitated.

"I don't know what to say to her." he said to himself. He couldn't give his little sister the same defense he gave his best friend. She looked up to him; there was no way he could admit he didn't put her feelings into consideration. He opened the door to see her staring at the ceiling. There was no sign of the little happy girl he had left behind.

"Hey lady, we brought food. Come in my room."

"Okay," she said in a hollow voice.

Lye walked back toward his room, and left the door opened. Contrary to her earlier comment, Felix had already awakened and got in her pajamas, and Bernabe was already eating food.

The door opened slowly, and teary-eyed Courtney made her way into the room. She walked slowly toward her brother and squeezed herself between Lye and Felix.

"What would you like to eat stank butt, we have more than enough burgers for you."

"A burger, she mumbled.

Lye laughed as he dug into the bag and pulled out a burger and a handful of fries. Lye began to chew his food before he realized it was too silent in his room. Usually silence while eating meant the food was good. But there was also the feeling he was being watched.

He looked up from his food to note that everyone had their eyes on him. After a few forced chews and a rough swallow. "What?"

"Well . . ." Felix began, " You haven't seen us in two months, and we were wondering if you would mind catching us up. if you're comfortable about it. If you're not, then we can wait."

He looked around his bedroom. For once he noticed the full manner of the tired faces looking around him. He owed them that much.

He took a deep breath and began since the moment he was thrown into the cop car. He told them about the cell phone, about the prison, and about his cell. He told him about his manic days and his depressed days. It became hard to speak when he reached the topic of Aesop.

They won't believe you

But they were his family. They weren't just him, they loved him. He took a deeper breath and told them about the weeks of hallucinations. About the terrors that he was given. He told them about the therapy, and how he ended up with a pardon.

Unbeknownst to him, his leg had been shaking since the middle of his speech. He looked around again, and noticed the tears in Bernabe's eyes, the worried look in Felix's face, and the increased pressure of Courtney's arm around his waist.

"I'm sorry to hear that." they all said, and took turns hugging him.

Lye, never wanting the subject to be on him for too long, decided to change the subject. "I do have to ask, how's Michelle?"

"She told me she's not my friend anymore." Courtney said. "She didn't want to talk about what was going on with you, and she said you got with you deserved. I didn't like that. she called you a menace to society."

"Those are quite harsh words coming from a friend." Lye said.

"She stopped talking to me as well; told me the same thing." Felix said.

"And how is Elsa?" Lye asked.

The girls burst out in laughter.

For the first time in his life, he saw Bernabe turn red. A sight that made prison time worth it.

"Wait, what did I miss?"

Even as he asked, he wished he had waited a few seconds before asking. The question stopped the laughter he had missed for all those months. He missed seeing his sister's face crinkle as she laughed, and the way she started to wheeze if she didn't get enough air. He had missed the way Felix brought her head back and let out laughter. For a second half of the people in the room were laughing.

It stopped much sooner than he had wished it to. Courtney was the first to recover and begin her story.

"Well, your best friend. Your brother, your amigo-"

"I think he remembers who I am-" Bernabe butted in. Lye noticed the snarl on his face as he spoke.

Lye chuckled a little bit and gestured for her to continue.

"Anyway, your boy thought it would be funny for him to bring a girl over. I mean, we all knew you were too broken and bruised to try anything with Felix, so there was never any worry with y'all. But Alexis thought he could do the same thing. So, mom, Felix, and I walk into your room to see him and making out with her on the floor."

Felix decided to take over from there. "And Mrs. Davis pulled off her belt and spanked him from your bedroom to the door. And when he tried to run, she chased him around the entire neighborhood."

Courtney laughed so hard she fell back onto the bed.

Bernabe said nothing, he simply ate his food and went downstairs. With the break of the hard times, the Davis children went to Courtney's room. As he hugged her asleep, she grabbed on his shirt.

"Promise me Lye, promise me you won't do anything like that again?"

He hugged her again. "I promise."

She looked at him, taking in her broken brother as

tears swelled in her eyes.

"I won't say anything when you decide to try to throw your life away again. I won't say anything." Tears began to swell as she looked at her older brother.

He hugged her once again, "Like I said, I promise. doesn't my word mean anything to you?"

She hugged him again and ran into her room, slamming the door. Lye heard nothing in the room, not even the sound of crying. He walked toward his room and closed the door.

His two accomplishes were in conversation with one another. Once he had turned on the light, they stopped and stared at him.

"What- never mind, I don't want to know."

He opened the door and walked down the stairs. There was a time where his steps were springy, even joyous. Now it felt his movements were filled with lead. He found it harder to move, and harder still to sit down. He walked into the kitchen and went for the fridge. He pulled out a coke and walked toward the front step to the house. He sat down and opened the can, drinking a large gulp.

"Are you going to tell them you still see me?"

He looked over to see Aesop, in the same attire and condition since he had blown his head out in his cell.

"No, I won't. it's none of their business."

"Why not? Did you see the way they were talking about you, about us, when we walked in the room? I'm just saying, two months is a long time to be away from a man as fine as us." Aesop teased. The idea of his friends committing such a betrayal was absurd.

"You really should get all of this out before tomorrow morning." Lye threatened.

"Why?" Aesop mocked. "I'm not going anywhere."

Lye thought about what he had down these past two months. How he had brought so much problems to his family, and his friends. It would be time before those wounds would heal, and even longer before he no longer felt the guilt of it.

He looked at the night sky. Of all the thing he had missed while locked away, the Alabama sky came to his mind first and most. It didn't mean that change would come over night; he knew the change that came in such a way was always torn twice as fast.

"I'm getting on medication as soon as I can." He finished the coke after a few minutes of enjoying the night air. Maybe it was the trick of his mind, but he was sure Aesop smiled as he drank the last drop.

Afterwards he went to the living room and sat on the couch. He didn't want to watch anything. His room was too small of a room for him to be comfortable at this time. He had been in a small area for long. He laid down on his couch, the softest piece of furniture that didn't resemble a bed. For the first time in two months, he finally got a good night's rest.

***

It had been weeks since his release, and Lye stared at the ceiling above his bed. He looked at his dresser, the two pill bottles stood in honor, the pills diligently waiting to take on their duty as soldiers fighting the imbalance of Lye's mind. He yawned; everyone had gone out an hour prior to him waking up. They had told them they needed to leave. He walked down the stairs, the springy step once again returning to his body, and sat in the living room. He dared not turn on the television. Lye knew if he did, he would want to look up the news. It had been too long since he looked at the news and didn't hear his name or see his face. Videos of him played on air almost hourly. Bernabe had told him more about what he heard over the radio the night he was released.

Many of the teenagers in the country took his words closer than the older demographics. But some had misunderstood his message. Violence had blossomed across the states. Violent riots and bombings took away from the message of equity and understanding. Even series of school shootings, terrorist attacks, and other terms of violence that had nothing to do with his message was soon being tied to him. A lone wolf shooter, if he was old enough to have cared about Lye's words, was just another soldier of Lye Davis.

Lye plopped himself on the couch and turned on the television. The house was too quiet for him to be alone with his thoughts. Boredom trumped guilt. Though it had been days since he had to worry about Aesop, the thought process that created the hallucination was always under the surface, looking for a break in his defense to cause him to slip into his own mind once again.

The only thing on his mind now was the itch of

forgetting something important. The harder he thought about what he was forgetting, the harder it became to remember it. He turned on the latest football game as a way to distract his mind. He had never had any opinion of football, he didn't understand all the rules, but he watched. He even stood up and yelled when a team scored a touchdown. It didn't matter which team won; the excitement of the game was infectious.

The sound of the door opening alerted him. He had not been away from his prison long enough to believe a door opening was benign. He walked in to see his family coming in, holding various bags.

"What's going on?" he asked.

Bernabe was the first one to look at him in a confused manner. He almost looked insulted. "Did you forget what today was?"

"I have had my mind on other things lately. So naturally, yes." Lye answered. He thought back at the forgotten important thing he was trying to hold on to.

That didn't stop Bernabe from having a confused look on his face. "It's our *birthday*."

Mrs. Davis followed suit, with her husband at her heels.

"The Bernabe family is going to be here at seven. I'm going to need you not to look like a jailbird by the time they get here."

Lye looked down. His t-shirt had multiple stains from it; he hadn't changed it in two days. A piece of every meal he had eaten had latched on his shirt. His shorts had followed suit, and he did realize he smelled a little ripe.

"Thank you, will do." He turned to Bernabe. "Happy birthday homie."

They embraced, and he went to shower. Only after he was sure he didn't smell did he enjoy the company of his makeshift family.

"Why were you watching sports?

Lye turned to Courtney.

"Well, I'm still in the news, and I didn't want to watch myself. So, I went to watch some football. Did you know, in ancient roman times, the people of power would have a great competition to distract the roman citizens from what they were doing. I always think about that whenever I watch football because of the super bowl."

"You have a weird brain." Felix said.

They all laughed as they continued to watch the game. No one had the heart to admit to Lye that he wasn't watching football at all, but rugby.

The hours flew as they prepared for the party. Mr. Davis and Bernabe stayed in the kitchen cooking food while Felix and Courtney handled the decorations. Lye was wrapping Bernabe's presents, while Mrs. Davis was in the next room was wrapping Lye's.

The bell rang, and from upstairs Lye heard the sound of recognition and glee. He came down the stairs to see the Bernabe and some of his extended family at the door.

He gave everyone a hug and walked toward the front door. In the front yard he noticed one his birthday gifts.

"Abuela!" he yelled. Before he knew it, he was in a race with Bernabe to see who would get to the phenomenal old woman first. To those who were watching behind them, they must have looked like a of five-year-old's running to see their grandma. That was exactly what they felt like. They all had to slow down before they got to her, afraid that the force of them hugging her would knock her over.

"I'm so happy to see you, my loves. More than ever happy to see you together. There are very few things better than a friend." she smiled. She walked with the help of a walker, and even though she had an oxygen tank on her, she looked strong. Her smile was radiant, and she looked as though, for the moment she smiled, that she could do anything.

"When did you get out of the hospital?" Lye asked.

Bernabe was the one to answer. "She's been moved into a home. She's doing a little better, but we thought it would be better for her if she had twenty-four-hour assistance."

"It's not that bad. I've made a few friends. I'm popular there."

There was a twinkle in her eye that made both boys afraid to ask why. They led her in to the house, and a chorus of happy birthday tore through their conversation with the matriarch.

The party commenced when Lye and Bernabe sat down to blow out their birthday cake. As tradition, Lye blew out the candles on the right and Bernabe blew out the candles on the left. They grabbed each other by the back of the head and smashed their faces into the cake. Laughter roared, and pieces of icing flicked from their lips as they enjoyed themselves. As what was to happen whenever the sides of the makeshift family got together. They laughed and told stories, and everyone asked about Lye's well-being. Cousins and aunts and uncles shared the table with Bernabe's family. Everyone was merry.

"I swear, you'd think that Bernabe and Lye were getting married."

Lye looked to see the source of the voice. Courtney had been speaking to the matriarch of the party. She said something in Spanish, which made Courtney laugh. Lye didn't know that his sister was able to speak Spanish. After a few hours everyone grew tired and said their goodbyes to go home. Bernabe and Lye had gone to do the dishes, and everyone else started to clean the house.

"What's on your mind?" Bernabe asked.

"Huh?" Lye said, coming back into reality. He realized he had been drying the same dish for two minutes now.

"You seem distracted. At least more so than usual." The time they spent together had put weight back on their bodies; so, the grin Bernabe offered looked familiar once again.

"I looked more into what the news have been saying about me. Not that I care about the media, but I

317

think the message I was trying to get across at prom had been lost. That the vilification I'm going through is causing the people to believe I want them to go out and start blowing up buildings. Not that I can say I am against blowing up buildings."

He looked at the blinking camera in his kitchen. In the first few days since his release, they had agreed that if they were to talk about anything that had happened the night of prom, they would put all blame on Lye since he had already been pardoned for those crimes. No one else was ever arrested, but that didn't mean they could test their luck with a sadistic government.

"And you're trying to figure out what you can do about it. I mean, that may be a little hard for you to do at the moment, you can't actually go on television to yell 'do as I say, not as I do'. It would be hypocritical."

Bernabe passed him another plate, Lye stayed quiet for a bit as he thought about a solution for the answer.

"I mean, you're right. I don't know what I can do about the situation." he lied. Bernabe passed him another plate as he continued to talk. "And I know you told me that I shouldn't go out trying to get beaten again, but there has to be something I can do. Something."

Bernabe looked at his best friend. It was obvious his input in the conversation was only to keep the conversation going. Lye may had been in the room with him, but his mind was miles away, putting together pieces of a puzzle no one else saw because no one else saw an unfinished picture.

He dried off the last plate and looked at his best friend.

"Could I borrow your truck? I just want to go on a drive." he said.

"I'm not exactly sure I should let you do it. At the moment, Lye Davis saying he's going to take a drive could translate to 'I'm going to build an army and bum rush the state capitol."

"I'm taking Felix with me, if she wants to go."

Bernabe shrugged. "You say that as though it is a good thing. She may be the voice of reason in this pack of ours, but by no means does that mean she'll keep you out of trouble if anything goes bad."

Bernabe grabbed the broom, and Lye went to grab the dust pan. As he swept Lye leaned over the counter, watching his friends and family clean the house. Though it was a minute thing, it did warm him people of different races could laugh together under one roof. Everyone was happy, and everyone was able to know that the other person, even if they did not look at him, was filled with love for the other.

"Alexis, can I ask you a question?"

Hearing his first name from Lye's voice made the boy jump. He looked at him with horror. In the time since thy had known each other, Lye might have said his first name five times, and each time ended with someone bleeding. It wasn't always one of them, sometimes it was a third party, but nothing good ever came out of hearing his first name. There would be no sarcasm or jokes in whatever came next out of his mouth.

"Of course, what's up?" he said, not taking his eyes off his task.

"Have you ever thought, since me and Felix had been a thing, that being with a white girl takes away from my message?"

He spoke in a low voice, making sure his words, which would naturally project, would stay in the confines of his embarrassment.

"Why do you ask that?" Bernabe questioned. Though he didn't know what to expect, the question wasn't on his spectrum of topics he would expect from Lye.

"I'm afraid my message would be tarnished by the idea I am not marrying someone from my own race. Sometimes I feel people will believe I'm playing both sides. I love her, I do. But I just wanted the opinion of someone else."

"So, you choose the other non-black person in your life? I'm joking." Bernabe brought the pile of dirt to Lye, and Lye bent down in order to catch it with the dustpan.

"I think you can want the best for what your people need. I think you can feel the pain that those who look like you feel, and still want to do something about it while loving someone who doesn't look like you. There's nothing wrong with that. Now if you went around saying you liked Felix because she didn't look like a black chick. Or something like you don't like black women because they're too ghetto, or too loud, or whatever you could think of in that situation, I would smack you myself. I don't think you remember this, but someone asked you the same question you just asked me. I think you said 'I can have love for a white girl while still having love and respect for my black women. How can I, a black man, who came from a black woman, say that I don't like black women? How could I hate what birthed me?'"

Lye coughed to hide his laughter. Bernabe did a terrific job in imitating him. He hugged his brother and went to pick up the rest of the dust.

"What would I do without you?"

Bernabe put his hand on his chin, acting as though he was thinking about the question. "Get shot. Like a lot."

Lye chuckled. Months ago, it would've been impossible for Bernabe to make a joke about the drastic changes in their lives.

Felix came over and kissed Lye on the cheek. She stopped once she realized the serious faces on her friends.

"Anyone wanna talk?" both of the boys looked at one another and shrugged.

"Would you like to take a drive with me?" Lye asked.

"Sure, I'll get my keys-"

"I want to drive Bernabe's truck." Lye said. "I apologize if I sounded rude. It's just a desire of mine."

"Uh... sure." She waited for Lye to explain more but shrugged when he said nothing. They expected that from one another. If other wanted to explain, they would explain.

Bernabe handed him his keys and they said their parting words to the family. Lye and Felix climbed into the cab of the truck. It didn't take long before they found themselves thinking of the last time, they rode in this truck together, and the consequences of that night.

"So where are we going?" Felix asked. They had been driving for a few miles in silence.

"Whataburger."

"We just ate."

"I know, but I have to talk to someone."

"Alrighty then."

At times, the fact Felix understood sometimes Lye didn't want to explain everything, meant more than he thought it would. Everyone in his life seemed to want a detailed description about his movements. He understood why. Sometimes his thoughts would take him off course of his actions. But understanding and agreement were two different things; he never liked his every action second guessed.

He parked gangster style in the parking lot, peering his eyes to see if a familiar face was there.

There was still enough sunlight in the sky for his plan to go through.

"Are we looking for someone in particular?" Felix asked. Lye looked around at the workers in the restaurant, trying to find someone he noticed the last time he was here.

"Yeah, that girl over there. I'm waiting for her to get off?"

"So, we've succumbed to stalking teenagers?"

"One: we are teenagers ourselves. Two: technically, I'm the one stalking her, you're just a peace offering. And three: I just want to talk to her." Lye said, not taking his eyes the front of Whataburger.

"Weird flex, but- wait, how am I a peace offering?"

"It's evening time, if a teenager just walked up to a girl out of the blue, she might think I have bad intentions. But if you come out, she might not feel the same way."

"I'm so happy to know to know I've become a racial shield." Felix teased

"We all know I only keep you around to confuse the government on my taxes."

Before she had a chance to continue the banter, the girl in question walked out of the restaurant. She walked with two of the three coworkers he had seen that night. They stopped for a second when one of them looked toward the truck. Once Lye was sure they had at least mentioned the truck looked the same as the night they had seen him, he hopped out. The teenagers started a race to come over to him, and by the time Felix got out of the car, they had reached it.

"What're you doing here?" asked the teenager who caught up to him first.

"I wanted to ask a favor from the three of you."

The trio of teens took in Felix as she walked around to stand by Lye. She waved at the group. "Hello, racial shield and peace offering, Felix Cambridge."

She smiled as the teens looked at her with the same amount of awe. The leader of the miniature pack regained her composure and directed her attention toward Lye.

"Wait, you need our help?"

"Yes." Lye admitted.

"Of course."

Lye looked up in the sky. As expected, a black bird was hovering over the parking lot.

"Before I tell you what I am going to ask of you, I need you to understand something. You're going to be watched a lot more by cameras like black birds since you're talking to me. And if you do what I ask, it might be even worse. I don't want you to get involved into something you might not want to do. Are you sure you want to help me?"

A few moments passed as the group thought it over. The middle one, the one who had noticed Lye from the window, was the first to nod.

"One of the books I read said something along the lines of 'people who see oppression and do nothing are just as evil as the oppressors.' I would love to help." Quickly the others agreed.

"Bet. I want you to take selfies with me. And then post online I told y'all that I'm going to be giving a speech in the Justice High School parking lot three Saturdays from now."

Their eyes widened at the idea. "We get to take pictures with you?"

"Do you need me to post it everywhere?"

"We get to hear a speech?"

Lye still felt the unwanted attention nagging at his mind. "I would appreciate it if you didn't put as much weight on my words. I'm still human. I bleed as much as you do. Actually, given the last few months I do hope I've bled a lot more than you guys. Are you in?"

Their phones were out by the time he had finished the sentence.

On the ride home, Lye felt a little relieved. At least it would give him a chance to correct the message that he had meant to give.

"You know that, if they blast that on social media, it will be more than your supporters who know what you're planning. Like those who would wish to do you harm or the prison guards you so effortlessly decommissioned. Isn't it illegal to do such a thing?" Felix asked.

"The Constitution protects us to assemble and protest. Even though most of us are too afraid of the punishment from law enforcement. What I'm doing is completely legal."

"What about those who wish to do you harm?" Felix asked.

"Hopefully they wait until the end of the speech."

"Do you care about the people who care about you?" Felix muttered. There was no playful banter in her voice.

The question threw him off, so much that he had swerved a little as he looked over at her. The sign announcing they had entered Justice passed swiftly by.

"What do you mean?" he pleaded. The accusation had hurt his feelings.

"Do you ever put our feelings into consideration before you make these crazy decisions? If I had known you were going to bring more people into this. To ask them to announce you were going to do something stupid. I would have never agreed to get into the car with you. I have to ask again; do you ever think about anyone besides yourself?"

Lye gripped the wheel until his knuckles turned a different shade. He couldn't tell why it angered him so much. But it did.

"To answer your question . . ." it was hard to keep the anger out of his voice. "No, I don't think of anyone besides myself, because I'm not thinking about myself. I haven't done anything I have done since I learned about the idea of being Lord President because I wanted to think of *myself*. I didn't get shot, arrested, and put in prison because it would make me happy. I didn't help burn down the only place that meant something to me these years because I woke up and realized that I was a masochist. I am thinking about everyone but myself. Do you know how easy it would be if I just thought about myself? I would kill for just one day where I'm not thinking about injustice. When I can think about how children can grow up in this nation and not feel the need to act. I would love to be someone who was so comfortable in their own mediocrity that they didn't care. I am thinking about every single last person in this country *besides* myself. And I apologize if I hurt your feelings along the way. I apologize if breaking my body causes you pain. It causes me pain as well. Has anyone ever thought about that? I was the one who got shot. I was the one who kept having dreams his family was being killed while he was incarcerated. I was the one who became a damn guinea pig. But I still kept on with what I thought was right. Not because I thought it would be a great prank. Because I don't know if anyone else will do it if I don't."

He took in a deep breath in order to stop any of his next words from stemming from anger. "And since we're on the subject of how one another feels. How could you ever think I would want to cause any of you pain? Do you think so little of me?"

Felix answered quickly, none too softly. "Nobody is angry about your passion. We're not angry you want to change things. Hell, we're not even mad that you went to jail with the intention to have a psychotic breakdown! We're all upset about the fact you shut us out. That you don't allow us to know what you plan to do. You just give us these half plans and these half-truths. Do you think so little about us? Do you know what *we* have sacrificed for *you*? My family won't even talk to me because I stood by your side. Bernabe and I have been with you every step of the way, and you treat us as though we're just minor characters to the Legend of Lye Davis. We're not pawns. We are partners. So, do I think of little of you? I have. I have since we picked you up from the same prison, they had me in. Remember? I've gone through the same thing. I feel right now it's just something personal. As though you're going to tear down the entire government. The same government we've had for centuries, by flicking your wrists and saying a few words. Think. And allow us to know what you plan to do. That's all. "

"I worry-"

"Lye No one in their right mind asked you to worry about us! Don't give me the whole chauvinistic 'I didn't want you to worry' 'I had to carry this burden alone'. That's bull and you know it. That's not why you hide things. You hide things because you don't want us to try to stop you. You hide things because a big part of you thinks your plan gonna work. So, when we hear about it, everything is already in motion. You make sure it's too late to give rational thought into that head of yours. that's why you don't tell us."

She didn't raise her voice. She didn't scream or yell insults at him. And that's what made her words hurt more. If she had been angry, it would have been easy to slide them off as her anger, that she didn't mean them. There was no emotion in her voice. There was simply cold fact. He stole a glance to look at her, and her face matched her voice. Emotionless. Nothing but truth.

"You're right."

"What?"

"I know that I haven't been rational. I know you won't believe me until I show that action."

He didn't finish the sentence. He looked up and realized he had driven all the way home without remembering any part of the drive. He got out the car and opened the door for Felix.

As they walked in, the other family members noticed the tension from the two. Some tried to ignore it, while others waited to be informed.

"I- I want y'all to know I am going to be doing a speech three weeks from now. And before you give me reasons not to, I'm doing this in order to set the record straight."

"If that, the case, why do you have a sour face?" Mrs. Davis asked Felix.

"I don't know what to do with your son."

Mrs. Davis shrugged. "I don't either at times, but his heart is in the right place. I just try to look after him."

FOURTEEN

Felix's prophetic words soon came into action. The buzz of Lye's final speech spread across all means of media faster than the flames of his beloved memorial. Each hour a member of his circle would give testament to another soul who wished to hear his words up close. None of them cared it would take place in the parking lot of a school. While his words were targeted for those of his age- the teenagers that had yet to accept their lives did not belong to them- there were others who wished to hear from him. The oldest member of is future congregation was celebrating her ninetieth birthday (she had her grandson post she would be there.) But with every mention of appreciation of an addition of the audience, there were two comments found that told him to stop what he was doing. Many comments were filled with hate and derogatory words. The house favorite was "Take yur ass bak to where u come from."

This was the only one in which Lye had replied to,

explaining in the most foolish way possible that since he had been born and raised in Alabama, he had done exactly that once he had come from prison. He smiled when they said nothing in response.

There were serious claims, claims that made even his mother, who rightfully believed in his cause until now, wonder if she should allow her son to go through with the plans he had. The one that scared her the most was a claim that a man 'and his buddies' would come to his house in the dead of the night and shoot his house up. The claim would have gone through as nothing important if not for the fact that he had correctly posted Lye's address online.

Lye came in the house from checking the mail. Of the thirteen parcels in his hand, twelve were labeled for him. If the past few days were anything to go off on, four of them would be from a high schooler that had seen all the information about him online, two of them would be queries about a book they had read, and the rest would be filled with threats on his life. Though most of them were written in black ink, the most colorful words were those that spoke about how they would kill him for tarnishing the American name.

"Are you sure you will be okay with me leaving?" his mother asked. She gripped the handle of her luggage case. The contents were only enough to hold a few nights worth of clothes, but she pulled on it as though it weighed a ton.

"I'll be fine ma; they can threaten me all they want."

Worry carried on her face, not willing to move unless she could put her son in the luggage as well. "Is Alexis going to be here?" she pleaded.

Lye wasn't mad. He understood, and more so expected, her to act this way. She had to leave the state for a business trip, and his father would spend most of his time at the hospital. He had taken too much time off during Lye's incarceration, and he had to make up for lost time. Even though he appreciated the worry, he knew she would very easily miss her flight than leave without knowing she would be safe.

"No ma'am, Abuela is in the hospital again, he's going to spend a few days with his family. I don't know the details, but he was rather worked up when he left, he told me he'll call when he's coming back. It'll just be me and Felix. Courtney is staying at Aunt Miriam's since it's summer."

Mrs. Davis opened her mouth to talk, but before she could utter a sound, Lye put his hand up. "She's been living here for months ma, and right now she's only here to play Jiminy Cricket. You don't have to worry about us disrespecting your house, I can promise my ribs are much too bruised for me to be doing any thrusting."

Nervous laughter came from his mother. It wasn't much, but it was enough to lighten the load of her luggage. He kissed her goodbye and walked her to the car. Only after he saw her gray sedan turn on the corner did he let his smile down. As carefree as he tried to act, he was completely terrified. Six days from now he would be standing in front of dozens of people in order to try to change a narrative that has been the same for centuries.

He walked inside the house and locked the door, then checked to make sure the door was locked an extra three more times before he left the foyer. He climbed the steps to the only sanctuary he had left and opened the letters. He scanned them for a moment and sorted them in their rightful place on his dresser. A mountain of hate mail towered the far-right side of his dresser. The puddle of fan mail stood on the far-left side, and in the middle was a plateau of neutral mail. It was not threatening or happy, they simply wished to talk to him. On his nightstand stood the mail he had responded to. In order to keep a low profile (ironic as it may sound) he only answered a small percent of his mail. The recipients of those letters would usually post the letter online, making the past two weeks of his life incredibly transparent.

He sat on his bed and let out a hard breath. It was Sunday, and for the first time in years he wished he had gone to church. For two hours it would be nice to believe that a higher power was at work here. Even at this moment he felt at times he was only a teenager acting out because he didn't like the job he was given.

"I wonder what I will do for the rest of my life." he spoke to himself; the chance that he will still be Lord President was slim to none. In the past week, the vice president had taken the place of Lord since the resignation Lye helped produce.

Lye looked around his room and realize he had little to do in his room. The idea of having fun had become asinine in the last few months. He wished he had a new phone, that way he could text Bernabe, but decided it wouldn't be polite. While Lye knew that Bernabe was more than willing to answer his calls or his texts, he would feel less than right to bother him now.

"I know you're going through a tragedy right now, but I'm bored." was the only message he would relay, no matter the actual words that was sent. Felix was out with her little sister. In the past day she had been allowed to visit Michelle, but only if she met her mother at a predetermined destination. She wasn't allowed to return to the mayor's manor, and by no means was Michelle allowed to be at the Davis House. In the past weeks Lye learned the mayor was only there to pick him up because he knew how to get there without directions. The mayor was understandably mad at Lye, once he realized Lye had no intentions on becoming Lord President, which meant his promise to give him a job had been an empty one.

He peered out his bedroom window. The amount of black birds staying in his neighborhood had decreased since his incarceration, but ever since the declaration of his final speech, they had increased dramatically. There were now seven black birds in his neighborhood sky. More than he had ever seen in his life. The number of blackbirds had nothing to do with the idea more black birds would help keep down the tension that surrounded the house. It was in fact the opposite; the amount of black birds kept the tension alive. It was a very simple and expensive message. A message that everyone had dutifully ignored until now.

Your government is always watching you

He yawned. Not a yawn of tire, but one of boredom. He simply could not find him something to do.

As the minutes passed, he wandered around the

house aimlessly. Within ten minutes he had stepped foot on every square foot of the house three times in a way to pass the time.

Sooner than later the regressed memories of things he had forgotten.

He ran to his room and grabbed his backpack and took the backpack to the bathroom.

He pulled out his lead box, and from his lead box he pulled out his copy of Hamlet, the only piece of his memorial that had not gone up in the fire.

He greedily ran through the words, happy to find a distraction. Too soon did he finish the book, and at the end of it, he simply stared at the cover. "I hate to admit it Hamlet, but I am still happy I don't have your life. I feel you with the whole 'to be or not to be' thing though." his head snapped up once his brain caught up to what he was doing. "I'm talking to fictional characters- now I'm talking to myself." He let out a frustrated yell and went to the kitchen. He opened the refrigerator door...and stared at the contents for five minutes.

His ears picked up once he heard the sound of a key going into the lock, he turned his head to watch the intruder, and his face perked up as he saw Felix walk in the house. He galloped toward her, ignoring all the constant cries from his body not to muster anything faster than a brisk walk. He fell to his knees and wrapped his arms around her waist.

"Thank God you're here!"

Felix, who had been preoccupied, suddenly grew

into a state of alarm. "What's wrong? Are you okay? Are you hurt? Did someone come here?!"

Lye brought his head back in the most dramatic way. "I've. Been. So. BORED!"

After a few moments of silence, he opened his eyes to see Felix's deadpan face.

"What?" he said.

"I'm here thinking you're dying and you're sad because you're on punishment. You've been through this before. I've been through this before."

"Y'know, it's really hard to use solitary confident as a punishment with you. It's almost not fair, so, whatcha wanna do today?"

After a few more minutes, Felix helped Lye up. "We can go to-"

"No, we can't." Lye said in a monotone voice.

"What do you mean?" Felix asked.

"Mom said I can't leave the driveway."

"You're a-"

Lye put his hands out in a submissive gesture. He no longer had to wear his sling. "Listen, by all means, I will go up against the American government. But by no means will I go up against that crazy lady I call mama. Not happened. I can't leave."

For a second, Felix's face showed she wanted to laugh, but as she thought more about the types of punishment they could ensue, she decided against it. "You're right. It's in our best interest to obey." She looked around the house.

"What do you want to do?"

"Not sure. How was the visit?"

Felix shrugged, "It feels weird to have visits with my sister. I feel like I just divorced my dad, which sounds a lot worse than it did in my head. Too many Alabama jokes there. But she's okay. She's still pissed at me, but it is what it is."

"Why don't you just go back?" Lye asked.

Coming from anyone else, the question may have sounded smart. Even more so there might have been malice behind it. But they had known each other for a long time, and she knew that there was no malice behind his question. It wasn't a question out of spite, and it might have not even been a question out of concern. It was simply a question of curiosity.

"To explain myself, I'm standing for what I believe is right. I am not here standing just out of blind love or loyalty, but I do believe in the message. Please take that smile off your face, most of the time I think you're a chicken running around with his head off. But I believe in what you stand for. And if this is the consequences for believing for what I stand for-" she paused in order to pull up her shirt, showing her branding. "I have a permanent reminder I have had worse."

Lye walked over and kissed her. "You're such a badass, wanna get married?"

She smiled. "I'll think about it, but the way it's going right now, we're gonna have to wait until my father dies to wear the ring."

He kissed her again. "Not if the government has any say about it."

She returned his kiss. "We can watch a movie? How's the attic?"

Lye walked toward the couch, thinking about her question. "It's a little cluttered. Though there's no rodents in there. I can finally think freely. Nonetheless, I would rather not talk about my mental health right now. I would much rather enjoy the time we have with one another. This is one of the few times I have alone time with you since we learned we were partners."

Felix sighed. "Fair enough, let me change."

Lye turned on the tv, looking for the allotted movies the Common Connector had. Lye hadn't taken off his pajamas all day, and Felix went upstairs to follow suit. When she came down, they cuddled on the couch. Giving he was the host, Lye decided that Felix could choose the movie.

"What do you want to-"

"Transformers."

"We've seen it for-"

"Transformers."

"I'll put on the movie."

The couple watched the latest remake of transformers (which was surprisingly worse than the Michael bay remake) happy to be in one another's company. There was no political talk, no schemes, no fears of bullets. At least out loud, even as he watched the movie, Lye's mind would not allow him to forget about the threats he had made everyone believe he cared nothing for. Frequently he looked out the window, making sure there was no foreign car in his driveway. Letters that contained details on how they wished to bomb his house kept his nose out for the smell of almonds, hoping he would detect c4 before anyone tried to bomb his beloved house. His outward appearance resembled nothing but calm, but that was the total opposite inside his body. Lye looked around to every window and every door he could see from his space on the couch. Trying to make it appear as though he was only stretching.

Lost in his track of though, he felt Felix's lips on his, bringing back to reality.

"What was that for?" he asked.

He looked down to notice her fingers were upon his wrists, the entire time she had been checking his heart rate.

"You said we wouldn't worry about anything but the movie, and here you are, worrying about everything but the movie."

"I'm sorry, it's just."

Immediately she jumped from the couch, looking inside the pantries and other rooms for something of importance.

"What are you doing-"

He didn't have to wait long for the answer. Felix came back from her search with a metal trashcan. Afterwards she went upstairs, and only came back after she had filled the can with letters. He assumed it was all the hate mail. She opened the back door and beckoned him to come.

"I need you to watch this." She said. pulling out a thing of matches.

"Why do you have-"

"Bernabe's been chain smoking since you were arrested. In order to hide it from you and Mrs. Davis, he asks me to hold his matches." She said, lighting the packet and dropping it into the metal trash can. It did not take long for the dry paper to catch; the ink of the paper turned the fire into a calming purple color.

"Alright, we have no more threats, you don't have to think about it. Can we go back and watch the transformer movie now?" he nodded. He couldn't explain it, but watching them burn with his own eyes eased his worry. He happily agreed to watch the movie.

The following days were ones filled with peace and laughter. They spent the day Monday coloring and cooking. Tuesday, they slept in until three in the afternoon and stayed up until three the following morning. Wednesday, they watched even more movies, and they practiced law terms for Felix on Thursday. On Friday Felix woke up to an empty bed.

Lye had finished putting the last light up when she

came down from the bedroom. When he saw her, he smiled in acknowledgement, and passed her a plate full of eggs, bacon, and sausage.

"I didn't know you could cook." She said, she looked at the plate with caution.

"There's a difference between not being able to cook and being too lazy to cook. Don't worry. I promise everything on the plate is edible. Trust me. I licked my own fingers."

She looked at him quizzingly. But she sat down at the table and ate her breakfast.

"I figured you would remember that quote. Shakespeare said you shouldn't trust a cook who won't lick his own fingers."

"It's actually pretty good, but I have to ask you, what's up with the Christmas lights? You know it's nowhere near the holidays?" she said.

Lye was focused on how the lights look. He had managed to move the furniture in the living room to the edges, so the middle of the floor was empty. He had set the Christmas lights around the living room, creating a warm glow in the room.

"I know. But every day is a holiday when you're sure people are out to kill you."

"You're still planning on going out tomorrow? Lye, have you been online lately? People are talking about shooting you where you stand."

"I no longer have a working phone. And my laptop

was destroyed with the Common Connector. I haven't seen any of the comments online unless someone else told me about them." He lied. The truth was he had spent the last night on his sister's computer. The closer the days passed to Saturday, the more the threats overwhelmed the messages of encouragement. Matters were made worse when Lye identified some of the people who were talking to him with tongues filled with anger. A group of guards from the prison that once held Lye, and Felix, had spoken their claims. They hated their unemployment, and they blamed no one but Lye for it. The profile picture of the guard who walked him to the rec center carried the message he would shoot Lye as he spoke.

"Those messages will not stop. The threats of death and punishment will not stop. If hate screams it will not stop, then I am obligated to tell them love will not be hindered by their threats."

He turned his attention to Felix. Once she was done with her meal, he took the plate and cleaned it, and then put it up. He grabbed her hand and led her to the living room.

"Before it went up in flames, the Memorial held some old CD's. I'm not sure how to describe them, they're little disks that hold information. But the CD's held music on them, and I found a CD player. I had been holding this for a long time, waiting for a good time to admit that I had it. I guess today would be the best day to do so."

On the mantle was a dust covered antique. Lye had to find an extension cord in the laundry room in order to keep in plugged in that position. There may had been lights that came on when the music player was turned on, but the bulbs had died out decades ago.

"What's the name of the CD?"

Lye concentrated on putting the CD in the small slit on the front of the music player. "If I'm reading it correctly, it's called *My Way* by a man named Usher? I'm only going to play one song on it. It's called *Slow Jam*? I really don't know what a 'jam' is, but I'm quite sure it has nothing to do with preserved fruit."

After a few minutes he found how to play the song and put the song on repeat. By the time the first words of the first verse had started, Lye had turned off the central lights, so the only light source came from the Christmas lights.

"I couldn't do much dancing at prom since my arm was in a sling. May I have this dance, Felix Cambridge?" he asked, his hand outstretched.

She laughed and shook her head. Soon she walked over and gave him her hand.

"What's with all of this?" She asked, afraid to know the answer.

Lye looked at her with a smile as he pulled her close and kissed her. Soon they swayed to the rhythm of the song. He kept his head down as they dance, afraid to make eye contact with his lover. "I feel that this story is going to end soon. And I'm not sure how tomorrow will go, so I wanted to make a nice memory to compensate for whatever pain may happen."

They complicated the swaying into the waltz. Lye

found the courage to bring his head up and made eye contact with her.

"Lye, I'll always be with you. You know that."

He smiled again, but the smile never reached his eyes. As much as he tried to hide what was going on in his mind, his eyes continued to water. He knew his face showed his own fear, his tire, his need for everything to be over. He continued to smile as they dance, but tears gently ran down his face. In that moment he wished he could go back, to never had complained, to had kept his head down all those years, because that would mean they could dance as they were the next day. And the next day.

"I love you Felix. But with the type of person I am, there is no guarantee that I will always be here with you."

He silently begged her not to ask what he meant by those words. He didn't want to admit what he was afraid of. Thankfully, she never did. She simply freed her hand from his grip and wiped the tears from his face. After which she kissed him and held placed her hand on his cheek.

"What would you have me do?" she asked. Her voice was so tender, it seemed out of place. He wanted to apologize for all the things she had been through in his name. But he knew that this was not the time and place to do so.

He let out a dry laugh as he looked into her eyes. "My life will never be a fairy tale. So, before everything goes to shit, I only ask that you allow me to have a fairy tale until the music stops playing."

She nodded in agreement. Lye and Felix held each other close and danced the morning away. They spoke about nothing that had to do with what they knew might come the following day. They danced, they embraced, and they kissed until the music player played its last repetition of the song, and finally submitted to the call of old age.

The rest of the day was spent watching movies, and cooking.

A sense of unease woke Lye up in the middle of the night. He looked over to see Felix was sleeping peacefully. He pulled out her phone and checked the time. The time read half past midnight. It was the day of his final speech. He couldn't tell what woke him up, so he peered out of the window.

On the curb sat a black car with tinted windows. A look into the sky showed no black birds. He nudged Felix awake.

"Huh?" she said, the strain of being awake evident in her voice.

"I need you to walk downstairs, go into my parent's bathroom and hide in the tub."

The words woke her up in alarm. "What's going on?" she asked. She quickly began to rub the sleep out of her eyes.

His heart began beating out of his chest. "I think someone is here to shoot me."

He turned his neck to look at Felix's car. Sure enough, two of her tires had been slashed. The full moon was the only witness besides him to what he was seeing.

"And don't turn on any lights." He said urgently. "Yell at me when you are safe."

He didn't move as she got out of the bed and hurried down the stairs. He slowly climbed out of his bed, making sure not to make any sudden movements to alert whoever sat in the car outside his home. Once he was out of his bed, he went to his dresser and pushed it toward his bed, until it was parallel to how he would have been sleeping. His body had healed quite a bit since his incarceration, and even more so since he was shot. But the urgency of the situation almost angered him when he thought about how long it took him to move something that should have taken three minutes.

Lye looked at his handiwork while he heard Felix yell that she was okay in hiding. The yell scared him. He jumped; thankful no one had seen what had happened. He quickly ran across his room to open the door again. He turned on the light in his room, and ran down the hallway, covering his head from any debris that might occur.

Within seven seconds he heard the first gunshot break his window and thud into the dresser. His heart raced in his ears, but the bullets raced across his room faster. He risked his safety to turn around, lying on his back to see plywood and plaster fly across the hallway as bullets ate at his bedroom wall. Some were stopped by the objects in his room. From his position he could hear bullets eating at his furniture and clothes, ripping apart his bed, and finding their mark on the wall. The rays of light that followed the exiting wounds on the wall abruptly stopped once a bullet hit the light in his room.

Three minutes later, there was nothing but eerie silence and dust in his hallway. He had prepared for this moment, but it didn't stop him from throwing up the remains of his stomach. After a few minutes he received another yell from downstairs.

"I'm alive, and I called the cops. Are you okay?" Felix yelled. He quickly responded he was okay. A lot better than he would have been if he had not been so paranoid. He crawled the rest of the way toward Courtney's room. A few stray bullets had entered her room, but it was obvious he was the intended target for the overkill.

Sirens soon woke up the night, and from the window he could see the blue lights down the road. Many of his neighbors had woken from the sound of bullets, and the slowly began to form a crowd outside his house, looking at the damage.

Once he was sure he was safe to move, he ran down the stairs to check on Felix. There was nothing wrong with her.

"You're bleeding." She gasped.

He looked down toward her line of vison and noticed a trail of blood crawling down his leg.

"I've only been licked. A bullet grazed me. I'm fine."

The couple walked out the front door toward the crowd and blue lights. Two police officers walked toward the front of the house with their weapons drawn. The younger cop looked at the couple, looked at the blood coming from Lye's leg, and quickly reached for his handcuffs.

"What the hell are you doing?" yelled a voice from the crowd. The officer, not yet accustomed to his authority being questioned, looked toward the crowd to find the source of the voice.

A frail old lady walked up. Her hair was in curlers, and her hand rested on her hip. Though she was unarmed, Lye felt more of a threat from her than the two officers.

"Young man, don't you hear me talking to you? What are you planning on doing? Are you trying to arrest that boy?"

"Ma'am . . ." he said, completely ignoring Lye and Felix, "I am just trying to do my job. There had been a crime here-"

"And you're going to arrest the victim?!" she screamed, appalled at what she was forced to look at. "That boy has lived in that house all of his life. The damn house has been shot up, and he comes out bleeding. Where in that dull head of yours does it look like he did it? You think he would shoot up his own house? While he's sleeping?" she looked around the yard, and her eyes fell on the slashed tires. "Did he slash the tires too? For fair play?" she hurried to the cop, the speed of her house slippers surprising everyone. "Your job here is to arrest the criminal, not the darkest person at the scene. I don't care what you think of the boy, he's innocent. Do you job correctly or so help me God."

She never finished her threat, the two cops remembered why they were there in the first place and walked to the couple. Lye recognized the old lady as he gypsy that had given him a ride months ago.

"Ma'am, can you tell me what happened?" they said, turning their attention to Felix. Without a word, they tried their hardest not to notice Lye and his bleeding leg. Felix, aware of both sides of the interaction, simply crossed her arms.

"I don't live here, why don't you ask the man who was shot at?"

With dozens of people in the audience, and a growing silence not even the sirens were defying, they turned their attention to Lye. Given his expectations of the officers, he quickly explained what had happened.

"You were the antagonist in the situation?" asked the older cop. Since his eyes were on Lye, he didn't notice the house slipper whizzing pass his head. Nor did he see the two men having difficulty holding gypsy lady back.

"The constitution protects my right to protest, even if people have forgotten about that. And a protest doesn't justify that SOMEONE TRIED TO KILL ME IN MY OWN HOUSE."

"Sir, if you raise your voice again, I will have you arrested-" Neither cop noticed as the companion of the first house slipper barely missed their heads.

Lye's anger flared up, but he quickly dampened the fire. While he talked to the officers, Felix alerted his parents.

Before long an ambulance, followed by Mr. Davis'

car, parked in front of the house. The large man seemed to get out of the car before the car had stopped moving. The speed of his steps, along with his size, caused the crowd to part as he ran up to Lye. Without a word, he grabbed his son and embraced him.

Mr. Davis' concerned face then flashed in anger. "You are not going anywhere tomorrow. At all, do you hear me?!"

Lye watched as the blue lights flashed across his father's face.

"Yessir, I promise I won't go anywhere." The feeling of emptiness he tried so hard not to pay attention to burst toward the surface. He found it hard to maintain eye contact with his father. It was the first time he had ever lied to his father with the intention of lying. The lie didn't feel right in his throat.

The police began to do their job, looking around the house and asking questions. Lye paid no attention to the cops or their questions, and rarely did they pay attention to him. They asked his father, or Felix, about what had happened. Lye didn't mind, his mind was elsewhere. He walked into his room, looking at the shattered mess of the bullets.

Splinters and broken pieces of wood littered the floor. Some of his clothes had made it out of the now broken dresser, and his bed was barely recognizable. Bits of spring and foam spread across the room. His room looked the same as every other room in the neighborhood as far as the blueprints went. But this was still his room. He had lived in this room for the better part of seventeen years. He found it hard not to cry, not to shed a tear, as he looked at his busted windows and the glass on his once tidy room. He shuffled through the debris, careful not to cut himself on any glass shards or lethal looking splinters. He pulled out an outfit and walked toward the laundry room.

After accepting the damage of his room, he felt nothing. There was nothing to feel. He absentmindedly watched the lone outfit swirl around in the circle of water. The police had confirmed the bullets had stayed confined in his room. The only bullets that strayed from the concentration was done by accident. It was obvious he was the lone target of whoever a shot at his house in the dead of the night. The police, for once, agreed with Lye the slashed tires had been done in order to stop him from escaping. His only concern was, why in the world would anyone dare run toward active fire? The logic escaped him, but he mentioned it to no one.

"Are you okay?" said a weak voice.

Lye didn't take his eyes off the washing machine. The suds had obscured the view of his outfit, but he still watched the bubbles as they raced around in the circle.

"I find it weird that everyone tends to ask if I'm okay, when all reason would show that I am far from being okay."

"Son, are you okay?" followed a deeper voice.

"See what I mean?" He finally took his eyes off the laundry. His father and Felix both stood in the door frame, both afraid to come closer. He wished his mother was here. His mother would not have hesitated to come in to the room and hug him. She would understand what he was feeling without him having to explain himself, but she was hundreds of miles away. At least she was now, word would have reached her, so she would soon be on the next plane to Alabama.

"Has Bernabe answered your texts?" Lye asked in the hollow voice that no one wanted to be on the receiving end of.

"He hasn't answered any of my texts." Felix answered.

In a normal occasion, the idea that Bernabe didn't answer a text that had to do with Lye was alarming in its own right. It meant that something tragic must have happened to his best friend. Something that outweighed his own trauma. But this wasn't a normal occasion, his wet blanket of nothingness would not allow him to feel anything, to register any emotion that did not correspond with the dull swirling of the water.

"What are you going to do?" he said, keeping his eyes directed at his father. Unlike his mother, unlike Bernabe, they kept their distance from Lye. The overwhelming feeling of defeat leaked from him, causing the air of the laundry room to weigh down on whatever body part they allowed to shy into its reach.

"I- Well I'm going to stay here for the night." His father said. Lye put up his hand to object.

"You don't need to. There's no way for me to leave, they slashed the tires. And I doubt they will try to do it again since the whole neighborhood was roused up in this. It would be foolish, almost fatal for them to try and shoot me again tonight. Trust me, if anything bad happens, I will call you." There were no self-depreciation jokes, there were no smirks of humor, there was nothing but an empty voice. The sight made the observers' eyes water. They wished to see the Lye full of life, full of vigor and revolution.

Mr. Davis' phone rang, and everyone could hear the voice of Mrs. Davis. His father tried his hardest to keep up with what she was saying, to answer every question she asked. In a hurry he tossed the phone to Lye, still afraid to enter the newly found vault of depression.

"Were you hit, honey?"

"No ma'am. I was grazed. I noticed the car before they started shooting and I was able to get out safely."

There was a silence on the other line.

"Do you want me to go home?"

"No ma'am, I'm sure you know why."

His mother understood. Her leaving home would show there was a concern for his life. That would be documented, and whoever sent those bullets would feel better with the knowledge they had subdued Lye.

"Are you still going to go to the speech?"

"No ma'am, I'm not going to go and do the speech tomorrow." he lied. Of course, he was lying, but this was his mother. She knew he was lying, and after a few moments of silence, asked a question that proved his superstitions.

In a lower voice she asked. "Is your father in ear shot?"

"Absolutely. One hundred ten percent."

She went silent for a moment, deciding what was more important to her. "Your bike is behind the house; you might have noticed it if you went to the backyard. Put me on speaker."

He did as she asked.

"Can everyone hear me?"

They confirmed in chorus.

"Okay, Felix, I'm happy to know you're okay, but I do need you to do me a favor sweetie. Watch over him tonight. I know you're stressed, and your nerves are shot, but please look after yourself and my son. Baby, I talked to him, and I don't think you have to stay home from work tonight. But I will need you to head to my sister's house. I'm going to let her know to stay away from the house, and to keep Courtney for another week. Please make sure you don't act like we just got the house shot up. Lye, look after Felix. You can sleep in our room tonight, just don't do anything too crazy while you're there. "

They said yes ma'am in chorus as well, Lye let out a small chuckle as he thought about the fact of his father saying yes ma'am to his wife. As the meeting adjourned, Mr. Davis slowly made his way to his car, afraid to leave his son to his own devices.

That night, he heard nothing from Bernabe.

That night, as they lay in his parents' bed, Felix

cried in her arms. His only wish was that she had not been there to witness, that he would have to had shouldered this burden by himself. But he knew he was wishing to a false reality. Even as she cried, he could do nothing to hold her. Not because he couldn't find anything to say; because he still felt nothing.

Felix finally fell asleep around seven in the morning, at that time Lye inched out of the bed to put his outfit into the dryer. He took a shower in his parent's bathroom, and when he left, he was amazed at how soundly Felix was sleeping. He licked his thumb and wiped the salt trail of dried tears on her face. She didn't move an inch.

He made himself breakfast, and did a few light stretches to warm up his muscles. After he was done, he looked to see if she had moved. Nothing. He used her phone to call his parents to update them, he called Bernabe with no answer. His worry for his friend soon eclipsed the worry he had for his own life. Bernabe was never one to not answer a call, even, no, specially, if Lye had left voicemails before. He grabbed his clothes out of the dryer and dressed himself. Though he had sifted through his clothes to find something less damaged. The shirt had two bullet holes in it. After some time, he realized this was the only clean shirt he had, so he quickly put it on. He looked at the time to see it was only an hour away from noon.

He swiftly waked into his mother's room, half-expecting to see Felix sitting up angry. But there was nothing, she hadn't moved a centimeter since the last time he checked on her. He closed the blinds and quietly closed the door.

He made his way to the backyard. It somewhat surprised him not to see angry faces pointing guns at him as soon as he opened the door, but he was relived altogether not to see anything. He saw his bike. He hadn't seen it since the day he was shot, since the day that caused this crusade of his.

"Hey, I missed you." he said to his favorite inanimate object while he readied himself. As he started to pedal, he listened to hear for any sounds that Felix was awake. He heard nothing, and he quickened his pedaling.

The roads leading to the school was packed with traffic.

He had never seen so many cars in one place in his life, at least not in real life. For a moment he couldn't think of a reason as to what could be going on to cause such havoc. Until someone rolled down their window.

"Look! Look! it's him!"

Teenagers waved at him as he rode pass. Only then did it occur to him that he was the cause of all of this. He had expecting to see a few people, maybe a couple dozen, but not nearly enough to cause city-wide traffic.

He zoomed past the cars, every now in again someone would roll down their window and send out a chip of appreciation and encouragement.

Once he reached the school, his bewilderment continued to cascade. The ruins of the Common Connector had been cleared out, and people began to use it as a parking lot. Those who had gotten there earlier waved at him. He was astonished to see, as he parked his bike in his usual part of the bike rack, that there were three other bikes there. People of different ages smiled and waved at his confused face. He walked toward the back of the school toward the parking lot, and his mouth hit the floor.

In all honesty, he had no plans once he had made it to the school. If worse came to worst, he would simply stand on someone else's car and yell through cupped hands. But the parking lot was full of people. The different colors of everyone's shirt turned the scene into a rainbow. There had never, and there will never be, so much colors in this parking lot like this.

They all focused their attention on the stage. Lye was too far away to see where anyone would have found an actual stage. There were at least fifteen rows of people on all sides of the stage. And there were various microphones coming from the center.

"Er...excuse me?"

The person in front of him looked behind him with a smile. Recognition spread over there face. "Good afternoon, how are you doing? Do you need to get by?"

Lye tried his hardest to cover up the recoil of hearing another accent. He couldn't tell where she was from, but he knew they weren't from Alabama.

"Yes ma'am, excuse me."

He watched as the others looked back to see the conversation, and they all began to part to make room for Lye. Once he made it to the stage, he realized he had spoken too soon. The stage he thought he saw was three desks pushed aside. The charred wood made him guess that it was some of the debris from the Common Connector. He stood on the stage, looking at the hundreds of people standing in his high school parking lot. Officers stood at the edge of the big circle, some willing to listen to what he had to say, some waiting to find a protester that had gone too far.

"Uhh . . ." he said into the mike, realizing the sound had reverberated throughout the crowd. He noticed there were multiple cameras from different networks trying to get the first scoop of the news. The flash of cameras solidified the "uhh" he had started before. He noticed the lack of Bernabe, but he was glad to see the different shades of faces in the crowd. The rainbow of shirts corresponded with the different shades of skin., The different ages, the different genders. The diversity of his crowd renewed his strength and washed away the emptiness he had the night before.

"I know some of you may have heard there was an attack on my life last night. Someone had tried to kill me, to stop me from talking to all of you. I wish you to know no one was hurt. Their action of hate was stopped and thwarted. All of us are safe." the crowd cheered. As much as he tried to smile, the cheering didn't sit with him. There was no part in him that wanted to be celebrated.

"I want everyone to know that, because of this, I don't have words for those who tried to kill me. Who tried to do me wrong."

He looked around at the crowd. Looking once again at the uniqueness of everyone. The contrast of old white men standing near pre-teen Hispanics. Of black and white, yellow and brown, all standing together to listen to what he had to say. He readied himself, the wind blew through the holes in his shirt, but he ignored it as he began his final speech.

"These words were not meant for creatures whose hearts are filled with malicious intent. These words were never meant for those whose love for profit has dwarfed their empathy for their fellow human. These words were not meant for those whose self-righteousness has set them on a pedestal above God himself, waiting to cast judgement on everyone unlike them. I have given you words before, and the words I speak now, are not for you.

"These words are for those who must live with the policies of those who govern them, knowing their welfare was never put into consideration. These words are for women whose body has become reason for political forum by men who only wish her to be a machine to crank out babies. These words are for people of color, people of poverty who live under a foundation designed to keep them in their place. For those whose mental welfare is at risk because they do not know whether they can find something to eat for the next day. These words are for those who have been denied love because of their sexuality... these words are for you.

"You digest these words hoping to find a way to avoid a dystopian America, an America void of hope and joy. You eat these words hoping to shy away from a country that no longer loves her citizens. I must ask you, how are we not? We live in a country where our every action and transaction are watched. A country where our national debt is only dominated by our national incompetence. We once were a country that boasted in our desire to help. Our great country now cannot feed the homeless, but our senators live off six figures for inadequate jobs. Police are governed by police, and the country pays for the lawyer, so police brutality goes unpunished. A country in which the system we rely on is the same system that restrains us. Our country is a place where we are taught we must be good people but are reminded police bullets cannot tell the difference between heroes and villains.

"This is a dystopian nation we live in. Because of that fact, my words are not for those who benefit from this dystopia. I am not giving you the words of those who wish you to be nothing but emotionless parts in a machine that profits them. I do not wish you to be things! You are not things! You are beautiful creatures with emotions and free will and your own, valuable thoughts! We must unite against this dystopia. The love we have for our fellow man must override the default setting of hate we have been conditioned to feel. We must continue to strive, united in our differences, and we must remind those who believe they hold no power who we are. We are not simply numbers on a piece of paper. We are not just information passed on to win elections, no, we are much more than that. You are much more than that!

"These words were never meant for those who will only believe what their parents have believed. I ask you to step away from what has always been, for it has never been always right. I say we remind those who sit in their lofty chairs that we will not be silenced. That we will have our demands met. And I will remind you, that we have no leaders in this country. We have representatives, and like any employee who has not done a good job, we must terminate those who have failed us. Reelect no one.

Money and power are corruptible, and therefore we must limit them; to make sure the people come first. People should always tower over profit.

"Friends I ask you in complete irony, not to be satisfied simply by words. The most wretched of us still had enough power over the English Language to make you believe he is your ally. So, think. Think. Think! Unlike those who have come before us, do not forgot the responsibility of thought. Do not believe for a second that your government has our best interest in mind. As long as we think, resist, and unite. As long as we talk to one another with the goal to convey and not to persuade. As long as we listen with the intent to understand and not to response, then we shall see change. We shall see change when we allow our hearts to beat as humans do. When we let our emotions flow as humans do. When we show empathy, and understanding, and compassion, as humans do. We shall see change. Our government treats us as animals, as machines. YOU ARE NOT MACHINES! YOU ARE NOT ANIMALS! None of you are called to be a beast of burden! So, remind yourself that, and with that, remind others too that they are also human.

"And to those who sit in their gated communities without the experience to understand the problems of the projects. The people who don't understand the racism because they are unaffected. The people who see no wrong in our system because they benefit from it. I wish you to know we don't hate you. We extend our hand to you. we don't hate the ignorant, we simply despise your ignorance. but if you are willing to understand, we are willing to teach. We were taught to hate one another to keep us contained. For if we are at the throats of one another, we will not notice how many of us are taken for slaughter. So, we extend our hand to you, we wish to come together. Let your labels be what defines you, not what separates us. Let our beliefs be what holds us together when things are array, not the thing that destroys our bond with fellow humans. We do not have to be alike to enjoy the merit of one's company. We are America, and we are a nation of love. The road to understanding will be long, but we can overcome if we all-"

Lye never finished the last sentence. He didn't feel the bullet, but he heard the gunshot. He remembered the familiar pain of being shot as his shirt turned red and he fell to the ground.

Acknowledgements

Of course, the first I would like to acknowledge is my God for giving me the idea and talents for this book.

Lye's the first protagonist I ever made- throughout the course of this book- and by default, his life- he's dealt with the same mental illnesses his creator goes through. With that being said, I thank my support team for allowing me to lean on them through every episode of mania and depression I had. Every tear-filled night I never thought I wouldn't finish; every day I barricaded myself in my room in order to write. Each time I thought a sleeping may be a better outlet than talking. Over the course of writing this book; I've been a blessing and a burden to all of you. You've been nothing but blessings to me- helping me become a better person and a better writer. I thank all of you; you're amazing- and without you I'd probably still be editing chapter two for the umpteenth time. Trash Cat, the biggest of thanks goes to you. You looked after the thing most important to me when I was too weak to care for myself.

Special thanks goes to my cats. I have countless pictures of you sitting on me while I slaved away on this spawn of mine. You are the greatest editors I've had, even though you can't never read. If this is a success, I promise I will buy you all the fresh fish your little hearts could desire. There's been too many nights you've fallen asleep by my laptop waiting for me to go to bed; you will receive the ultimate level of head scratches.

My Real Life Poets family, and all those I met because of you, I have to say we've come a long way from the high schooler who wrote love poems in Algebra class. You've been with me every step of the way, and honestly I don't think I could have made it this far without your help. With the tips and lessons you've given me- I've learned that my passion for writing could be used for bigger issues than puppy love. This isn't saying I'm done writing love poems

when I'm smitten- just not as much. We don't need another 2016 on our hands.

To all of my comrades that know the split, and all my friends in Calera- thank you. You taught me lessons I still use in my work and my life. Thank you for listening to my ramblings at times when breakfast was energy drinks and cigarettes.

And since the story of Lye Davis is one of a teenager creating change in spite of his mental illness. I thank you, the reader. Thank you for going on this adventure. I believe in you, you are amazing. Even if you didn't agree with every thing I put in this book; I thank you for hearing the idea that you can do anything, no matter what's in you head.

ABOUT THE AUTHOR

Ra'Quann Randle-Bustamonte lives in Calera, AL with his cat and all unfortunate enough to live with him. When he's not writing or sleeping, he's trying to bestow sentience to crows.

CPSIA information can be obtained
at www.ICGtesting.com
Printed in the USA
BVHW071609180619
551321BV00001B/168/P